A QUESTION
OF DESPAIR

Maureen Carter

CRÈME de la CRIME

This first world edition published 2011
in Great Britain and the USA by
Crème de la Crime, an imprint of
SEVERN HOUSE PUBLISHERS LTD of
9–15 High Street, Sutton, Surrey, England, SM1 1DF.
Trade paperback edition first published
in Great Britain and the USA 2011.

British Library Cataloguing in Publication Data

Carter, Maureen.
  A question of despair.
  1. Women detectives–England–Birmingham–Fiction.
  2. Women journalists–England–Birmingham–Fiction.
  3. Kidnapping–Fiction. 4. Detective and mystery stories.
  I. Title
  823.9′2-dc22

ISBN-13: 978-1-78029-000-3 (cased)
ISBN-13: 978-1-78029-500-8 (trade paper)

Except where actual ... his ... ... characters the pub-
described for the sto ... ...
publication are fictit ... ...
is purely coincidenta ... ...

All Severn House tit ... ...

Severn House Publis ... ...
the leading internatio ... ...
are printed on Green ... ...go.

MIX
Paper from
responsible sources
FSC
www.fsc.org
FSC® C018575

Typeset by Palimpsest Book Production Ltd.,
Falkirk, Stirlingshire, Scotland.
Printed and bound in Great Britain by the
MPG Books Group, Bodmin, Cornwall.

ONE

They heard the mother before they saw her. Two streets away, through the open windows of an unmarked police motor, and they could hear the screams. On what felt like the hottest day of a baking summer, the sound was chilling and incongruous. To Detective Inspector Sarah Quinn's way of thinking, the flawless turquoise sky called out for ice cream, paddling pools, children's squeals. Not this cry against nature.

Maybe it was the cooling sweat trickling down her spine, but Sarah shivered again as she reran mentally what little they'd picked up on police radio. Scanning the surroundings, her shrewd grey eyes took in a stream of probably inconsequential images on the way to the bigger picture: a whippet trailing after a fat man with a ponytail, an old woman dragging on a cigarette as she tugged along a tartan shopping trolley, a chav yelling into a mobile, while pushing a double buggy one-handed.

It was force of habit for Sarah, the constant observing, recording, filing for possible future use. Anyway, detail via the radio had barely provided crumbs let alone food for thought, it had been sparse to the point of useless; the original triple-nine made from a call box, anonymous and garbled: a missing pushchair, White's newsagent just off Small Heath high street and a young mother who, quote, needed a good slapping. Sarah arched an eyebrow: the tip-off was right on that score – the hysteria was evident and she hadn't even seen the woman.

She wasn't alone. Passers-by turned cocked heads trying to pinpoint where the screams came from. Sarah glanced at her sergeant, part of her willing him to drive faster, the rest scared they may already be too late. Either way, picking up speed wasn't an option on inner city streets heavy with traffic and heaving with people. It was uniform's shout by rights. Sarah and Hunt just happened to be in the vicinity when the call came in. She'd suggested taking a quick look, was already beginning to think better of it; quick was likely the last thing it would be. Thursday evenings were French conversation class – she was lucky if she got to one in three. *C'est la vie.*

'Next left, John.' Her clipped tone verged on curt; tight vocals the only sign of stress. It certainly wasn't a case of least said soonest mended. If the screams were anything to go by, the damage had already been done. The feeling was so unlike Sarah; she didn't do instinct, sixth sense, whatever. So why couldn't she shake off the uneasiness?

John Hunt's muttered, ma'am, articulated more than her senior rank. Born and bred in the second city, the detective sergeant needed directions like Delia Smith needed cookery lessons. Registering his pale face and pinched features, Sarah realized this call-out could be a too-close-to-home nightmare for Hunt. He and his wife had lost their first baby in a cot death just before Christmas.

Focus woman, she told herself, curling twitching fingers to stop them tapping; it wasn't even clear yet that a child was missing, let alone permanently. Even before Hunt cut the engine, Sarah was out of the Vauxhall, long legs striding towards a growing crowd of gawpers. Through a sea of jeans and shorts, saris and salwar, she caught a flash of yellow. The warrant card and her air of seemingly effortless authority were enough for most spectators to step aside and for the first time Sarah saw the woman.

Down on bony knees in the middle of the dusty pavement, she was oblivious to the curious stares and occasional asides, to the fact her bright yellow sun dress had ridden up, exposing hollowed white thighs. Head cradled in her hands, she rocked and wailed as tears dripped from her chin, spotting a paving slab already mottled with discarded gum.

A man crouched at her side, his hand hovering but not quite making contact with her bare shoulder. The concerned glances he cast at the open door of the newsagent's, as much as the biro tucked behind his ear, suggested he was the eponymous owner.

Sarah stopped just short, rapidly deciding on the best approach. The woman's misery was almost palpable but it wasn't getting anyone anywhere.

'Took your time didn't you?' The biro man had a voice. And a point. Sarah was well aware the traffic had held them back. Five to four now – the call had come in eleven minutes ago. It was a long time in policing. It could be a lifetime if they didn't act fast.

'Mr White, is it?' Over his shoulder she glimpsed Hunt in conversation with a couple of uniformed officers. He'd be briefing them; they'd start questioning people on the street, all potential witnesses.

'That's right.' White staggered to his feet, the brusque tone slightly mollified. Sarah heard relief in it as well. Like most people he was happy to let the cops deal with it, whatever shit it was. 'Can't you do something for her?' He jabbed a thumb at the hunched figure as if there was any doubt, as if Small Heath was a hotbed of women on the verge of a meltdown.

'Let's get inside. I can't do anything here.' The noise was grating and the woman needed to get out of the heat, drink some water. They'd have to call an ambulance soon if she didn't get a grip.

'She won't budge. I've tried.' White's bald pate was surrounded by what looked like a fallen halo of wispy cotton wool. He pulled dung-coloured slacks over a middle-aged paunch. 'She's terrified to move in case the baby comes back.'

Comes back? Suppressing a growing sense of urgency, Sarah moved in closer. 'Calm down, love. Take some deep breaths.'

Maybe the girl hadn't heard. The rocking and wailing continued. Her sallow complexion was marred by twin trails of shiny mascara-blackened tears. Staring straight ahead now, she seemed oblivious to the crowd, to Sarah, to anything but her own misery. She was obviously in shock, but had she witnessed something vital? Or someone?

'We're wasting precious time, love.' Sarah's patience was at a premium, too. It took an effort not to show it in her voice. For a few seconds, the woman appeared to focus on Sarah's face and the screaming stopped. In the brief period of eye contact, Sarah was surprised to see how young she was: sixteen? Seventeen? Not much more than a child herself. She managed a tight smile of reassurance, encouragement, but the girl started screaming again.

Conscious of Hunt at her side, Sarah snapped a command. 'For Christ's sake, John, stop her making that sodding noise.' The words came out louder than intended and sounded harsh even to her ears. Hunt failed to hide his reaction. She didn't care if he was appalled; if a baby was missing hurt feelings were neither here nor there. Without a word, he went to the girl, squatted beside her and laid a strong arm around her scrawny shoulder. His six-two well-padded frame made her appear even smaller, even frailer. 'Come on, sweetheart. Let's get you inside. See what we can do to help.'

Hunt was good at the touchy-feely stuff; unthreatening despite his bulk; a passing resemblance to David Tennant didn't hurt. It was enough to silence the girl, she cut Sarah a glance that was difficult to read, then allowed him to half carry, half steer her into the newsagent's. White must've retrieved the girl's bag from wherever it had fallen. He clutched it self-consciously as he showed them through to a cluttered storeroom then slipped it on the floor near the only chair, an upright that had seen better days. Hunt gently lowered the girl onto the seat where she hung her head, curtains of dull mousy hair concealing her face.

'What's your name, love?' Silence. Sarah tried again. 'I'm Detective Inspector Sarah Quinn. This is DS Hunt. Can you tell us what happened?'

The girl raised her head, stared sullenly at Sarah for a few seconds before pleading with Hunt. 'Find her, please find her.'

'You have to tell us what happened first.' Sarah softened her voice and moved closer. 'We're here to help . . .' Neither words nor action bridged the gap. Despite the girl's anguish, her animosity towards Sarah was glaringly obvious.

'Get out there and find her then.' She licked dry lips, froze Sarah out again, turned to face Hunt. 'Please find her, mister. She could be with anyone by now. They could have taken her anywhere.'

Sarah balled her fists, knew she was getting nowhere. The girl had been distraught outside, but clearly not deaf. Her uncharacteristic outburst was regrettable, and already proving an obstacle to communication when it was essential to get through to the girl. She nodded at Hunt to take up the questioning.

He got down on one knee and gently lifted the hair from her face. 'Come on, sweetheart. We can't help, if you don't help us. We don't even know your name. Or baby's.'

The word brought it back in an instant. She sat bolt upright. 'Oh, my God. They won't hurt her, will they?' Wide hazel eyes begged for reassurance, which he gave – too quickly.

'You're just saying that,' she snapped back. 'Tell me they won't hurt her. Tell me she's safe.' She placed trembling fingers on his arm.

Touching scene it might be, but Sarah wanted to shake the girl. Her attitude – self-indulgent and over-the-top to Sarah's eyes – was slowing down the police response to what was probably a major incident. She felt a tap on her arm and absently accepted a bottle of water from White. Offering it to the girl, she said, 'Have a drink, then talk us through what you know.'

Still no movement. Hunt unscrewed the cap and passed her the bottle. 'Inspector Quinn's right, sweetheart. We have to know what happened. What she looks like, what she's wearing. And we still don't know your name. Or hers.' His smile was reassuring, dark brown eyes warm and friendly. Sarah mentally rolled hers. Where did Huntie get the patience? He must have taken her share when it was being doled out. Her nickname round the station was the Ice Queen. She rarely saw it as a failing.

The girl gave a quick nod. 'Evie. Her name's Evie.' She reached for her bag as she spoke. 'She's six months old. God, she'll be starving. Will they feed her?' Head down, her hand was scrabbling inside the cheap white plastic bag. The photograph wasn't in a wallet. When she took it out, it was flecked with tobacco and fluff. But the girl's sharp features softened as she blew the surface, and for the first time there was a glimmer of a smile on her face. 'Beautiful, isn't she?'

Sarah stepped forward for a closer look, but the girl's focus was on Hunt, searching his face for the slightest sign of disagreement. There was none.

'A right little smasher,' he said. 'Gorgeous.'

Despite the reply's speed, no one could doubt it was genuine. Sarah was no big fan of babies, but with huge blue eyes, pink peachy cheeks and one tiny-toothed smile, Evie could do TV commercials for Mothercare.

And now she'd gone and the clock was ticking. 'May I?' Sarah reached for the picture. 'When was it taken, Miss, Mrs . . . ?'

'Lowe. Karen Lowe.' Reluctantly she let the picture go. 'And it's Miss. I'm not married.'

There's a surprise. Sarah made no comment, didn't even tighten her lips.

'And when was it taken, Karen?' Hunt prompted.

'Last week. In the park. I took a load but I only got that one printed.'

'And the others are still on the camera?' Sarah asked.

'Yeah, most of them.'

Sarah nodded at Hunt who took his cue. 'OK, Karen. Now we need to know what happened.'

The young mother swallowed, took a deep breath. 'I'd run out of nappies. There's a place up the road sells them a bit cheaper. I nipped in here on the way home for a mag and a packet of fags. I've never left the pushchair anywhere before. But there's no room in here – you can see what it's like.' She paused, seeking approval, perhaps. 'I was only going to be a few seconds. Had the money ready and everything. Course there's an old dear ahead of me. Buying up the shop, moaning about the weather. Y'know the sort . . . all the time in the world.'

The words must have hit home. She clamped her hand to her mouth, a look of what Sarah interpreted as absolute terror on her face. Maybe she had an image in her mind's eye of Evie being wheeled away by a stranger, some sort of monster. Her face froze, her slight frame shook, and in between heaving sobs, her rasping voice broke through in utter conviction and deepest despair.

'They'll kill her, won't they? They'll kill her. I'm never going to see my little girl again.'

Evie was screaming, her tiny face red and shiny with furious tears. The kidnapper didn't realize the baby was hungry. Would lifting her out of the pushchair, giving her a cuddle, stop the crying? The racket was getting on the kidnapper's nerves. Hush there hush. The screaming stopped, but only for a second or two, then returned louder than before. Ear-piercing, it was doing the kidnapper's head in. Shut up, for God's sake. The kidnapper pulled Evie closer, tightened the embrace, then walked slowly away.

TWO

When a child goes missing every minute's precious; when a baby's snatched each second counts. Police treat both incidents as major crimes from the get-go even if there's ground for doubt and an innocent explanation emerges. Toddlers can occasionally wander off for a short heart-stopping while then turn up unharmed. But statistics show that a child taken by a predatory paedophile dies within three to six hours. There was no evidence either way yet, but Evie Lowe had gone nowhere without a helping hand.

Which was why less than an hour after the alert was raised Operation Bluebird had been launched: more than sixty officers – uniformed and detectives – were in or on the way to Small Heath; the newsagent's in Prospect Road was now a designated crime scene and Sarah Quinn was at her neat-ish desk in Lloyd House tetchily twiddling her thumbs. She'd been called back to police headquarters to address a hastily-arranged news conference. Detective Chief Superintendent Fred Baker had wanted the media on board immediately. Not surprising. Given the family's circumstances, a ransom demand wasn't likely. Whoever had taken Evie wasn't after cash. It made the abduction more sinister; the need to catch the perp more pressing. As senior investigating officer, Baker would get top billing. Sarah had no problem with that. So long as he didn't faff around as per, and she could return to the action.

Fanning her face with loose papers, she ticked mental boxes, running through the well-established police procedures that she knew were kicking in across the city: a mobile major incident unit was in the process of being set up on site, officers carrying copies of the baby's photograph were flooding the streets, a specialist search team was combing – initially, at least – the immediate area. Behind the scenes scores of checks were being made: sex offender registers, hospital maternity units, CCTV footage. Operational overkill was acceptable – if it saved a child's life. Better safe . . .

Sarah blew out her cheeks, couldn't get Evie's image out

of her head. Or that the young mother's histrionics had wasted
a fair number of those priceless early moments. She'd asked
Huntie to drive Karen Lowe home, stay with the girl until a
family liaison officer arrived. Hopefully, he'd elicit more information. Either way, calling in at the Small Heath bedsit topped
Sarah's list of priorities. Assuming she ever got out of this
place. She glanced at her watch, where the hell was the chief?
Baker was a difficult bloke to get a handle on. He could be a
lazy sexist sod, and definitely was coasting to early retirement
and a fat pension. Why she had the occasional soft spot for
him, God only knew. Maybe because he didn't pay lip service
to all the isms? What you saw was usually what you got? A
decent-looking bloke in a fat suit? More likely because he
wasn't a bad detective. When he put his extraordinarily devious
mind to it. And he'd have to. Baby snatching was still rare
but thanks to the occasional high-profile case, the critical eyes
of both the media and the man and woman in the street would
be on how the police handled it. Baker was nobody's mug
which was why he'd wanted a full briefing from Sarah before
addressing the pack. She'd delivered it five minutes ago, so
what was the old devil playing at?

Impatient, she rolled back the chair, walked to the window
and stuck her head out to catch the breeze. Chance would be
a fine thing. There was just a wall of heat, stale air, exhaust
fumes. Tendrils of hair stuck damply to the back of her neck.
They'd escaped from the customary bun, worn – perhaps
deliberately – to reinforce the ice maiden image. Her hair was
white blonde and almost waist length, though only a select
few at work knew that.

Give the blokes an inch . . .

She jumped a mile when what was most likely a fist
hammered at the door. 'Come on, Quinn. Get your ass in gear.'

That would be the chief, then. Made Gene Hunt look like
a new man.

Caroline King was her own boss. Self-employed, freelance,
lone operator, call it what you will, she was a reporter, roving,
but definitely not one of the pack. She wouldn't even want to
lead it. Designer-suited, and tanned shapely legs crossed, she
sat on the front row, dead centre, in a conference room at
police HQ set aside for the press. Her chiselled features and

square jaw line were softened by immaculate make-up and a chin-length glossy raven bob. Part of her confidence came from knowing she looked good. But how was the competition shaping up? Glancing round apparently casually, she took in every detail, reckoned there was no contest.

ITN's Midlands correspondent Phil Birt was sprawled in a seat next to her, she didn't recognize the blonde from Sky (they all looked the same to Caroline). One or two of the local print and radio guys she knew by sight. Around twenty in all. And her film crew summoned from the Mailbox, the BBC's Midlands headquarters, was in pole position. Naturally. It was a decent turnout. No surprise. A baby snatch was potentially big news.

Assuming the kid didn't turn up any time soon. She skim-read her draft script waiting for the conference to kick off.

'Slumming it, are we, Caro?' Phil winked. With those teeth, she'd keep the smiles to a minimum.

'Did you say something?' Like if he had, it wasn't worth hearing.

'Suit yourself.' Shrugging, he turned away but not before she'd seen his jaw tighten.

As for suiting herself, that was a given. Though she had to cede it was pure chance she'd decided to stay on in Birmingham for a few days, not return home to Fulham. She'd been working for the Beeb on an expenses scandal item. The intake editor at TV centre was more than happy when she rang offering to cover the baby story. It had barely hit the wires then, but a journo was only as good as her contacts. Her mouth moved in what could have been a smile. Caroline's sources were the best in the business. She'd had what you might call a head's-up. Just the bare bones; the meat she'd have to sniff out here.

Unlike her colleagues she didn't react when the double doors swung open, nor did she glance across as three or four cops filed towards the front and took seats behind a black table so highly polished their reflections were visible in the wood.

So that's why they're called woodentops. She dropped the smirk, stiffened almost imperceptibly as she registered the female cop in the line-up.

Well, well, well. Sarah Quinn was on the case. Quinn was

no woodentop. She was more ice cap. And she'd just clocked
Caroline. The reporter held the detective's glacial grey-eyed
gaze for a few seconds before glancing ostentatiously at her
nails. To say the women's paths had crossed was like saying
water's wet. They had more history than the Magna Carta.
And none of it good.

Caroline straightened her spine, recrossed her legs and circled
a pointy-toed Jimmy Choo. This may not turn out the doddle
she'd foreseen. On the other hand it looked as if the fat guy
was in charge. The name plate read Detective Chief Superintendent
Fred Baker. His suspiciously black hair was shot through with
white streaks. He put her in mind of a badger. She watched him
rise heavily to his feet and wipe a checked handkerchief over
a visibly damp brow. Feeling the inquiry's heat already?
Probably not. It was too early for that and he looked too experienced. No, he'd be suffering under the real thing, exacerbated
by a stuffy room full of stale bodies and hot air. Even the Ice
Queen looked as if she might melt round the extremities.
Caroline pursed full red lips. Nah. That was wishful thinking.

'Thanks for turning out,' Baker said. 'As some of you'll
have heard, a six-month-old baby was abducted in Small Heath
this afternoon.' He nodded towards the back and a lackey hit
a button. Behind the cops a wide screen now showed a blown-
up photograph of Evie's face. Sweet kid, Caroline thought.

'Evie Lowe was last seen around three forty-five. She was
asleep in a pushchair outside a shop in Prospect Road. There
were lots of people—'

'Seen?' Caroline cocked her head, arch, ingenuous. 'Do you
mean, left?' OK, it was early to take a pop, but what sort of
idiot leaves a kid on its own nowadays? Don't people watch
the news, read the papers?

Baker paused just long enough to cut her a contemptuous
glance. The point had hit home though, and the seed planted
among the other hacks. '. . . in the vicinity at the time.
Shoppers, school children, motorists, cyclists. It's now ninety
minutes since the pushchair with Evie in it was taken. It hardly
needs saying it's imperative we find her, fast.' Another nod to
the lackey at the back, and a second image hit the screen.
'This is the same model and colour.' A red and grey Mamas
and Papas. 'Someone must have seen it either outside the shop,
or being pushed away. We need to get the word out now.'

'How long was it there?' A young reporter asked.

Baker glanced at Sarah. 'Four, five minutes, no more.' Her tone was neutral.

'Five minutes?' Caroline shook her head. 'What leads are you following?'

Baker ignored the question. Either they didn't have any, or he wasn't prepared to divulge them. 'Obviously the priority's to spread the word, to get the baby's picture out there. We need witnesses to come forward.'

If it was that busy why hadn't people come forward already? Could be down to the area, Caroline supposed. It was single mum central out there, pavements chocker with chavs and babies in buggies. Even so . . .

She made a few notes, half listening to questions fired by other journos, questions the cops couldn't or wouldn't answer; they always withheld information, of course, it went with the territory. Like it was hers to dig it out. Baker raised both meaty hands when he'd had enough. 'I can't really add much more at this stage. But we'll be grateful for any publicity, and myself or DI Quinn are happy to do interviews if it'll help.'

Looked as if it was news to Quinn. Caroline stifled a snort of derision. As far as she was concerned there was only one person worth interviewing, one player worth pursuing, and it wasn't fatso or the Ice Queen. 'Where's the baby's mother?'

'Under sedation.' Sarah answered before Baker opened his mouth. 'She won't be—'

'Under sedation where?'

'At home.'

'Where's home?'

'We're not releasing an address at this stage.'

'Where's the father?'

'That information's not for release.'

Caroline was getting the picture. 'How old's the mother?'

'Eighteen? Your point being?'

Few would admit it, but a story involving an absent father and a teenage mother from an inner city back street wouldn't have the same punter appeal, the same sympathy factor, as a baby who'd been taken from a professional couple's home in leafy Edgbaston.

Caroline shrugged. 'You tell me, DI Quinn.'

THREE

Sarah strode along the corridor, headed for the squad room. Baker could barely keep up. She knew what she'd like to tell Caroline King. And it wouldn't be, have a nice day. Off would feature somewhere in the short phrase. The reporter's pointed persistent questioning had distorted the angle of the story, diminished it almost. And she, Sarah, had come off worse in what was little more than a less than subtle slanging match.

'What was that all about, Quinn?' Baker tugged angrily at his tie.

'I don't know what you—'

'The mother's not under sedation, and—'

'I don't want her hounded by rep—'

'Don't give me that crap. You're not talking reporters plural. And there's no percentage antagonizing them all. Whatever bad blood there is between you and that dark-haired hack, it doesn't get in the way of the inquiry. Got that?' Had it been so obvious, then? Maybe she'd not masked her feelings adequately, or the old boy could read her too well. He certainly couldn't know that King was one of the reasons Sarah had transferred from the Met four years ago. She opened her mouth, but Baker hadn't finished. Pausing at the door, maybe to catch his breath, he said, 'We need the media on side. One hundred per cent. Even Ms Smart-arse.' He tapped the side of his nose. 'At least until we find the baby.'

Half a dozen heads turned as Sarah and Baker entered the open-plan office crammed with desks and computers, printers and files. Most squad members were out, in and around Small Heath, but calls still needed making, answering and hopefully acting on. The faces said it all: there wasn't a lot to act on. Even those who didn't have kids looked grim.

'Anything?' Baker asked the nearest DC.

'Nothing concrete, sir.' No witnesses, no pushchair, no forensics, nothing on CCTV.

'What about the woman in the shop?' Sarah asked. The old

dear with all the time in the world, according to Karen. She was a regular customer; Robert White had provided a name. Dora Marple had left the premises before Karen, it was conceivable she'd seen something. 'Have we spoken to her yet?'

'She's out at the moment, ma'am. David Harries slipped a note through the door.'

DC Harries, relatively new to the squad. Sarah nodded. Still uneasy, still unable to shake off the bad feeling. Surely something should have moved by now? A baby can't just be snatched off a busy street in broad daylight. Unless . . .

'What is it, Quinn?'

'I think we should search the mother's house, sir.'

Baker didn't take a lot of convincing. Five minutes later Sarah was in a police motor driving to the girl's council flat in Victoria Terrace. She'd left the chief prepping the evening brief. If her suspicion was right, he could be wasting his time. Tapping the wheel, she muttered something about the traffic, though after her call to Hunt there was no rush, Karen Lowe wouldn't be going anywhere. She'd told him not to let the girl out of his sight. Maybe Sarah should have seen the possibility sooner?

Home was usually the first place police look when a child goes missing. But Evie had been snatched from outside a shop half a mile away. Allegedly. What if the kidnap was an elaborate hoax on Karen's part? A desperate bid to divert police attention from the truth. The histrionics had seemed over-the-top to Sarah. But if Karen Lowe had harmed her child, it could have been a fit of remorse. Either way she had questions to answer. According to Huntie, she'd refused to allow a family liaison officer into the house and was still refusing to name the baby's father. They could only hope that with the exposure the story was already getting, the guy would do the decent thing and come forward anyway.

She sniffed. Yes. And pigs might fly jumbos.

The block was squat and square, the grimy grey façade broken up by rusting iron railings and peeling balconies. Lines of limp washing hung in the available air space, splashes of colour were provided here and there by children's bikes, pedal cars, beach balls. Sarah gave a wry smile. Birmingham was as far from the sea as it gets. The search team's transit van was parked in a side road, two white-suited officers perched on the bonnet waiting for her.

The team leader approached as she locked the motor. 'Give me five, Ben. I need a word with her first.' Tact and diplomacy, Baker had counselled, kid gloves and pulled punches. Like she'd barge in and ask Karen where she'd buried the body. Broaching it either way wouldn't be easy, but that's what she was paid for.

The stairwell stank of lavender air freshener laced with urine and smoke, not all of it from cigarettes. Sarah hadn't used cannabis since her student days, still missed it occasionally. She bounded up the first flight two stairs at a time, the exercise wouldn't hurt and she couldn't remember the last time she'd hit the gym.

'Are you sure about this, boss?' Huntie was waiting at the door, he'd probably been at the window looking out for her. 'The girl's on a knife edge as it is.'

'Can't say I care much where *she* is, sergeant.' The corollary was tacit. He'd know it was Evie's whereabouts that were giving her grief. His eyes darkened for a second, but he stepped aside to let her pass. 'You know best, ma'am.' The 'ma'am' spoke volumes. 'I'll be in the kitchen if you need me. She's asked for a cup of tea.' Tactical withdrawal more like.

The small sitting room was spotless, everything in it pink: carpet, curtains, Dralon suite, half-a-dozen crocheted pink crinoline dolls were lined up on top of a gas fire. It was like stepping into Barbie-land.

Karen, still wearing the sun dress, was slumped in the chair nearest the grate. An ashtray with five butts lay at her feet. She glanced up, curled a lip when she saw who it was. 'What do *you* want?'

Sarah gave a tight smile. 'Same as you, I expect.' She perched on the settee, waited to see if Karen would take the cue. A clock ticked six, seven seconds. Mingled smells of toast and talcum powder lingered in the air.

Karen gave an exaggerated sigh. 'What's that, then?'

'To find Evie.'

'So what're you doing here? Why aren't you looking . . . ?'

'We are. We search everywhere.' She glanced round the small space. 'Everywhere we think she might be.'

The girl was sharp, sharper than she appeared. Staring at Sarah, she straightened slowly, folded her arms. 'You're not serious? You can't really imagine . . .'

Sarah's face was impassive. She didn't have to imagine – she'd seen it: the crimes people are capable of, the violence they inflict, the bodies beaten beyond recognition often by so-called loved ones. And she'd heard the lies. Being a cop meant trusting no one, taking nothing at face value, suspecting your own granny if need be.

'You're sick, you are.' The girl sneered. 'God, I'm glad I don't have your job.'

Sticks, stones. It was nothing she hadn't heard before. 'What job do you have, Karen?'

She narrowed her eyes, muttered what could have been bitch.

'So we'll take a look round if that's OK.'

'Please yourself. It's not like I can stop you.'

Sarah walked to the window, gave the search team a thumb's up. Still with her back to the girl, she asked, 'Where's the father, Karen?'

'Pass.'

'What's his name?'

'Pass.'

Sarah turned, gazed at the girl a while. 'What's your problem, love?'

'What do you think, *love*?'

'I think you have a bad attitude. You're doing yourself no favours. I'm not here to give you a hard time. That job you're so glad not to have? Right now, it's trying to find your baby. Why not help me out here?'

'This I will tell you.' Her hand shook as she reached for an Embassy and had trouble lighting it. 'I'd rather top myself than harm a hair on Evie's head. She means more to me than anyone in the world. Not that you'd understand. But the sooner you take that on board, the sooner you can get on and do your sodding job properly.'

FOUR

'I still think it needed doing.' Sarah sat across the desk from Baker. The wall behind him was covered in framed photographs; the boss posing with bigwigs in fancy costumes like the chief constable and the Lord Mayor. The one with the Queen was pretty prominent. You'd have to be blind to miss it. She tore her gaze away. He still hadn't responded. 'Are you with me, or what?'

The search team had just phoned in with the results from Karen's flat: nothing to suggest foul play. But two detectives were still questioning other residents at the block, finding out what if anything they knew about Karen, whether they'd heard rows, a baby crying, if they'd seen visitors, especially boyfriends.

Baker took a few swigs from a bottle of water. 'We're not getting fixated on the girl are we, Quinn?' It wasn't the royal we, he meant Sarah.

She wasn't prepared to grace the comment with a reply. It wasn't a question of obsession, though she did feel there was something odd about Karen, something she couldn't pin down. The girl certainly didn't seem big on people skills; she was apparently estranged from her own mother. At least she'd finally come round to the idea of having a family liaison officer stay at the flat. Jess Parry would be an extra pair of eyes and ears for the police, as well as providing emotional and psychological support for the girl.

The silent treatment had worked. Baker lobbed the bottle into a bin, leaned across the desk. 'Look, if I hadn't agreed, I wouldn't have given it the nod. It was a good call. You're a good cop. Christ, woman, what's wrong? You don't need me to tell you that.' She didn't much care for his intent gaze. 'Not losing that famous cool, are you, Quinn?'

Unblinking, she held the gaze in silence. One of these days she'd count the number of unanswerable remarks he came out with in these sessions. Again, he got the message. 'Come on.'

He scraped back the chair, grabbed his jacket, slung it over a shoulder. 'It's show time.'

The first brief in any major inquiry is vital. It sets the tone, defines the parameters, energizes and inspires officers. More than that it initiates early actions and assigns tasks to the detectives best equipped to deliver the goods. Make a bad decision, take a wrong turn – and the inquiry goes down a blind alley. Or a dead end. And it's only as good as the man or woman holding the floor. No pressure there, then.

Sarah had observed Baker in action scores of times before, of course. But right now he seemed sharper, more focused; he'd cut the customary banter and one-liners that were part of his style, designed to put officers at ease, dilute the tension. The boss's new sobriety could be down to the image dominating the whiteboard behind him of course.

Evie's one-toothed smile and gorgeous blue eyes stared – it seemed – at every man and woman in the room. Everyone of whom should be acutely aware that at 7.06 p.m., it was more than three hours since she'd been seen in the flesh by anyone but her abductor.

Millions of viewers had seen the baby's photograph by now. It had aired on all the major news channels, stories were running on the web, the front pages of the late editions had lead with it. Ditto, radio stations. Word was out, but no quality intelligence had come in. Six so-called sightings had been reported, none checked out. Hopes of an early breakthrough were fading fast.

Fears were heightened further because as the boss had said, they still didn't know what – and more precisely, who – they were dealing with. He'd virtually ruled out kidnap for ransom. Karen Lowe hadn't got two euros to rub together. It left a multitude of sins. Up there with the worst was that Evie was in the hands of a paedophile or that she'd been stolen to order. A childless couple, a beautiful baby, an unscrupulous broker. It happened. Not so far in the UK, but . . . Sarah shuddered. Dear God, give us a break here.

Sitting straight-backed behind a desk at the front, she glanced round at colleagues and not so familiar faces. Thirty officers had been drafted in from across the city's ten local policing units, making a total operation-force of around a hundred. Most were out knocking doors, canvassing passers-by, questioning drivers, but twenty-two detectives were currently hanging on Baker's every word. The shaft of sunlight pouring through a picture window added unnecessary drama. The atmosphere was emotionally supercharged already.

Sarah studied the main players, the squad members she'd work with most closely, those whose qualities differed from her own. The touchy-feely Hunt was still holding Karen Lowe's hand, of course, pending the FLO's arrival. DC David Harries was on the front row as usual. The young constable's nickname was the Boy Wonder. She'd taken him increasingly under her wing recently. Nothing to do with his dark good looks, though he was certainly easy on the eye; it was his empathy she admired, the ability to connect with complete strangers in potentially threatening situations. What she called verbal disarmament. Seated alongside was DC Shona Bruce. The tall redhead had an amazing ability to persuade witnesses, victims, even crims to open up; Shona was worth her not inconsiderable weight in gold in the interview room. Sarah reckoned the Bruce voice could tempt a Trappist to talk. Baker still was.

'We don't know where she is. We don't know who's holding her. So what we need to establish fast is, why?' In Sarah's book as well as Baker's crime always came down to motive. Except when they were dealing with madness. 'What we need to ask,' Baker said, 'is, was the abductor after any baby or Evie Lowe specifically?'

Frowning, DC Harries raised a tentative hand. 'I thought you'd ruled it out, guv? Evie being taken for ransom?'

'Keep up, lad.' Baker shook an impatient head. 'Doesn't always come down to cash. There's any number of reasons she could have been targeted.'

Sarah's list of possibles on the notepad in front of her made demanding money look like a benevolent act.

'Least worse scenario's the mother's pissed somebody off big time.' Baker motioned to one of the team for water from the cooler. 'They've taken the baby to scare the pants off her, teach her a lesson. Then they give the kid back. She on drugs, Quinn?'

Sarah shook her head. 'No sign of it.' She'd considered it briefly: a dealer with a warped mind exacting revenge.

'Maybe she dissed some buddy on Facebook.' Baker showed off what he thought was his street cred.

'Yeah right.' The sotto voce sneer came from one of the new officers. He'd yet to learn Baker's hearing was sharper than a bat colony.

'Well, let's hope so, sunshine. Cause if it is the case, Karen'll maybe have an idea who.' Hunt had already mooted the possibility to the girl that she might know the kidnapper; she'd dismissed it but as the hours passed, she'd be questioned more closely. 'If we're talking a complete stranger, a random snatch . . .' Baker sank both hands in his pockets, turned his mouth down. No one needed telling: it made a difficult job nigh on impossible until – make that unless – the perp made a mistake.

'It'll be some woman who's lost a kid, won't it?' The drawled assertion was made by Dean Lavery, a DC who was going nowhere. Lazy, been there, done that, Sarah wouldn't give him house room let alone a place in CID. The cynical assumption was off beam and no good to anyone. Cases of grieving mothers stealing replacement babies were rare and invariably involved newborns taken from hospitals. If Evie was a case in point, she'd be the first snatched from the street. The possibility couldn't be ignored, however slim, the line still had to be followed, but not as a foregone conclusion. A couple of DCs were running checks now in the squad room along the corridor.

'If you're so sure, Lavery, you can go give Jenny and Kim a hand.'

He dropped the slouch. 'But, guv . . .'

Baker jabbed a thumb at the door. 'Starting now.' Sarah caught the glower on the detective's face as he turned, doubtless it deepened as he headed out with Baker's words ringing in everyone's ears. 'No one assumes anything, right? Anyone with a closed mind, go join the priesthood. And what's on yours, Harries?'

Sarah masked a smile when the DC jumped, startled. But with furrowed brow and hand stroking chin, it hadn't taken a detective to work out he'd been deep in thought.

'What if it's down to kids, guv?' No one who'd seen the video footage of two-year-old James Bulger being led away by his killers Robert Venables and Mark Thompson would ever forget it. The image was certainly imprinted on every cop's brain. Birmingham had its share of feral youths from dysfunctional families, kids for whom juvenile court was a second home, but stealing a baby was a hell of a stretch from shoplifting or nicking cars.

'I hope to God it's not, lad. But we rule nothing out.'

They didn't have the moment – seconds more like – of Evie's abduction on CCTV. Unlike the shopping centre from where James was taken, Robert White's newsagent's had no security cameras. Uniformed officers had collected tapes from neighbouring premises and requests had been made for footage from cameras along all possible routes the kidnapper might have taken. Every man, woman – or youth – captured on tape with a pushchair any time around 3.45 was a suspect until traced and eliminated.

The brief continued for another thirty minutes. More theories were thrashed out, more tasks assigned, duties delegated. Paul Wood would be appointed office manager for the duration, experienced and an eye for detail, the sergeant was respected and well-liked. Not always a combination.

If nothing broke overnight, Baker said, the search grid would be extended at first light, posters of the missing baby would start going up across the city. Chairs were scraped back, files tucked under arms. Baker raised a staying hand. 'One more thing. We're going to need the media on board like never before. It goes against the grain, I know, but it's how we'll keep Evie's image out there. Not just this evening, tomorrow morning, but for . . . however long it takes. As deputy SIO, DI Quinn will take twice daily news conferences either here or at the incident unit in Small Heath. Ring the changes, eh?'

Wring his neck more like. Sarah opened her mouth, but Baker was still in wrap-up mode. 'I've got a good team here.' He ran his gaze over every officer. 'The best. Let's get an early result. She's out there somewhere. Let's find her, bring her home.'

Five minutes later, Sarah was alone in the room. She stood looking out through the window. Despite Baker's rousing words, she still wrestled with uneasy thoughts. What was it with her? Had Caroline King's presence earlier stirred a bunch of emotions she thought were buried deep? Or was it the continuing and surprising absence of a baby with a beguiling smile?

She glanced up at the sky. Divine intervention? No. She'd seen the evil people can do and that no god would allow. For the first time in what seemed weeks, there was a cloud in the sky. Small, white, wispy and were she given to flights of fancy, she'd describe it as shaped like a baby's hand.

Evie screwed her tiny fists into tight balls, damp hair was matted to her scalp, a pulse clearly visible in her neck as she arched her back and screamed. The abductor darted anxious glances round the room, dashed to the television and hiked the volume to drown out the baby's sound. She'd had milk, for Christ's sake, what more could she want? If she didn't look out, there'd be no more cuddles, no more sweet talk. Couldn't afford neighbours hearing a baby cry. Not with all the stuff on the news. There it was again. The baby's picture full screen, the newsreader telling everyone to look out for her. Eyes narrowed, the abductor approached the TV set and hit the off button. The picture faded to black. The abductor turned and walked back to the crying baby.

FIVE

L ying on her king-sized bed in the Marriott hotel, Caroline hit the remote to switch stations. Her piece had just gone out on the ten o'clock news. She'd have a quick look at ITN, seriously doubted they'd be carrying anything she didn't already know. Raising a glass, she toasted her performance with the remnants of a gin and tonic. 'Another day, another dollar, sweetie.' Her ironic smile faded as she sucked the lemon between her perfect white teeth. And it was nothing to do with the sour taste in her mouth. It was the thought of Sarah Quinn's arrogant intransigence. And given the bloody woman had blocked official channels, it was going to take a damn sight more than a buck to get to the baby's mother.

Eyes narrowed she pictured the Ice Queen, the cool grey eyes, impossibly blonde hair in that ridiculous bun, the severe charcoal trouser suit that on anyone else would look masculine if not butch. Caroline snorted. My God. The woman hadn't always been so bloody strait-laced. Pensive, the reporter swung her legs over the side of the bed, drifted to the minibar. Buttonholing Quinn after the news conference had been a waste of time. Caroline had asked a few questions on camera, the answers being so bland they were hardly worth using. Then she'd pushed the inspector for access to Karen Lowe. Quinn had stonewalled better than Hadrian, assuming the guy used stone. Caroline curled a lip; he could've used reinforced concrete for all she cared. What did concern her was that Quinn wouldn't even come up with a pic of the mother, let alone the means to a little chat. Well we'll see about that. She poured a second large G and T, carried it back to the bed. Her phone lay on the pillow. The number was on speed-dial.

'Caro, here. Can you talk?'

Of course he could.

'I know I shouldn't let it get to me.' Sarah nursed a dry white wine. It was gone 11 p.m., she was at home trying to relax. The Brindley Place apartment was off Broad Street, surrounded by crowded pubs, wine bars and still busy restaurants. The apartment was functional, unfussy; décor white, furnishings ivory. Through floor to ceiling windows, multicoloured lights reflected on the dark waters of the canal. Not that Sarah was admiring the view, she'd been on the phone for nearly half an hour. 'I'm just surprised it didn't get more air time, Adam.'

The abduction had made the late news, but it wasn't the lead item. Evie's picture had appeared, true, but to Sarah's mind, it had been given less screen time than Caroline King's piece to camera. As for the shots of a visibly self-important Robert White claiming he'd done everything in his power to calm the mother down . . . What earthly purpose did they serve?

'The baby could be anywhere by now, Adam. God forbid she could even be dead. And the main channel virtually ignores the story.' She sat back on the leather settee, bare feet curled under.

'Come on, Sarah. I saw it. Have to say, I thought it was a decent piece.'

The power of the press, or a pretty face. Grudgingly, she admitted to herself the coverage probably could have been worse. King was a sharp operator, had a convincing authority on camera. People actually believed her. Adam's voice was teasing but tender. She heard a smile in it, too. He could probably recognize the tension in hers, he'd be concerned. He was close enough to know it wasn't like her to be so down at such an early stage in an inquiry.

'I wish I was with you, Sarah.' She glanced at his picture on top of the bookcase: he reminded her of Che Guevara in the poster everyone had on their wall at uni. Except she couldn't imagine him leading even a student revolt.

'Yeah, me too.' The lie came easily. Adam would be a distraction she couldn't afford. He'd be going around taking her jacket from the back of the chair, tidying her shoes, straightening papers, plumping cushions. He didn't mind clearing away after her. She pretended she didn't mind him doing it. But the fussing irritated her. He knew it. But had no idea how much. It was one of the reasons they didn't live together. Adam's law firm was in Oxford, she always resisted the suggestion he commute. They joked about it to the few friends who still asked why. As in: some couples have his n' her towels, we have his n' her homes. It worked after a fashion.

'I have to go now, Adam. Need to call in, see if anything's broken.'

'Sure thing lady, take it ease . . .' Frowning, Adam stared at the receiver. Sarah had already ended the call. He gave a deep sigh. She'd looked tired on TV, the beginnings of shadows under her eyes, the light mauve shade would deepen if she didn't look after herself. And she wouldn't.

He'd heard faint noises off during the call, the clink of a glass, cutlery on a plate that meant she was still picking at supper. Or maybe it was lunch, or dinner, tomorrow's breakfast even. Work was her priority, eating didn't come close. She was committed to a job most people wouldn't even consider. And with her analytical, questioning mind, the ability to keep out emotion – she was damn good at it.

It was one of the reasons he loved her, and one of the reasons, sometimes, he did not. But even when he doubted he even liked her any more, he always wanted her. She wasn't the most beautiful woman he'd been in love with, but she was the only woman he never tired of. Just as he thought he knew her, she'd do something unpredictable and he had to think again. He was convinced he'd never meet anyone who meant so much, most of the time.

As for living together? He told himself it was no big deal, they were happy as they were. Maybe if children came along . . .

The storm broke in the night. Thunder woke Sarah, or maybe it was the rain pounding the windows. Had she left one open? She rose to check, stayed to watch the forked lightning streak across a velvet blue-black sky. Flash after brilliant flash, lighting up the night, reflecting in the ribbon of the canal, accompanied by the deep rumble of distant sound effects. Invigorating. Awesome. Intoxicating. Storms hadn't frightened her since she was a . . .

Briefly she closed her eyes. Evie's image was still in her mind. Did babies get scared of thunder, the dark? Was a little girl with big blue eyes out there now? Cold, wet, crying, hungry? Had some sick bastard taken her for kicks? Too crazy to know what they'd done and mad enough not to care? Or was Evie even now on the way to a new life with a new family? The police had issued alerts at all ports and airports, but if someone was despicable and desperate enough?

Raindrops ran into each other, raced down the glass. Sarah leant forward slightly, pressed her forehead against the cool surface, and whispered softly, 'Oh Evie. Baby Evie where are you?'

They found the pushchair first. A newspaper boy rang one of the police hotlines. Him and his mate had seen it on the Blake Street waste ground late yesterday afternoon. Hadn't thought anything of it then. But it was still there when they met for a ciggie first thing before they started their rounds. They'd seen on the news about the baby and all that, reckoned there might be a reward or something. A local patrol car was pointed in their direction and the lads led the driver to the spot. The pushchair lay on its side in the mud, rain still falling and pooling in the fabric.

SIX

'The pushchair's come to light then? It doesn't look too good, does it?' No preamble, no intro needed.

It was a phone call, though Sarah Quinn was barely aware she'd picked up the handset. She'd reached for it on autopilot from the depths of a troubled and too short sleep. Bed long gone midnight on a too large Armagnac was with hindsight not the answer to any problem. And certainly not Evie's abduction. Thoughts of the baby had kept her awake and were now forcing her alert. She glanced at the clock: 7.20. Jesus H. And bolted upright. She couldn't remember the last time she'd overslept. Sitting on the edge of the bed, she was growing wary as fast as she was becoming aware.

'Who is this?' She knew, of course. Was playing for time already lost.

'I haven't woken you, have I?'

'Don't be ridiculous.' She tried not to snap. The effort failed.

'I have, haven't I?' Caroline King didn't even attempt to hide the amusement in her snide tone.

Sarah took a deep breath, aimed at calming her rising fury. How the hell did the reporter get her number? More important, what was she talking about?

'You haven't got a clue what I'm talking about, have you?' The voice had a harsh edge now, contempt there, too. 'I thought you were *supposed* to be one of the senior officers on the abduction inquiry?'

Sarah shook her head hoping it would clear any lingering fog. There'd obviously been a development in the case and as deputy SIO she should have been informed. She'd be damned if she'd admit her ignorance to King.

'I'm making no comment now. Obviously, I'll issue a press statement later.'

'Better hope it won't be too late, eh *inspector*?' King hung up, leaving Sarah no opportunity to offer an explanation that even if she had, she wouldn't have given.

*   *   *

'What the hell's going on?'

The door slammed against the wall as Sarah, hair still damp from the quickest shower she'd ever taken, strode into a near empty incident room. It was fourteen minutes since the unwanted alarm call from King.

'Morning, inspector.' DC Dean Lavery glanced up from a monitor. 'I wondered when you'd get in. It doesn't look too good, does it?'

Lavery had unwittingly echoed Caroline King's opening line and – just for a second – Sarah thought he was being insolent.

'What did you say?' Her voice was quiet, each word chipped from ice.

Lavery raised both hands. 'Not you, I mean the pushchair, you know?'

Sarah dumped her briefcase on a desk. 'No. I don't know.' She picked up a sheaf of overnight reports, ran her gaze down the first page. 'But if you're saying what I think you're saying . . .'

Lavery clearly believed that when on thin ice you stand still. He didn't bat an eyelid. Not even when the door opened aided by the generous backside of DS Paul Wood. 'Morning, ma'am. Can I get you a coffee?' Wood's podgy fingers were clasped round two steaming mugs, perched precariously on top of one was a bacon sandwich.

'No. You can't. You can tell me why I wasn't informed about this.' She waved a sheet of A4.

Wood glanced at Lavery whose face gave nothing away.

'I thought . . .'

'I don't care what you thought, sergeant. I want you to tell me what you know. I want you to tell me where it was found, when it was found and who found it. And then I want you to tell me why the first I hear of it is when a bloody reporter rings me at home.'

A patchy pink flush was rising up Wood's bull neck. 'I asked someone to call you while I organized forensics and a lift for the kids.'

'Kids?' She raised an eyebrow.

'The kids who found it.' He ran his fingers through a thatch of dirty blond hair. 'Shit, ma'am, I'm real sorry.'

Her hand brushed his apologies aside. 'These kids, sergeant?'

'Right.' He offloaded the mugs and plate on a desk. 'A couple of paper boys. They live on the Paradise estate, do their rounds there. Irony is they saw it first yesterday afternoon. Didn't think anything of it. Well, they wouldn't, would they? Y'know what that waste land off Blake Street's like.'

'No, I don't. But I'll tell you what I think's ironic, and it's not a couple of kids failing to recognize the significance of an abandoned pushchair, a pushchair found in an area we were supposed to have searched. No, the irony's that I find out about it from a journalist.'

'I can't see how the press knows. We were waiting for you to get back from the mother's place, before releasing it. Didn't want her to hear it on the news first, like.'

Like? No, she didn't. She couldn't believe what he'd said. 'How does that work when I didn't even know myself?'

Wood glanced at the younger man. 'Dean?' And passed the buck-shaped baton.

Lavery frowned. 'I thought you rang her, ages ago.' Meaning Sarah.

'Fuck's sake, lad. I told you to.'

'No, sarge . . .'

'Shut up both of you.' Miscommunication? Right hand unaware of the left? Yes, both and it boiled down to a cock-up. 'Outside, Dean.' She spoke calmly to the young detective, her gaze fixed on Wood. She liked the big man. They'd worked together a lot. She knew Woodie was one of the blokes who thought she did a decent job. She expected the same from him. Ordinarily he delivered. This time he hadn't.

'You were the senior officer here. It was up to you to phone me. If that wasn't possible – and I see no reason why – you should have checked it had been done. And then checked again. This is slack, sergeant. And it had better not happen again. Do I make myself clear?'

'But, ma'am . . .'

'Do I make myself clear?'

'Absolutely.'

'We're now in a situation where a reporter knows the pushchair's been found and the mother's still in the dark.'

'Want me to . . . ?

She shook her head. 'I'll go. I take it Jess Parry's there?' Family liaison officer.

'Yes, ma'am.'

'Tell Baker where I'll be, OK?' Sarah picked up the brief-case and was at the door when she paused, frowning. 'How come everyone was so sure it was Evie's pushchair?'

'Her sun hat was in it. And the cardi with the pink stripes.'

She nodded, tight-lipped. As she turned her glance took in the sergeant's forgotten breakfast. The coffee would be stone cold. And the bacon fat was congealed like candle wax round the edge of the plate.

SEVEN

S arah could see at once what Paul Wood meant. The waste ground off Blake Street was used as a communal dump. The scrubby land was littered with detritus: two rusting bikes, a couple of supermarket trolleys, TV with a smashed screen, crushed drink cans lay everywhere. A row of black bin liners – mostly split – threw out a rank stench along with their foul contents. The rain had eased off now, but puddles of dirty water rippled across a surface scarred by potholes.

Two white-suited forensics officers were on the far side crouched around the pushchair, police tape cordoned off the activity. One of the guys raised a gloved hand in greeting. She nodded, but stayed where she was at the edge of the site. It was less than half a mile from Evie's home and not much further from where she was snatched.

One of the uniforms had told Sarah that a row of Victorian two-up-two-downs had stood here until a few months back. It stirred not particularly welcome memories. She'd been born in one not dissimilar in Hackney. The terrace would have housed scores of families over the years. Babies would have been born here, men and women lived here, loved and fought and laughed here. A few would have died here – peaceful deaths in their own bed. Now only ghosts remained.

And her presence wasn't needed. Detectives had already been tasked with house-to-house inquiries, other officers were on standby to conduct a fingertip search of the sodden ground as soon as it was given the forensics all clear. A search of the surrounding area was already under way. It was a large-scale operation, as well as more housing, there were small business premises, lock-up garages, a café, hairdressers. All were within sight of the park – and the canal. Divers had been called in an hour or so back.

Still Sarah lingered, needing to spend time here, to see for herself where the abductor had been. Here among the rubble and rotting rubbish, a man or woman had held Evie. Here, where scraps of wallpaper with faded pink roses still clung to a few jagged bricks, a man or woman had dumped the pushchair and walked away with Karen Lowe's baby. In her mind's eye, she saw a shadowy figure lifting out the child, perhaps hugging the tiny body close, whispering a few soothing words, then . . . what? Where did they go, what did they do?

She tightened the belt on her black trench coat, sank hands deep into the pockets. She wasn't fanciful enough to think the site would give away its secrets. She just wanted to be there, to stand in the same place, to get a feeling of something she couldn't even put into words.

She felt a profound pity. For Evie Lowe, surely. And, perhaps, for the unknown lives of the unseen families whose homes were now reduced to scattered bits of rubble and dust. Is this what it all comes to? Sarah, come on. She shrugged off the maudlin thoughts. Wondered what was the matter with her?

'Have they found her then, love?' An old woman in a purple mac and plastic rain hat stood at Sarah's shoulder, her narrowed gaze focused on the forensic team, obviously unaware she was talking to a cop.

'No, not yet.' Sarah wasn't going to enlighten her.

She sniffed loudly. 'I've told my daughter not to let her kids out a' sight till they catch the bugger. Not that she would. Well, you don't, do you? Asking for trouble, wasn't she, the mother?'

Interest piqued, Sarah turned. 'Do you know the mother?' The woman's skin was like deeply lined newspaper left in the sun. The jaw movement suggested dentures that didn't fit.

'Nah. Stands to reason though. What sort of mum . . . ?'

'I have to go, excuse me.' Even if one of the FSI guys wasn't heading over, she couldn't be doing with ignorant tittle-tattle. Walking to meet him though, she reckoned if the old

woman's thoughts were typical, that the viewing public had
already made up its mind about Karen Lowe's parenting skills.
So much for the news coverage Baker was keen to encourage.
And Caroline King happy to slant.

Closer now she recognized the lean good looks of FSI lead
manager, Ben Cooper. 'How's it going, Ben?'

'Done as much as we can here.' He swept a heavy straw-
coloured fringe out of chestnut eyes. 'Seems clean, but we'll
take a closer look back at the lab. Mind the rain won't have
helped.' She hid her disappointment but wasn't entirely
surprised. 'I'll give you a bell if anything turns up, inspector.'

'Appreciate it, thanks.' Head down she made her way back
to the car. The heavy downpour overnight would likely have
washed away any liftable trace evidence. Assuming any had
been left. She had her doubts. Given it was now eighteen hours
since the baby had been seen last, the abductor was either in
luck or knew enough to leave nothing to chance. Either way,
they were still desperate for a lead.

Family liaison officer Jess Parry opened the door at Karen's
first-floor flat. Pretty and trim, with sleek chin-length auburn
hair, she looked a fair bit younger than mid-forties. Her smile
was the first Sarah could recall seeing since the inquiry began.

'How goes it, inspector. Any . . . ?'

'Where's Karen?'

'In the sitting room. Why?' Smile faded, Jess placed a hand
on the side of her face; her anxious gaze searched Sarah's.

Voice lowered, she told her they'd found the pushchair and
some of Evie's clothes but there was still no sign of the baby.
Jess shook her head, folded her arms. 'God knows what that'll
do to Karen.'

'How is she?'

'Quiet. She talked about Evie for hours last night. She's
saying very little about anything right now. Mind, she must
be shattered. I couldn't get her to go to bed, so we sat up most
of the night, chatting, drinking tea.'

Typical Jess, Sarah thought. She'd served with the police
fifteen years, FLO for eight. She was in a career where cynicism
ruled and cutting remarks often mistaken for sharp intellect.
Jess had never bought into the culture, but was more than capable
of holding her own in the riposte stakes. Sarah envied what she

knew of the woman's life away from the job where she must
have to work just as hard to keep her marriage happy and three
kids content. Unlike a lot of cops, Jess acknowledged people
had feelings and fears and was smart enough to tap into them.

'Do you want me to tell her, inspector?'

'Thanks, but I'll do it.' She followed Jess into the small hall.

'Who is it, Jess?' Karen's voice carried through from the
sitting room.

Sarah paused, hand on the door. 'Five minutes. OK, Jess?'

'You?' Karen glanced up as Sarah entered. 'That's all I
need.'

Sarah bit back a response. From what she could see, the
girl needed a shower and a change of clothes, she needed to
quit smoking, sharpen her act and drop the slack attitude.
Apart from that . . .

'How're you feeling this morning, Karen?'

'How'd you think?' Sarah was beginning to think the girl's
sulky scowl was a permanent fixture. She let the silence hang
for a while expecting Karen to ask if she'd brought any news.
It was usually the first thing people wanted to know. A cursory
glance took in the rest of the room. Nothing seemed to have
changed since her last visit apart from a couple of photo
albums lying on the carpet. The stack of baby toys still stood,
untouched, against a wall. After an impasse of ten, fifteen
seconds the girl's indifference was needling Sarah. Slumped
in the chair, Karen studied her hands, chewed an already
badly bitten nail. Occasionally her glance darted to a corner
where garish pictures flashed across the TV screen. At least
the sound had been muted.

'Karen.' She cleared her throat. 'I need to tell you
something.'

'No,' she screamed. 'I don't want to hear.'

She took a step closer. 'Karen . . .'

The girl recoiled, clearly terrified. 'You've found her, haven't
you? She's dead, isn't she?'

Not indifference then? Defence mechanism? Denial? 'No,
Karen.' Sarah shook her head, spoke gently. 'We haven't found
Evie, yet. We have found the pushchair though.' Karen stared,
wide eyed. 'Some of her clothes were in it. But we're still
searching for Evie.' She paused, again waiting for Karen to
ask questions: where'd it been found? What clothes were in

it? Could she have them back? The lack of interest seemed strange, but was it suspect?

Sarah knelt to meet the girl's eye-line. 'Karen, is there anything you can think of that might help us? Did you see anyone, anyone at all near the paper shop?' Slow head shake. 'Have you been aware of anyone following you? Anyone acting strangely?'

'I'd've said, wouldn't I?'

Sarah raised a palm. 'Think about it, Karen.'

The girl sighed, closed her eyes, rocked back and forth. It looked to Sarah as if she was going through the motions. The sound of kids playing in the street floated through the open window; the cry of a seagull, a police siren. 'No,' the girl said eventually. 'Nothing. I told you everything yesterday. I went into the shop, there was an old woman there, I came out and Evie was gone.'

Had they spoken to the woman yet? Sarah made a mental note. 'I appreciate this is difficult, Karen, but can you think of anyone who'd want to harm you?'

Another shake of the head. 'The other cop asked already.'

John Hunt. 'And?'

'No one I know'd be that sick.'

'Where's her father?' The sudden change of subject didn't work.

'He's got nothing to do with this. How many times you need telling?'

'If he's got nothing to do with it, give me his name.' He'd have to be interviewed if only for elimination purposes. Sooner the better so they could cross him off the list. Or not.

'I don't know.'

'Oh come on, Karen.' Sarah was losing patience. 'You must know his name.'

'Yeah, maybe.' She reached for a cigarette, scowled when she saw the pack was empty. 'If I knew who he was.'

Was she lying? Or did she sleep around? Both probably. Sarah rose. It wasn't her role to sit in judgement. The priority was finding the baby. She'd ask Jess to probe further, try and get a list of boyfriends.

The news headlines were on TV now, a split screen showing the pushchair and Evie's pic. It had to be worth a try. Sarah narrowed her eyes. 'Karen, do you want to help?'

'Course.'

It was hardly a new idea, a relative making a witness appeal on camera. It wouldn't be what Caroline King had in mind, a weepy interview with moody shots and tacky heart-tugging voice-over. It would be a strictly controlled news conference and Karen would be properly coached. The fact it would cut the ground from under King's feet had nothing to do with it.

Sarah took the nearest seat to the girl, leaned towards her, hands between knees. 'I'll be honest with you, Karen, most criminal investigations rely on witnesses, information from people in the street. Tell you the truth I'm surprised no one's come forward already. We know there were lots of people around yesterday – we need to reach them.'

'Yeah?' The girl straightened, and for the first time met Sarah's gaze. 'And how do you do that?'

'*You* do it, Karen.'

'What d'you mean?'

Jess entered, picked up the vibe, placed a tray on the table and left them to it. 'I'll call a news conference,' Sarah continued. 'Later today would be best. I'll get all the papers and the TV people there and you tell them how much Evie means to you. How much you want her back.'

'No way.' Her hair swung like limp curtains across her face. 'I can't do that.'

'Course you can. Millions of people will see it. Just one phone call could give us the break we need.'

'I can't, I just can't.' What was wrong with the girl? The protest seemed way over the top.

'Why not?'

'I'd be useless.'

It's not about you. Christ, if it was her child, Sarah would do anything to get it back. Feelings hidden by a warm smile, Sarah gently coaxed. 'You'll be great. Don't worry, I'll help. You won't have to answer any questions if you don't want to. I'll write a few words for you to read out. That's all you'd have to do, read a few lines asking people if they have any information that could help. And appealing to whoever's holding Evie to bring her back.'

'Will Jess be there, too?'

'Sure, no worries.'

More dithering, but she finally agreed. 'OK. What do you want me to say?'

Sarah sat back. 'We'll work that out later. When it's set up, I'll send a car to drive you to police headquarters. Would you like your mother there as well?'

'If she's there – forget it.'

Hunt had mentioned something about them being estranged. It seemed a shame. 'I'd have thought you could do with your mother around at a time like this?'

'What would you know?'

Not enough. Not yet anyway. 'No worries. It's your call, Karen.' She pulled her car keys out of a pocket. Better to leave while the going was relatively good. She'd pursue the mother issue later. The girl either didn't hear or ignored the goodbye.

Sarah found Jess in the kitchen, brought her up to speed, said she'd call as soon as the arrangements were made. She was about to let herself out of the flat when the bell rang. To echo Karen's phrase: that's all she needed. What was Caroline King doing here? As if she needed to ask. She presumed the reporter's shock was mirrored in her own expression. This time her recovery was quicker. 'Ms King? What do you want?'

'I'm here to speak to the baby's mother.'

'Out of the question.' Sarah pulled the door to behind her, invaded King's space. The six-inch height difference didn't seem to faze the reporter.

'Perhaps we should ask her?'

'And perhaps we won't. How did you get this address?'

King smiled. 'I'm a reporter, remember. It's my job to find things out.'

'And I'm a senior police officer, and it's my job to protect the vulnerable. I say you're not talking to her. She'll be at a news conference later today at Lloyd House. Until then you won't even ask as much as her name. Is that clear?'

King shrugged. 'What time's the conference?'

'You're the reporter.' She clutched her briefcase under an arm. 'Find out.'

It was childish, a cheap jibe, nothing more than point scoring. Yes. Sarah smiled. But, boy, did it feel good. And she had ground to make up. She resisted the urge to wave as she watched King drive past in a black Mercedes sports. Checking the mirror, she pulled away from the kerb, pointed the motor back to base.

When had the sun come out? She lowered the visor, grabbed her shades. A quick glance at the dashboard clock showed 10.05. The early brief would be history now. If there'd been a major development, someone would have phoned. Yes, right. Recalling her rude awakening, Sarah used the hands-free to check in with the incident room. Woodie supplied a quick rundown: six iffy sightings, three women had reported seeing a 'weirdo' hanging round Small Heath park recently, two men on the sex offenders' register appeared to have gone AWOL. Officers had been tasked, it was all being followed up.

She asked if anyone had spoken to the old woman in the paper shop. Still no joy, there.

'Give me the house number, Paul.' She virtually passed the end of the street, may as well swing by on the way back. She made a quick call to Jess first. Told her the press was sniffing round. Just in case.

EIGHT

Caroline King sat in the parked Mercedes waiting until she saw Quinn's motor pass the end of the road. Difference between an amateur and a pro? Forget giving up after the first hurdle, pros persist after the last ditch. Caroline drove back to the flats, parked in the same spot, touched up the lipstick, smoothed the bob and applied the face that said she cared.

She did. Desperately. To talk to Karen Lowe. The reporter wanted an exclusive interview with the mother, not just a few trite platitudes wheeled out at a free-for-all news conference. Caroline didn't want a foot in the door; she wanted both Louboutins under the table. If she could forge some sort of relationship with Karen Lowe, depending how things panned out, there could even be a book in it. She'd covered a couple of similar stories in her career, but her intuition was telling her there was more in this one, a lot more. And she wanted it all.

It was déjà vu with the doorbell. But this time she heard a woman talking inside. The conversation sounded pretty one-sided, could be on the phone, of course. Caroline pressed her ear to the wood, waited until she heard the right noises then rang again.

The woman hadn't answered the door to put out the welcome mat. 'And you are?' Caroline busked, on the balls of her feet. 'Hello there. I'm Maggie Fearnley? Social Services? I thought I'd drop by see if Karen needs anything.'

In her line of work, Jess Parry knew a lot of social workers. Her cocked eyebrow and pursed lips suggested none looked like this. Caroline thought the Armani suit might be a giveaway. It said catwalk not council worker. Jess asked for ID.

'I'm so glad you asked.' Caroline smiled. 'Not enough people do. Some of us are too trusting these days, aren't we?'

Unsmiling, Jess held out a palm.

'Of course.' She reached into a taupe leather shoulder bag. Frowning, she dug deeper, careful not to over do it. 'I'm sorry. I think it must be in my other bag.'

'Course it is. And I'm the pope's god-daughter.'

'OK, you got me. What do I say now?' She smiled. 'It's a fair cop?'

'That would be particularly stupid, wouldn't it?'

She dropped the pretence. The woman was too hostile to be won round. Probably a cop, then. 'OK, fair dos. I'm not a social worker, I'm a reporter.'

From Sarah's description on the phone, it wasn't hard for Jess to work out who. 'Yes, and you've already been told to clear off once.'

'Come on. I'm only trying to do my job.'

'True. You're trying. I'm doing. And at the moment that means keeping you and your social work friends away from Karen Lowe.'

Caroline's toe was tapping. 'Go and ask what she wants.'

Jess made to close the door.

'Are you refusing to pass on my request for an interview to Miss Lowe?'

'Got it in one.'

'You've no right . . .'

'Miss Lowe will be at a news conference at police

headquarters this afternoon. Until then she's resting. She's got enough on her plate without answering stupid questions'

Caroline was angry now. She wasn't some run-of-the-mill hack, and she didn't ask stupid questions. 'You're the one being stupid. I'm the one who could actually help that girl get her baby back. I'm the one who—'

'Could stop wasting everyone's time.'

It wasn't the first time a door had been slammed in Caroline's face. She doubted it would be the last.

Sarah stepped back from the pristine front door with its shiny brass knocker and looked up at the neat terraced house. Dora Marple was a widow in her early eighties who lived alone. According to Robert White she rarely went out, a daughter did most of the shopping, Dora popped into the newsagent's now and then, more to pass the time of day than anything. So where was she? And where had she been when officers had called before?

Sarah took a business card from her pocket, scribbled a few lines, slipped it through the letterbox. She was almost at the car when something made her turn back. She knelt, opened the letterbox, and looked through the gap. It was the smell that hit her first.

NINE

B lood and human waste have distinctive odours, impossible to describe but absolutely unmistakeable. Sarah registered both even before her glance took in the body. Dora Marple's thin frame lay at an unnatural angle at the foot of the stairs. Blood had poured and pooled from a head wound. The dark almost black colour indicated it was a while since it stopped flowing. How long had the body lain there? More to the point, how had it got there? Eyes wide, Sarah gasped. Was that a trick of the light? She refocused. No. Another barley perceptible twitch.

Grabbing her phone from a jacket pocket she barked instructions while sprinting round to the back of the house. Paramedics would be on the way now, but if she could get in . . . Shielding her eyes from the sun, she gazed up at the property. Windows looked secure, back door was locked.

'Hey, you.' A man with white hair and beard, brandishing a garden fork watched from next door's fence. 'What's your game?'

'Police. I need to get into the house. Now.' Tone of voice, urgent air, whatever. It did the trick.

'I'll get the key. Meet you at the front.'

He was there in less than a minute. 'Here y'go love. Look out for each other me and Dorrie do.' Neighbourhood gnome?

She turned the key, glanced back. 'Thanks, Mr . . . ?'

'Trent. Stanley.'

'I'll manage now. Can you keep an eye out for the ambulance?'

The smell inside made her gag. The fact it could be a crime scene and she could be compromising evidence was secondary in her thinking, saving life came first.

Breathing through her mouth, she approached Dora, simultaneously darting glances round the hall. No obvious signs of a struggle, no handy blunt instrument, it was conceivable the old woman had fallen on the stairs, hit her head on the way down. Conceivable. And highly coincidental.

The left arm was broken, bone protruded through the skin. X-rays could reveal more fractures. No way could Sarah risk moving her, but she could at least talk to her. Squatting at her side, she brought her face close to the old woman's. 'Mrs Marple? Can you hear me?'

Brittle beige eyelids fluttered, the faintest puff of breath escaped through sepia lips. 'Help's on the way, Dora. Hang on in there, sweetheart. We'll soon have you taken care of.' Sarah stroked the woman's hand half afraid of snapping its small twig-like fingers.

'I . . . I . . .'

'What? You, what?' Sarah had to stop herself shouting. 'Talk to me, Dora?'

'I . . .' She rolled her head to the side.

Don't stop now for God's sake. 'Dora. Dora. Can you tell me what happened here?'

'Back off. Can't you see she's in a bad way?' Trent, the neighbour, had appeared in the hall.

She brushed him away with an impatient hand. 'Dora, listen, I'm a police—'

'Leave her alone for pity's sake.'

Sarah glared. 'Look, Mr Trent. She may have been attacked, she might have vital information . . .'

'Carry on like that, lass, and if she was attacked you'll finish off what the bugger started.'

She opened her mouth to remonstrate, but held back. Maybe he was right. However Dora Marple had ended up this way, she looked as if she was at death's door. Sarah had no wish to open it.

It was academic anyway: a couple of paramedics in green scrubs had appeared behind Trent. Sarah made a couple more phone calls as they worked. A crime scene team arrived as Dora was being stretchered to the ambulance.

'So, did she fall or was she pushed?' was Baker's line after Sarah brought him up to speed. It was neither original nor amusing. Perched on the window sill in his office, she rolled her eyes while ceding it was a key point. The bigger question was this: if pushed was it because she'd witnessed Evie's abduction and could supply a description of the abductor?

'Strikes me as a coincidence too far,' Sarah said.

He turned his mouth down, gave a one-shouldered shrug. 'How would they know where she lives?'

'Kidnapper could be local as well?' The upward inflection conveyed doubt. Not surprising given the injuries could still be accidental. And they were most likely grasping for straws in the dark. Baker tipped his chair against the wall. The balance looked pretty precarious to Sarah. 'So,' Baker said, 'he – or she – knows the old dear saw—'

'Dora.' Not old dear. 'Dora Marple.'

'Yeah, yeah. So they know she saw what was going on and decide to shut her up permanently?'

Sarah swung an impatient leg. 'Only they didn't.' Which was why she'd ordered a police guard at the hospital.

'And she could still hold the key?'

'Assuming she survives.' Sarah had had a word with one of the doctors. Dora was clinging on to life by the frailest thread. She'd lost a lot of blood, suffered two cracked ribs as well as the broken arm. At her age, the shock alone could kill her.

'I won't hold my breath,' Baker murmured. Christ was he trying to be funny? 'Anything back from forensics?' The team was still trawling and tooth-combing the house.

She shook her head. 'Not yet.'

Tipping the chair forward, he sprang to his feet, grabbed his jacket. 'Bloody good job we've got a prime witness then.' He turned at the door. 'Come on, Quinn. What you waiting for?'

One day she'd swing for him. Right now she closed her mouth and followed.

A thin man with centre-parted short black hair sat straight-backed, hands clutching bony knees, in an upright chair in Interview Room One. The shiny black suit and thin tie added to the Uriah Heep-stroke-undertaker look. Only the face didn't fit the funereal image, it resembled a strikingly unsuccessful boxer's. Observing through the spy hole, Sarah reckoned the guy's nose had been broken at least twice over the years, it had taken squatter's rights on sunken cheeks and made slanted eyes appear even smaller. Shifty glances at his surroundings were the only discernible movements he made. Not that there was a lot to take in: metal table screwed to tiled floor, shelving unit housing digital recording equipment and a police constable built like the proverbial leaning against the wall, beefy arms folded. The uniform's bulk and heavy brow would probably make an archangel nervous.

'Who is he and what's he seen?' Sarah asked.

Baker raised an eyebrow. 'Don't you recognize him?'

Peering through the spy hole again, she took a closer look. Her heart sank. The scarlet dreds had been ditched, he'd lost a bunch of weight but underneath the more conventional exterior, Eddie Flint was just about recognizable. He was better known round the nick as Edward. As in the Confessor, a professional time waster and thorn bush in the police side.

She very nearly stamped a foot. 'What the hell's he doing here?' Like they hadn't got better things to do than pander to some serial fantasist.

Baker jabbed a thumb towards the door. 'He's helping with inquiries.'

'You are joking.' It wasn't a question. Flint wasn't the only target in her firing line. Talk about raised hopes . . .

'Lighten up, woman.' He shoved a hand in his pocket.

'Don't talk—'

'He saw someone with the baby.'

She narrowed her eyes. 'Or says he did.' How could they believe a word the guy came out with when he held his hands up to just about every crime that hit the front page? It was pathetic, she almost felt sorry for him. Almost.

'He's the closest we've got to a witness, Quinn. Don't knock it yet.'

She took a step nearer. 'How close?'

'He's given a description of two people, male, female, both white, early thirties. She takes Evie, he's waiting in a motor round the corner. They drive off towards the Coventry Road.'

'And that's it?' She paused for more. It didn't arrive.

He peeled himself off the wall. 'Best find out, hadn't we?'

'Come on, boss. He gets off on this kind of thing. He'll be making it up. We don't even know he was there when it happened.'

Baker lifted a finger. 'That we do know.' The hand he took from his pocket now held a small piece of paper. A receipt for a six-pack of Four X, a bottle of Johnnie Walker and five Hamlet cigars. 'Right place.' The off-licence was across the road from the newsagent's. 'Right time.'

'And if he's lying?'

'He'll need a hell of a lot more than a small cigar to feel happy again.'

'Is there anything you'd like to add to what you've told us?' Sarah sat across the table from Flint, playing a pen between her fingers. Baker seated at her right, had left most of the questioning to her. After an hour-long session they now had detailed descriptions of the couple he claimed to have seen taking Evie Lowe. As for the car, he'd said he wouldn't know a Daimler from a Daewoo, only that it was dark blue with a National Trust sticker in the back window.

Creasing his eyes, Flint appeared to give the point some thought before shaking his head. 'No, inspector.' He clasped his hands in his lap. 'I've given you everything I can.'

Including a splitting headache. Sarah stroked her right temple. Try as she might, she couldn't get a handle on the man. In sombre tones, he'd claimed to have seen the light, turned his life round and was eager to make amends for his shady past. Born again Christian? Or another string to his fantasy bow?

'So why not give it a little sooner, Mr Flint?' The smile was not warm.

'If only I'd realized the significance at the time, inspector. It wasn't until I bought the newspaper this morning.' He ran finger and thumb along what could be the start of a moustache. 'Believe me, it's a stick I'll beat myself with for the rest of my life should anything untoward . . .' The bottom lip quivered, pale green eyes were cast down.

Sarah tapped the pen on the table. How come when someone said 'believe me', it was the last thing she wanted to do? She classed it in the same school of weasel words as 'with respect'. Either way, given the information Flint had supplied, she and Baker would have to take a decision pretty soon on whether it was worth getting a police artist in to work on a visual that could be released to the media. The drawback being, if Flint was making this stuff up as he went along, any duff information could hamper the inquiry if not steer it in completely the wrong direction. Sarah stifled a sigh. With so little else in the evidence basket, could they afford not to take the risk?

She jumped when Baker's chair rasped against the tiles. 'OK Mr Flint, you sit tight. DI Quinn will get someone to rustle up some refreshment for you then we'll see about getting an e-fit together.'

So much for consultation. Sarah pursed her lips. As for rustling up refreshment, boy was he in risk-taking mode.

TEN

'Where are you?' Sarah with mobile in a neck-lock was talking to DC David Harries. The manoeuvre enabled her to juggle printouts, a roast pepper and feta wrap, bottled water and simultaneously close the office door with her backside. Multitasking they called it.

'Small Heath park. Talking to parents.' It figured given the noises off, primarily what sounded like the tinny tuneless blare from an ice cream van. She offloaded the late lunch on her desk, sank back in the chair and slipped off her shoes. 'A few of us are here,' he said. 'Chasing up the suss per?' Police speak for suspicious person. God knew why when the full version was easier to say.

'Can you get away any time soon?' She ran a nail under the cellophane to open the wrap.

'Sure. Why?'

'I need someone to drive by Karen Lowe's place, bring her in for a news conference. Half three kick-off. How are you fixed?' Not just anyone. Harries with his boyish charm and empathy might succeed where Sarah had so far signally failed: persuading Karen Lowe to open up, drop her guard. She'd also seen potential in him as a detective and thought it time it was tapped. Truth to tell, John Hunt was turning into a plodder. She sensed the older man's disapproval at times and in this case she wanted to work closely with someone who'd be fully on side.

'No problem, boss. Want me to try and get her to talk?'

'No, I want you to take her to salsa classes.' She injected a smile in her voice. Humour wasn't her strong point. He probably thought she was having a go. 'Course I do, David. Good thinking.' *What else would I want you to do?*

'What a relief. Two left feet me, boss.'

'Later.' Smile broadening, she placed the phone on the desk. Yes. She'd definitely made the right call.

By three-twenty, doubts began stirring in Sarah's mind. Her misgivings weren't centred on David Harries. The young DC freely admitted the initial contact with Karen Lowe hadn't elicited anything earth-shattering, but their conversation had at least been two-way. He felt it worth pursuing. That was fine by Sarah. No aggrandizing bullshit, just a fair take on the encounter. No. Her uncertainty was on the wisdom of serving up Karen Lowe even to a fettered press pack.

Gazing down from her office on to the station car park she was, to coin a paraphrase, counting them all in. Not war planes but a convoy of media vehicles: TV vans, radio cars, hacks' motors. Her calculations didn't include those journalists who'd arrived early to bag a decent seat and whose banter was loud enough even now to carry from the conference room along the corridor.

Sarah, accustomed to dealing with the media, was aware her palms were moist and heart rate slightly raised. What chance the naïve and gauche Karen Lowe? The girl wouldn't have a clue what was about to hit her. Sarah grimaced. *And Caroline King hasn't even arrived yet.* Turning away from the window, she aimed for a smile and affected a confident tone. 'OK, Karen? Are you good to go?'

A sheet of A4 paper shook in the girl's hands as she glanced up from her lines, a carefully scripted appeal produced by Sarah over her working lunch. 'I guess.' She looked calm, almost too calm. Sarah wondered if the girl was on medication. She'd certainly made an effort, washed the hair, applied make-up, swapped the skimpy sun dress for a pink shift. Deliberately going for demure? The girl was cannier than she looked. Tucking a couple of files under her elbow, she steered Karen towards the door, and hoped hostilities weren't about to commence.

One friendly face was guaranteed – Jess Parry was already in situ. Sarah acknowledged the family liaison officer's fleeting smile with a brisk nod as she led Karen to the business end of the room where sunlight streamed through open windows. A press officer whose name she could never remember was there shuffling papers, and a uniformed officer with a jug edged along the table pouring water into a line-up of glasses. Sarah frowned. So where was Harries? She'd told him to be here to hold Karen's other metaphorical hand, press whatever advantage he'd forged earlier.

The buzz faded and slack posture sharpened when hacks spotted the main players entering. It wasn't far off pin-drop silence by the time they reached their seats. Jess patted one next to her for Karen. Sarah sipped water as she cast a glance over the pack. Its focus was exclusively on the young mother. Unsurprising given this was the first time they had her in their sights. Not that they could see much, Karen's head was bowed, the long mousy hair virtually covered her face.

Still sipping water, Sarah took a rough headcount while they reeled off a few shots unleashing a chorus of clicking shutters. She reckoned there were sixty odd here: the major TV channels, half a dozen radio stations, thirty-plus print journalists. She couldn't recall a bigger turnout for a crime story in the city. Make the most of it, she thought. In a few days they'll move on, set up camp in some other sucker's soul.

Harries came in through a side door, mouthed a sorry, sidled in next to the press officer. Sarah tapped the glass on the table and cleared her throat. 'Ladies and gentlemen.' She knew if Baker were holding the conference, he'd add: 'I use the term loosely' then flash what he thought was a winning smile, the DCS never failed but pandering to the press wasn't her style. She ran through introductions, then: 'The sooner we start the quicker we can get on with why we're here.' No reminder was needed: the missing baby's photograph provided a telling backdrop. Karen's head and shoulders partially obscured the image, but not the sparkle in Evie's eyes.

'Miss Lowe will have a few words to say shortly, before then I'll outline the state of the inquiry and bring you up to date with developments.' She registered several reporters exchange less than thrilled glances. She knew they found her phraseology formal, stilted. Knew she was the sideshow. 'It's nearly twenty-four hours since Evie Lowe's abduction by a person or persons unknown.' Slight pause for the import to sink in: a six-month-old child out there with a stranger. 'As you know, she was taken—'

'Persons?' A thin guy on the front row pounced on the plural. 'The thinking is there's more than one kidnapper?'

'The thinking is we'll get on a lot faster if you let me finish.' She wouldn't and couldn't be drawn on it. Baker hadn't authorized the release of Flint's dubious intelligence about the couple he claimed to have seen. The e-fit would be ready in an hour or so, the decision would be taken then.

'But two kidnappers suggests—'

'Suggests being the operative word, Mr . . . ?'

'Beck, Will Beck. *Daily Mail.*'

'We've no proof either way, Mr Beck. But as in any inquiry we keep an open mind to any possibility. Now, if I can get on . . .' She continued with a summary, on the off-chance the salient facts weren't already known and in the hope they'd be reported accurately. Eyes glazed over, pens were chewed. Tough. She wasn't here to entertain. On the other hand she didn't want to lose them. Statistics always went down well, she threw a few out: a hundred officers on the case, more than two hundred statements taken, getting on for five hundred premises visited. 'As to developments . . .' She paused. The hush wasn't breathless but interest was piqued. 'I can confirm reports that the baby's pushchair was found on waste ground on the Paradise estate in Small Heath this morning.'

'Who by?'

'Where exactly?'

'What time?'

'How'd you know it's the right one?'

Sarah raised both palms. The flow ceased. 'Certain items were found . . .'

'What items?'

She folded her arms, waited until they got the point. 'I'm not prepared to go into detail at this stage, but there's no doubt it's Evie's. We need to know how it got there, when it was left. I'd ask anyone who was in the Blake Street area yesterday afternoon from around four onwards to contact the inquiry hotline, or call their local police. It's possible someone witnessed something without realizing the significance. The pushchair's now with our forensics' people . . . it's one of several lines of inquiry we're following.'

'But you're no further forward?' A voice gloated from the back. Sarah knew who it was without looking, should've known Caroline King would do her bad penny act. 'Is that a fair assessment?'

Wondering when the reporter had slipped in, Sarah kept a straight face, neutral tone. 'A fair assessment's that we're making steady progress.'

'Plod, plod.' The tone was scathing – for those close enough to hear.

'What did you say?' The bait was too strong to resist.

'Thank God.' King flashed a smile that fooled nobody. 'This great progress? Are you going to share?'

'Misquoting already, Ms King? I didn't say great, I said steady.'

'We're all ears, DI Quinn.'

Alongside Sarah, Karen was anything but steady. She saw the girl's hands shake, heard her short breaths, feared she'd hyperventilate if they didn't get the ordeal over soon.

'Well?' King persisted.

How could the bloody woman be so insensitive? More to the point, why? It wasn't doing her any favours, unless there was an unwritten agenda. 'I've no intention of taking questions now.'

'A word in private later?'

The reporter was pushing it. As for private: 'I'd have thought privacy was an alien concept to you, Ms King.' Sarah frowned. What was that noise? 'Either way, it isn't going to happen. Miss Lowe will now read a short statement then we can get on with our jobs.'

'No interviews?' A couple of reporters moaned.

'You heard.'

Karen's knees were trembling, knocking the table, rippling the water in the glasses. Jess leaned across, put an arm round the girl's shoulder. 'You'll be fine, Karen,' she whispered. 'Don't worry.'

'I can't do it. I feel sick. I'm going to throw up.'

'No, you're not, Karen.' Sarah's turn for soothing words. 'Remember, you're doing this for, Evie.'

Karen picked up the script but the tremor in her hands was too great. She dropped it back on the table, dragged it close, then voice devoid of emotion began reciting the words written by Sarah.

'I'm Evie's mum. I'm appealing to the person who's taken Evie to look after her. Please don't hurt Evie. I want my baby home where she belongs.' The frequent name check was deliberate. 'Please contact the police, tell them where Evie is, or think of a place where she could be safely left and the police could pick her up and bring her back to me, her mum. If anyone knows anything please, please tell the police.' She stifled a sob, shoulders heaved, teardrops formed damp spots on the paper. Through the window, noises off: the slam of a car door, tuneless whistling, ordinary life.

At least she'd got through it. Sarah started gathering files. But Karen hadn't finished. 'Evie and me've never been apart before . . . I miss her like mad. She's my precious little baby. I'm crazy about her . . . love her more than anything in the world.' The words were unscripted, heartfelt, heartbreaking. For the first time since entering the room, Karen lifted her head. 'Please, please help me get Evie back.' The emotion absent from the voice was etched on her ravaged features as the cameras went in for the kill.

ELEVEN

Caroline King studied her pointed scarlet nails as she waited for her prey. Leaning casually against an outside wall at Lloyd House, she was banking on Karen Lowe leaving by the back entrance and being led to the same car that had whisked her in. The assumption was reasonable; the reporter had been in place an hour ago and witnessed the arrival, filed it away. Timing is all. Actually, she mused, timing plus groundwork plus contacts were the real deal, the full package.

She now knew the girl's frump of a gatekeeper was a FLO called Jess Parry. She'd come across the dishy driver David Harries before. Not that it was something they broadcast. She also knew after watching Karen Lowe perform that the young mother was the only angle worth pursuing. But it had to be up close and personal. Caroline wanted more than Quinn's meagre offerings, more than the run-of-the-mill pack's pickings. Idling here in the car park, she'd observed the competition leave, journalists racing off or drifting away depending on their deadlines. Each to their own.

Sighing, she checked the time, answered a couple of messages on the BlackBerry. How long was this going to take? The temperature was rising and she had a bunch of other stuff to get through. Delving into the shoulder bag for her shades, she missed David Harries' approach until his six-two frame towered over her blocking the sun anyway. 'Miss King.'

A raised eyebrow. Give her the vertically unchallenged any day. Showcasing perfect teeth with practised smile, she peeled herself off the wall. 'Hi there.'

The handshake was fleeting, the eye contact intense. 'I'm sorry, but you're not supposed to be here. Now the news conference is over, it's a restricted area.'

'Sure thing.' She flapped a vague palm. 'I just need to grab a few words with Karen.' Like it was a given.

'That's not possible. 'Fraid, I'll have to ask you to leave.'

'OK . . . if you say so, David. But we did arrange to meet outside.'

His tightening jawline suggested she'd misjudged. Thinking on her feet, she lowered her eyeline a fraction, toed the ground to display what she hoped was some fancy footwork. 'That was a lie. I'm sorry. It's just . . .' Contrite, confiding. 'I truly believe Karen would want to speak to me, if I was allowed anywhere near her.'

'It's a policy decision. It may change over time, Ms King.'

'Problem being time's in short supply, David.' She raised her gaze, held his for three, four seconds before elaborating: 'How long's it been now? Twenty-four hours plus. I keep thinking of that little baby out there with God knows who doing God knows what.' Deepest of sighs. 'I've covered stories like this before. I know how they can end. But, David, I truly believe if I speak to Karen on camera, a sensitive in-depth interview, it could help get her baby back.' Her dark eyes shone with what could be tears. Unless she could turn them on at will. 'It's got to be worth a shot, surely?'

He appeared to be wavering slightly, but: 'It's not down to me. I can have a word with the boss, if you like.'

'DI Quinn?' Hopeful lilt to voice. Then reluctant resignation. 'I guess. But I don't think it'll do much good. Don't get me wrong, David . . . I think she's a fine police officer, tough, intelligent, gutsy, but I know from past experience she doesn't trust the media. She lumps us all together which is a shame . . . not all of us are out for what we can get. All I want is to help.' Tight smile. 'Still, I'm sure she knows what she's doing.' It was archetypal King, almost the full works. And it did the trick. As she turned to leave, he touched her sleeve.

'Leave it with me, Caroline.'

'Leave what with you, Harries?' Sarah's narrow-eyed gaze on the reporter's sashaying rear was considerably less approving than the young officer's.

'Ma'am.' Startled. How long had the boss been there? 'I didn't see . . .'

'Quite.' Tight-lipped. 'So what's she left you with?'

'I said I'd have a word with you, ma'am.'

'And?' Sarah nodded towards the back door and they fell into step across the tarmac.

'She's asking if she can interview—'

'Karen Lowe.' Sighing, she said, 'What part of no way can't King get her airhead round?'

Harries turned his mouth down. Caroline King might be a lot of things but, from what he'd seen, being a lamebrain wasn't one of them. And how come the boss was making personal remarks, sweeping statements? She was usually pretty reasonable, rational, not over-emotional. 'Have you even consid—?'

'Are you questioning me, constable?' She cut him a withering glance. The 'constable' was telling. He dropped the 'boss'.

'No, ma'am.'

'Well, maybe you should.'

'OK.' He held the door, waited for her to go through before taking her at her word. 'I don't think anything should just be dismissed out of hand.'

'That's what I do, is it?' Now she sounded faintly amused. Harries frowned; couldn't get a handle on the woman.

'I didn't say that.'

'Then what are you saying?'

'I can't see it'll do any harm.'

She turned to face him. 'Then I suggest you look further, a darn sight further than Caroline King's backside.'

He shook his head. 'That's so not fair, ma'am.'

'What's unfair DC Harries is a mother grieving for her missing baby and some ego-heavy reporter seeing it as a career move.'

For the second time in as many minutes he stood and watched a woman walk away.

By late evening millions of people had seen Karen Lowe's grief. It had been the only image to go for, and every media outlet had gone for it. Karen's misery beamed into countless homes across the UK. The kidnapper had recorded the item, a freeze frame now filled the wide screen: Karen's face distorted with strain and pain, a tear about to drip from her chin. Smiling lazily at the set, the kidnapper resisted the urge to hurl a brick through it. It'd make too much noise. Christ. The baby hadn't long gone down, if she woke bawling like before . . . Didn't bear thinking about.

Sitting on the edge of an armchair, the kidnapper hunched forward, remote in hand and played the recording for the fifth, no, sixth time. Hadn't had such fun for ages. Not. All that banging on about wanting the baby back. Evie this, Evie that, Evie the other. As for the stuck-up copper. It was blindingly obvious the woman didn't have a clue. Not much cop there, then. Both were in dire need of a helping hand. Sniggering, the kidnapper pressed pause, froze Karen's misery full frame again.

'Want your precious little baby back? See about that, shall we?'

As if on cue, Evie snuffled and cried out. Scowling, the kidnapper cut a glance at the makeshift cot. False alarm. The baby was still asleep, thank God. Mind, it'd be more of a surprise if she'd woken. The last bottle had contained more than milk. Kids need their sleep, don't they? Lots and lots of sleep. Beauty sleep.

Karen's image was still on the screen. Everything was ready for what needed to be done. Strolling across the room, the kidnapper lifted Evie from the cot, placed her in position. She didn't make a murmur as the kidnapper adjusted the cushion, reached for the camera.

TWELVE

By nine p.m., reported sightings were being chased in Bristol and Bath, London and Leeds, Durham and Devon. Sarah had little confidence in any of them, couldn't shake her conviction that the killer was closer to home. She was sharing a late supper with Baker in the canteen. Fried onion and stewed coffee odours lingered in the still warm air, they had the floor space virtually to themselves.

As well as a no-holds barred spat with Adam on the phone, Sarah's excuse for not-so-fine dining was an empty fridge and bare cupboards. Glancing at the boss, she suspected a home life that was equally barren emotionally. Sighing, she played a preoccupied fork through sausage, chips and beans. Nursery food, she thought of it: naughty but nice. Somehow her appetite had gone.

'Come on, spit it out, Quinn. I can see you've got something on your mind.'

She frowned. Not for the first time thought the old boy must be more sensitive than he looked. Mind, it wouldn't take much. 'Nothing, boss . . . in a way.'

He shovelled in a mound of shepherd's pie and peas, talked through the mush. 'That'd be a first.'

'I mean it.' Laying fork on plate, she pushed both away. 'Twenty-eight hours down the line and there's nothing. Not one decent lead.'

'Way it goes sometimes. You know that. It's not an episode of *The Bill.*'

'Yeah, yeah.' How many times had she heard him say that? 'But baby cases, boss, they usually generate so much intelligence.' Even villains come forward with information when child crimes are involved.

He glanced up, brow like a ploughed field. 'Tell that to the boys in the back room, Quinn. The phones haven't stopped.'

'*Quality* intelligence.' *And there are women slaving away in there too, dummy.*

He sniffed. 'We've got Flint's works of art.'

'The Mr Men meet L.S. Lowry?' God, she wished the canteen was licensed, she could murder a drink.

'L.S. who?' The suggestion of a wink implied the ignorance was feigned. At least she hoped so; surely he couldn't inhabit a cultural desert as well? 'OK. They're not Gainsborough but they're not that bad, Quinn.'

She shrugged. The e-fits weren't brilliant either. Baker had passed them round at the late brief. Opinion was divided. Sarah thought they were universal-one-size-fits-all, though with hindsight the woman did bear a passing resemblance to Cherie Blair. Either way, he'd decided to hang on to them until the saturation coverage of Karen's witness appeal dried up. Not quite an ace up the sleeve, more a means to gain further media exposure, keep the story out there and in people's minds. Sarah hoped the visuals didn't turn into jokers in the pack, and add yet further to the usually well meaning but often time-wasting flood of calls coming in to the incident room. Overload after airtime, was a risk they had to take. But as she'd told Karen, one steer in the right direction could lead to finding Evie. Sarah just wasn't convinced it would come from Eddie Flint.

Baker moved on to a mountain of custard-coated spotted dick. And changed tack. 'What about the old dear . . . Dora . . . she still out of it?'

Sarah nodded. 'Critical but stable.' She'd checked with the hospital half an hour back. Even if Dora came round spouting fluent Greek, there was no guarantee she'd be able to add anything useful to the inquiry. The FSI team had found no signs of a break-in at the house, nothing to indicate a struggle; the daughter had checked the place, didn't think any property was missing. Dora had definitely hit her head going down, but it could be she'd missed her footing. They hadn't completely ruled out an intruder – professionals cover their tracks or don't leave traces in the first place – even then it didn't necessarily follow that a putative perp was also the abductor.

Baker glanced up, wielded a spoon in casual greeting. David Harries was heading for the hatch. Mildly surprised, Sarah pursed her lips: Friday night and the young DC didn't have a home – or hot date – to go to.

'Keeping an eye on him are we, Quinn?' Baker's innocent delivery was at odds with the speculative pout.

She shifted her gaze ostentatiously to the window. High above, jet trails criss-crossed an almost Mediterranean sky, five geese flew in formation like avian red arrows. Sod Baker. The dig was uncalled for: her interest in Harries was purely professional. She'd kind of admired the way he'd stood up to her earlier. A yes-man was no good to anyone. He'd just needed putting straight on the shortcomings of the media in general and Caroline King in particular. He'd seemed to take it on board, they'd even had a laugh about it. As for the chief, he'd clearly had enough of the silent treatment.

'OK, Quinn, you win. Tell me: what aren't we doing we should be?'

She shrugged. Every box was being ticked: house-to-house inquiries and street interviews were continuing, already extensive searches would be expanded further at first light, paedophile checks were ongoing, CC footage was still being monitored, the mobile incident unit was up and running, Evie's missing poster was plastered across the city. So what was the persistent niggle at the back of her mind that try as she might she couldn't pin down? 'I wish I knew, boss.'

'So quit worrying, woman.' He scraped back the chair, slung

jacket over shoulder, slurped the dregs of his tea. 'We're doing everything we can. Something's gotta give.'

The withering look was wasted on his departing back. Was it a man thing, she wondered? She could have consulted Harries, but it looked as if he'd left too. Shame. She might have suggested they go for that drink. Unless she was wrong about that hot date.

THIRTEEN

'Going up in the world are we, ma'am?' A smirking Dean Lavery, arch of voice and eyebrow, dropped a pile of post on Sarah's desk. She glanced up from report-writing – the third that morning – not amused. The toast she'd grabbed from the canteen still sat on a plate. She reached for a slice, thought better of it, slipped it in the bin at her feet.

Saturday before seven was way too early for what passed as Lavery's humour, especially enigmatic one-liners and especially after another night lying in bed staring at horror movies on the ceiling. Would that they were. Even with eyes tightly closed the images played in her head. Most cops she knew had a macabre mental cinema, dick noir, Adam called it.

'I'm not with you, Dean. Enlighten me.' Or maybe not. As far as Sarah was concerned, in a drawer of blunt knives, Lavery wouldn't be the sharpest.

Sniggering, he pointed to the letter on top. 'As long as you don't expect us to curtsey, eh?'

She felt more like telling him to fuck off. His cheap after-shave was getting up her nostrils – it was almost as pungent as Baker's. 'I'm sure you have better things to do with your time, Dean.' Fake smile. 'Was there something else?' She hadn't a clue what he was going on about and didn't give a toss either way.

He shook his head, mumbled 'ma'am' and headed out. She sighed. *No wonder they call me the Ice Queen.* Tiredness did nothing for her temper or tolerance and both were in pretty short supply. An inquiry that was going nowhere and a personal life that appeared stalled didn't help.

When he'd closed the door, she picked up her pen, cast a cursory glance at the envelope. Dead funny, Dean. Someone had got her name wrong, written Queen instead of Quinn. So what? She shook her head, muttered, 'Boy, did you miss your vocation.' The guy ought to go into comedy. Then she took a closer look. 'Personal' had been written and underscored three times. It rather belied the misnomer: Inspector Sarah Queen. Curious, she ran a letter opener under the flap. The Polaroid fell face up. Sarah's features froze in shocked disbelief as she reached for the phone.

At the same time, four miles away, Karen Lowe opened a similar envelope. The young mother didn't freeze, she fainted but not before her screams woke several neighbours. Still wet from the shower, Jess Parry ran to the kitchen and found Karen unconscious on the pink lino. It was twenty minutes before Jess alerted the incident room. She had to call an ambulance first.

'Dean Lavery picked it up with the rest of the stuff on the front desk. He assumed it came with the regular post.' Sarah's steady grey-eyed gaze was on DCS Baker. She bit her lip. She'd seen enough of the image to last a lifetime. Suit jacket agape, the boss stood across the desk from her, his podgy fingers straining latex gloves that barely touched the edges of the evidence bag let alone the Polaroid it protected. He'd nicked his neck shaving; she saw a dried bead of blood near the collar of his shirt. The line of perspiration above his top lip was more recent; she'd watched it seep through the pores, doubted it was heat induced even with the temperature rising.

Baker's focus was exclusively on the picture, a sick parody of the Madonna and child. Hazel eyes creased, he ran his gaze over the surface, scanning it to memory, scouring it for clues. She hoped he'd have more joy than her. He hadn't uttered a word since taking it from her, though his breathing was audible and eloquent enough.

Karen Lowe had been reunited with her baby. Except Karen was on TV and Evie was propped on a cushion in front of the screen God knew where. Nothing peripheral was visible, no wall, no carpet, no curtain. And the proportion was all wrong: Karen's face was massive, dominated the shot. Incongruously, it put Sarah in mind of *1984*, Big Brother; all seeing, all powerful. It couldn't be further from the truth. Karen Lowe was currently under observation in hospital. Concussion, bruising. The baby's arms were splayed, ankles crossed, eyes closed. Sarah hands were fisted at her side. She prayed Evie was only asleep.

'Bastard.' Baker seethed. 'Fucking sick bastard.' Turning, he handed the evidence bag to DC Harries who'd been keeping a low profile by the door. 'Get it to the labs, Dave. Tell them I want everything they can give me now. Make that yesterday.'

'Sir.'

The envelope was already with forensics. It was bog standard self-seal, so no saliva, but there could be prints, sweat, fibres; hopefully in addition to Sarah's and Lavery's. The envelope would be passed to a handwriting expert as and when. The boss agreed it had been addressed to Sarah as the public face of the police inquiry. Like her, he doubted there was anything personal in it. As for getting the name wrong, maybe the kidnapper had misheard.

'OK.' Baker stood legs astride, hands on hips. 'Where are we at, Quinn?'

'John Hunt's going through our CCTV footage.' It was the first task she'd assigned in the half-hour it took Baker to get in from Erdington.

'Fucking arsehole.' Not Huntie. Sarah knew where Baker was coming from but turning the air blue didn't get them anywhere. Like Sarah, the chief suspected the kidnapper had paid them an out-of-hours visit. There was no stamp on the envelope, no frank, it was what you might call a special delivery. And it could be the kidnapper who'd made it. She'd requested the station's tapes immediately and Hunt was in a viewing suite along the corridor.

'We've also got a team of DCs knocking doors at Karen's block of flats. Jess Parry says there was definitely no post on the mat when she got up this morning.'

Baker loosened his tie. 'Time?'

'Quarter to seven. She took Karen a cup of tea, heard her get out of bed a few minutes later.'

He scowled. 'Shame that's all she sodding heard.'

'Come on, boss. Don't lay this on Jess. She was in the shower.'

'Yeah and the bastard gets clean away.'

'Don't. Try. And. Be Funny.' The icy glare reinforced the clipped cool tone.

The finger jabbing was perilously close to her boob. 'I'm not the comedian round here, matey.' She forced herself not to recoil but, boy, when he blew, he blew. Spittle glistened in a corner of his mouth, an unhealthy blush spread across the quivering jowls. She rarely crossed the superior officer line so overtly. She opened her mouth to apologize but he flapped a hand. The anger wasn't directed at her. 'The sick sod holding the baby's the one having a laugh . . . at our expense. Taking happy snaps and dishing them out like Smarties. What's the shit playing at?'

Not Happy Families for sure. She shook her head. 'I don't know, but at least we've got something to work with now.' A time frame for one thing: it was possible a neighbour had witnessed the drop off at Karen's or at least seen a stranger hanging round the flats. More than that. The kidnapper had made contact. OK, coming to police HQ was dicking them around but it also smacked of arrogance to Sarah. A perp who thought he or she was smarter than the cops. By handing in evidence, they'd taken a hell of a risk – it could turn into the second biggest mistake of their life. The first was snatching Evie. Perhaps unwittingly, Sarah's glance fell on the newspaper on her desk: the baby's photograph splashed across the front page, her beguiling one-toothed smile.

'And the pic sent to Karen's similar?' Baker asked.

'I haven't seen it yet, but from what Jess says it's virtually identical.'

Baker paced the floor, bottom lip protruding, hand sunk in trouser pocket. Sarah had had longer to mull it over. She let him think it through prior to pooling ideas with the squad. Taking a can of Coke from a drawer, she sank a few mouthfuls watching him wear out the carpet. He'd be oblivious to her attentions; his ability to focus – blank anything extraneous to the case – was legendary round the station. Married to the job the cliché ran. She didn't see it that way: Baker had a wife, he just loved the job more. At least they were still together.

'Well, Quinn . . .' He'd stopped pacing, stood stroking his chin. 'They've certainly got it in for the mother, haven't they?'

The idea had more than crossed her mind. 'You can say that again, boss. But, why?'

'Best find out, hadn't we? Come on, let's hit the brief.' His earlier outburst was history. Another good thing about the boss: he got whatever was bugging him out of his system, bore no malice. Unlike some senior officers she could name, and junior come to that.

She grabbed her jacket: the charcoal linen suit was going to be way too hot on a day like this. He was already holding the door. 'I know one thing, Quinn . . . I was right last night when—'

'You said something's gotta give?' She gave a wry smile. 'In spades, boss. But I bet even you didn't know who'd be handing out the prizes.'

'I know something else, Quinn. You should smile more often.'

Caroline King's smile morphed into a scowl as she approached the Mercedes. Bloody traffic wardens: hadn't they got better things to do? Still, in the wider scheme of things a parking ticket was a minor irritant, it could be written off on expenses – after she'd written up her exclusive. The hot tip had given her more than a steer. All she needed was a quote from Quinn. The scowl was now a smirk; sorry, make that, *Queen*.

'What the . . . ?' Whatever was tucked under the wiper wasn't a ticket. She eased out a cellophane package, eyes narrowed, breath on hold. Inside was a folded sheet of A4, on it three words cut and pasted from a newspaper. Caroline gasped; felt her heartbeat take a hike. 'My God.'

She'd no doubt who it was from. It wasn't just the message – it was the lock of fine blonde hair nestling in the cellophane. Caroline leaned against the motor, thoughts racing. Of course it couldn't have been a parking ticket, she realized now. This was the Marriot's car park and she had a resident's pass. So how come the kidnapper knew where she was staying, had she been followed? Casually she glanced round the cavernous interior: gleaming bodywork, concrete pillars, concealed cameras, the occasional glinting lens revealing locations.

She tapped her fingers on the driver's door. Why had the kidnapper singled her out? She snorted. Stupid question. Class will out. The question now was how to capitalize on the unexpected gift, the kidnapper's calling card. Eyes narrowed, she traced top lip with tongue. There'd be no mileage pissing off the police too much, but maybe it was a ticket after all. A ticket to ride.

In the car, she checked the mirror, winked approvingly, awarded herself a perfect ten. Either way a King beats a Queen hands down.

Laughing aloud, she hit the ignition, put her foot down as well.

FOURTEEN

Sarah couldn't recall seeing a squad so hacked off. Leaning against a desk at the front, she'd been watching reactions as Baker brought them up to speed on the Polaroid. The news had left stony features, slumped posture. It was hardly surprising, most had families, all had feelings. Forty plus detectives were in the room, as many again out in the field. Everyone had worked their butt off since Evie's abduction and forty hours on had little to show for it. Even the normally dynamic DC Harries looked a touch downbeat. The current despondency wasn't just down to a sense the perp was yanking their communal chain, though Paul Wood had expressed that view, it was more that the baby was still out there, in the hands of a kidnapper who also held all the cards. And if the attitude displayed here was anything to go by, he or she had just played a blinder. Sarah willed the boss to nip it in the bud; negativity was bad for morale.

'So that's where we are.' He parked a haunch on her desk, ran a keen gaze over the troops. They'd been briefed on which tasks were ongoing, what steps had been taken. 'Where do *you* reckon we should be going?'

The silence wasn't far off complete. A fan whirred, papers were shuffled, there were rustles as one or two officers shifted in their seat. Baker let the silence stand until just about everyone was on edge, expectant.

'That it, then?' He turned his mouth down, swung a chunky casual leg. 'Dumbstruck? Cat got your balls? Great.' He clapped his hands slowly. 'The perp'd love to see this . . . it's just what he was after when he sent that pic. It's called demotivate. Demoralize. Dispirit. Discourage. Dishearten. Disparage. Anything you like beginning with diss. That's diss with two s's, by the way.' For a fat man, he jumped off the desk surprisingly quickly. Papers wafted in his wake. 'Know what I call it? I call it pissing people off.' He cocked his head at Sarah. 'Pissing people off royally.' Her slightly curved lip acknowledged the not so subtle allusion. Baker's pause lasted three, four seconds, then: 'And I don't like people pissing me off. Specially villains.'

He was hamming it up, but seemed to have the audience with him. Sarah spotted fewer sprawled legs, folded arms.

'This guy thinks he's smart,' Baker sneered.

'Or she.' Ventured a female officer near the front.

Baker flapped a hand. 'I can't be doing with this he/she, his/her business. We'll stick with bloke 'til we nail the bastard . . . And believe me – we will.' No argument; the conviction was absolute. 'He *thinks* he's smart – I *know* we're shit-hot. What's the old saying: "Don't get mad get even"? Well I say: go ballistic and get one up on the buggers. And take it from me, I know where I'll be shoving it.'

'You and me both, gaffer.' Wood's crooked arm illustrated the point. A few officers echoed the sentiment. Sarah had to admire the old boy. A macho pep talk peppered with expletives, and though – in concrete terms – nothing had changed, the atmosphere was lighter, the mood less sombre. Detectives started throwing out questions, chipping in ideas. Only Lavery looked less than impressed but he'd still be miffed from the bollocking the other day.

'Why show his hand now, sir?' Harries asked.

Baker shrugged. 'Arrogance? Control freak? Nutter?'

'If you ask me, it's sadistic.' DC Shona Bruce. When the tall redhead voiced an opinion it was generally worth hearing. She'd certainly vocalized Sarah's thinking. 'The kidnapper didn't just target us.' Shona didn't elaborate, they all knew the other recipient on his hit list was in hospital. Tucking a strand of hair behind her ear, Shona said, 'Sending Karen a picture of her baby posed like that smacks of sheer cruelty to me.'

Several heads nodded. A phone rang on the desk near Harries.

'Dave? Get that, will you?' Baker nodded at Shona. 'Carry on, lass.'

She smoothed non-existent creases from a blue serge skirt. 'Karen goes on telly pleading to have her baby back. And he sends a photo? How vicious is that?'

'Not just vicious.' Heads turned as Sarah spoke. 'I think it's personal not random. Not spur of the moment. Planned to the last detail.' She'd suspected it from the start. Babies aren't just snatched from the street in broad daylight. And why had Karen been so convinced of the worst? More than once she'd said, 'They'll kill her, won't they?' They. Not he. Not she. As far as Sarah was concerned, the girl knew more than she was letting on. 'I think we need to dig . . .'

'DI Quinn,' hand over mouthpiece, Harries interrupted. 'It's for you. Urgent.'

She rolled her eyes. 'Who is it?'

'Caroline King.'

For Christ's sake. 'Not now, Harries.'

'She says it's vital—'

'Tell her I'll—'

'. . . she speaks to you now.'

'I'll speak to her when I'm ready,' Sarah snapped. 'Savvy?'

'Fine.' By now his tanned complexion had a pink tinge. 'But she says—'

'Read my lips, Harries: I don't care what she says.'

Baker mimed a slammed phone. 'You think we need to dig where, Quinn?'

'Karen's background, family, mates, boyfriends, anyone she's associated with recently. We need to find out if she's ever worked; where and how she spends her time. Does she go on-line? We need to know more about her than her own mother. Which is good a place to start as any.' Given Karen was in no condition to be questioned any time soon. 'When we're finished here, I'll get over to Harborne.' Harries could tag along, too.

It was nearly a wrap anyway. Further background checks were assigned to four detectives, others still had reported sightings to chase, a number were following up calls to the hotline. Everyone knew what they were doing and there was an eagerness – absent before – to get on with it.

'OK guys.' The door opened as Baker was shucking into his jacket. 'Anything else before we nail his sorry ass?'

'Guv.' John Hunt hovered in the doorway, CCTV tape in hand. Normally unflappable, the DS's hair was mussed, tie askew. 'Get the hammer. I think we've got him.'

Within minutes, half the squad was crammed in the viewing suite. Sarah and Baker, hunched close to the monitor, had ringside seats, their pupils reflecting the flickering colour images playing out on screen. Breath bated, palms moist, Sarah watched a tallish guy lope along the pavement outside the granite and glass façade of Lloyd House. His clothes were in monochrome: black combats, white T-shirt, grey hoodie. A logo emblazoned across the chest read University of California. Sarah sniffed, doubted he'd been within spitting distance of the campus. Either way coming here wasn't a sharp move. There was nothing furtive in his approach and force HQ CCTV was state of the art. She allowed herself a thin smile. All Postman Prat had to do was show his face.

'You can see he's carrying an envelope, guv.' Hunt leaned across the desk, tapered finger pointing. 'It's definitely the one. Personal's underlined three times and it's addressed to Inspector Queen.' Hunt's running commentary she could do without; the action was unfolding less than a foot away.

The guy paused briefly at the main entrance, bent slightly to make the drop. The digital clock read 06.35. The guy had his back to the camera at this point. Christ, Sarah thought. A couple of minutes earlier and she might have bumped into him. Five seconds passed, ten, fifteen; all they could see was his back.

Sarah fanned her face with a file. Baker tapped testy fingers on the desk. 'What the fuck's he doing?'

'Lighting a fag,' Hunt said. 'Don't worry, guv, it gets better.'

And then he turned. Taking a deep drag, he tilted his head back and blew three perfect smoke rings. The picture was so sharp, they could see the tendons tauten in his neck, then the glint from a nose piercing. The hood had dropped back to reveal wavy black hair, lots of it. He looked pretty fit; regular features, decent bone structure. Sarah estimated his age at late-twenties, early-thirties. She exchanged glances with Baker who was smiling too. *Gotcha.* ID-ing the guy should be a piece of cake.

Could it get any better?

From the back, a voice piped up, 'Gaffer. I know him.'

FIFTEEN

'This is Caroline King, BBC TV News, Birmingham.' Pink lip gloss glistening, the reporter gazed earnestly into the lens for a further five seconds or so, then: 'Got that, sweetie?' They were shooting in the Marriot's underground car park, Caroline's staged re-enactment of discovering the kidnapper's note was already in the can. The young woman behind the camera answered with a thumbs-up and a 'No worries'. Caroline was slightly uneasy though.

It had taken nearly all her considerable powers of persuasion to convince several editors at TV Centre that they run footage of the kidnapper's message prior to bringing in the police. Persuasion and precious time. What if the kidnapper had contacted other journalists? What if a rival station got the news on air first? God, no. It didn't bear thinking about. She checked the BlackBerry for messages or missed calls, breathed a sigh of relief.

Toe tapping, she watched 'sweetie' scrawl King PTC in black marker pen on a tape case. Not that her bitch was with the crew. It was the desk-jockeys who were a pain, soon as they came off the road they lost their edge, the thrill of the chase. As for the Beeb's lawyers . . . She curled a lip. *Do me a favour.* Christ. Favours didn't come much bigger than the kidnapper's. Talk about gift horse and mouth. Of course it had to be broadcast: the public had a right to know. After all Caroline had given the cops a crack at the whip, it was Quinn who'd refused to take the call. Or bothered getting back.

Stiletto heels clacking pitted concrete, she strode over to a despatch rider propping up the nearest pillar. With a winning smile, she handed over the tape. 'Soon as you can, honey.'

'For you . . .' He saluted with gauntleted hand before mounting the bike, the straining black leathers left nothing to the imagination. It brought tears to the eye. Caroline averted her gaze. She'd used only a little imagination to furbish the gaps in the story. She hadn't actually *seen* the Polaroid sent to the police. It had been described well enough for her to paint a word picture though.

The piece-to-camera had completed the sequences already shot. Editing would be done at the Mailbox: a short package for rolling news, extended pieces for the main bulletins. They might want a live two-way later. It might be Saturday, but news was 24/7, thank God. She fumbled in her bag for the car keys, then smoothed her immaculate bob. There were other fish to fry. Maybe grill was a better word, given the lengthy list of questions she had in mind. Chuckling to herself, she headed for the Merc. If poss she needed to collar Quinn, before the story broke. When the excrement would really hit the extractor fan.

When someone's *known* to a cop, it doesn't necessarily figure they're bosom buddies. There's no sharing popcorn at the cinema, going on for a curry and a couple of Cobras. They're known, as in: POI. Person of Interest. And the closest contact normally is feeling a collar, or eyeballing each other across a metal desk in a police interview room.

Which is where DS Reg Proctor had last seen Todd Mellor, in the flesh. Only Mellor's face was currently on show, a close up on the monitor in the viewing suite.

'I think he quite enjoyed the attention, guv.' Proctor was certainly under the metaphorical spotlight. He'd been giving rapt colleagues an account of his dealings with Mellor. A couple of years back, Proctor and his then partner had apparently brought the guy in for questioning. A few parents and teachers at a primary school near where Mellor lived had complained he'd been hanging round, taking pictures of kids. Mellor, Proctor said, had come in voluntarily, answered all questions satisfactorily, agreed to a search of his house, allowed them to take his computer. 'Came out cleaner than Persil, guv.' Sarah sniffed, cut a glance at the screen. Or he'd rumbled they were onto him.

Proctor mopped his shiny brow with a crumpled hankie. He was early thirties, but born middle-aged and wore the uniform: tweed jacket, leather elbow pads, trousers with a killer crease, neatly knotted knitted tie. His horn-rimmed glasses were getting the hankie treatment now. 'He didn't have so much as a box Brownie squirrelled away.'

'Yeah, well, we'll see about that.' Baker leaned back in the swivel chair, fingers tapping both chunky thighs. 'How'd he strike you, Reg?'

Hopefully, Baker would soon form his own assessment. An unmarked car had been despatched to Mellor's last known address in Aston. If he'd done a bunk, a picture would be circulated to officers across the city. If need be, they'd release copies to the media, issue an all points bulletin.

'He seemed pretty straight to me, guv.'

'Cocky?'

Proctor chewed a rubbery lip. 'More what I'd call laid-back.'

So Mellor had done nothing wrong or he'd destroyed anything incriminating. Sarah checked her watch. Coming up to half-nine, they needed to get on. Couldn't rely on Mellor holding up his hands. Either way, Baker wanted first interview-shot at the guy.

According to Proctor, apart from being questioned under caution Mellor had no previous and back then had no job, no family, no partner. He lived alone in a crummy one-bedroomed flat over a fish and chip shop. 'As I say, guv, he seemed to enjoy the attention.'

'Christ, Reg.' Baker whacked the desk. 'The guy was accused of having an unhealthy interest in little kids.'

Mouth turned down, then: 'He reckoned it was a case of mistaken identity, guv.'

The boss jabbed a thumb at the screen. 'Yeah? Well, he won't be getting away with that one this time round.'

SIXTEEN

A subdued DC Harries drove down a tree-lined street in Harborne. Dappled light flickered across the planes of his face. Sarah glanced at his profile. Hoped he wasn't smarting from the slapping down at the brief. Not that she regretted the rebuke. He was a cop for God's sake. If he took offence that easy he was in the wrong job. John Hunt had already had a moan because she was working more and more with Harries. Sarah reckoned the DS resented what he saw as being sidelined. Registering Harries' tight lips, white knuckles, she hoped she'd made the right call. Couldn't be doing with a sulker.

'Something on your mind, David?' Light tone, casual query.
'No, ma'am.'

She doubted that. He was bright, too bright to share his current thinking if hers was correct. He certainly had the gift of the gab when he needed it. Harries had graduated in law but after two tedious years defending petty crooks decided he'd be better off detecting the criminals. She also knew the old school guard at Lloyd House had initially given him a hard time. He'd told her a while back he realized early on the only way to deal with the sly digs, carping comments, was to laugh them off. Or crack even better ones himself.

Sarah pursed her lips. Since they'd got in the motor, he'd yet to crack a smile.

'There is actually, ma'am.'

Frowning. 'Is . . . ?'

'Something on my mind.'

She waited for him to share. Waited some more. 'Is it going to stay there?'

'You won't like it.'

She held fire while he manoeuvred round a dust cart partially blocking the road. 'Shouldn't I be the judge of that?'

'That call at the brief? Caroline King . . .'

'Spot on, David. I don't like it.'

'I think she's on to something.'

'After something more like.' Derisive snort.

'She said you'd regret not hearing her out, actually used the words: "on her head, be it".'

'Sounds like a threat to me.' They were at a red light.

'It did to me, too.' She sensed his gaze on her. 'I'm only the messenger ma'am. But what bugs me is this: if she was that desperate to talk to you . . . didn't you say she had your mobile?'

Karen Lowe's mother lived in a detached double-fronted red brick: neat garden, net curtains, number nine Wisteria Lane. Sarah twitched a lip: very *Desperate Housewives*. The ivy-laden property was immaculate and looked late-Victorian. Sarah imagined antimacassars and aspidistras, lace doilies and lavender bags. Even before her hand reached the gleaming brass knocker, the door opened a few inches. A woman's head appeared in the gap, hair like a steel grey skull cap.

'Didn't you see the sign? No circulars. No junk mail.' The thick Birmingham accent wasn't brusque, it was bloody rude. Sarah bristled. 'And definitely no cold callers.' The woman made to close the door.

Warrant card thrust in gap, Sarah just about managed to keep a civil tone. 'I'm Detective Inspector—'

'Why didn't you say?' Like there'd been a chance to get a word in? 'Come in . . . come in.' She swung the door wide before turning on her heel and traipsing down a long tiled hallway that smelt of lemons and pine, the chemical kind. Sarah and Harries exchanged bemused glances as they trailed in her voluble wake. 'We get all sorts here trying to sell stuff, double glazing, patio doors, new drives.' The hair was actually pulled tightly back in a thin ponytail, everything else about the woman was fat, bordering on obese. Given the swaying haunches, the beige sweat pants were not a wise choice. 'And don't get me started on the God botherers. You name it, we've had 'em. Jehovahs, Mormons, Baptists, Evangelists, happy clappers, I call 'em.'

Was this woman real? Granddaughter missing, daughter hospitalized and she was blathering on about reps and religion.

'It'll be Mrs Lowe you want. She's just through here.'

Sarah arched an eyebrow. Real then, but the genuine article lay on a cream leather Chesterfield in one of the chicest sitting rooms she'd seen in a long time. Thin silk curtains partially drawn, wafted in a gentle breeze, half a dozen marble lamps cast subtle lighting over clean lines, cool pastels, pale woods. Sarah couldn't comment on the owner. Deborah Lowe was under a satin quilt, a magazine over her face. 'Who is it, Cath?'

'The police, Mrs Lowe.' Cath mouthed, 'migraine' at Sarah. 'Shall I make us a cuppa?'

Deborah Lowe slung the quilt over the back of the settee then made heavy weather of sitting up. The glossy magazine slipped to the plush carpet at her feet: *Vogue*. Sarah recalled the dog-eared copies of *Heat* and *Closer* at Karen's tiny flat. *Like mother, not like daughter?* 'I don't think so. I'm sure this isn't a social call.' Thick blue veins stood out on the thin hand she raised to smooth her brow. The hair was an immaculate if suspiciously blonde page boy, the subtle mascara slightly smudged. Sarah wondered idly if the woman's clothes always coordinated with the décor, the ivory linen shift dress certainly

did and looked equally classy. 'Do sit down. You're making
me nervous.' The laugh was girlish and brittle. The woman
though well-preserved was no spring chicken. Late-forties?
Early-fifties?

Straight-faced Sarah ran through the introductions before
taking the nearest armchair; the cream leather looked more
comfortable than it felt. Harries sat opposite, slipped a notebook
from his pocket. He'd be observing, too. Body language could
convey more than words.

'This is about Karen, I suppose.' Mrs Lowe reached for a
slim silver cigarette case from a side table. *No. The European
Exchange Rate.*

'I don't know whether you've heard, Mrs Lowe, but Karen's
under observation in hospital.'

She clamped a hand round her throat. 'Why wasn't I told?'

Sarah explained that Karen had fainted after receiving a
photograph of Evie sent by the kidnapper. 'They're keeping
her in as a precaution.'

'Poor girl, as if she hasn't got enough to cope with.' *And?
What about Evie?*

'Our main concern is your granddaughter's abduction.' It
was difficult to keep the censure from her voice. She'd taken
an instant dislike to the woman. Making snap judgements was
unlike her and not helpful in any inquiry.

'That goes without saying, surely?' The pale blue eyes
seemed to contain a challenge. Maybe she thought better of
it. She broke eye contact, fumbled in a handbag for a tissue.
'When I think of that little baby . . . If there's anything I can
do to help . . . anything at all.' She dabbed away a tear, further
smearing the mascara. 'I only wish Karen would let me . . .'

What? The woman seemed incapable of finishing a sentence.
Sarah opened her mouth to speak but Mrs Lowe continued,
'We're not close, Karen and I. It tears my heart, but I may as
well tell you that now.'

'Why is that?' Sarah asked. 'You and Karen not being
close?'

Five-, six-second pause then: 'It's a long story, inspector.'
Fingers trembling slightly, she lit the cigarette she'd been
toying with. Her eyes were moist.

'Take your time, Mrs Lowe.' Harries' softly-spoken interjec-
tion took both women by surprise.

Mrs Lowe acknowledged the sympathy with a tight smile. 'It's the usual thing, I suppose. We gave her everything we could. Nice clothes, lovely holidays, generous allowance. But she got in with a bad crowd, started staying out late, running wild. When money began disappearing from my purse, I gave her an ultimatum. I'm sorry to say she . . .' Her head gave what looked like an involuntary jerk.

'What?' Sarah prompted.

'She attacked me. Threatened me with a knife.' She crushed the cigarette in an onyx ashtray. 'I told her if she couldn't respect the house rules, she had to leave.'

Sarah had heard similar stories, dysfunctional families weren't confined to sink estates. 'Where was her father in all this?'

'Thomas left when Karen was fourteen.' Head down, she started shredding the tissue. 'It was around then she—' A door opened, interrupting what was hardly a flow.

Cath stepped in, shucking on a coat. 'I've done the bedrooms, Mrs Lowe. Finished the ironing. If there's nothing else?'

'No that's fine, Cath. Your money's on the side in the kitchen. Thanks.'

Tight-lipped, Sarah hid a growing impatience. 'You were saying it was around then Karen started . . . what?'

'Going off the rails, isn't that the expression, inspector?' Another brittle laugh.

'When did she move out?'

She turned her mouth down. 'A year ago? No, two.'

'Where did she go?'

'I imagine she went to live with friends.'

Imagine? 'Does Karen still see her father?'

'I shouldn't think so. Thomas lives up north somewhere.' She slipped her feet into gold satin ballet pumps. 'I'll have that coffee after all. Would you like something?'

I'd like you to answer the sodding questions. Was the woman being deliberately evasive? Keen to put some distance, some thinking space between them?

'Coffee would be good,' Sarah said. 'We'll give you a hand.'

Her mouth tightened but she gave a brisk nod of assent. Standing, she was almost as tall as Sarah but stick thin. 'You'll have to excuse the mess.'

The kitchen was spotless, stainless steel sinks exactly that.

Shining appliances looked brand new, pristine fittings as if they'd just been installed. Sarah sniffed. Mess was a relative thing then. She watched as the woman ground beans, poured water and came out with a stream of banal small talk. She let the woman twitter on, fascinated not by the facile tosh but by the fact that every fifteen seconds or so, Mrs Lowe's head jerked, one bony shoulder shrugged. The movements were minuscule but appeared compulsive. She seemed oblivious, inured to what had maybe started as a nervous tic? Now it was as if her body provided punctuation to the conversation. The best place to buy coffee – jerk shrug. The price of beans – jerk shrug. Harries had clocked it too. He glanced at Sarah, quickly looked away. They both found it hard to take their gaze off the woman.

She'd removed obviously clean mugs from the dishwasher, rinsed them under the hot tap and placed them on a draining rack. Now moving to a drawer, she took out a neatly folded tea towel and dried the crockery. Harries looked to be making notes, God knows what about. Using the same cloth to wipe the rack and draining board, Mrs Lowe then held it out in front of her, smiling. She might have forgotten the police were there, she was certainly oblivious to the dubious fascination fixed on their faces. Sarah doubted the woman was admiring the cutesy cat and kittens depicted on the tea cloth. All around the border in bright scarlet lettering were the words, I Love Mum. She gave another jerk shrug then bundled the cloth into the washing machine.

Sarah pulled out a stool and sat down. OK, they'd cut her enough slack. 'Karen's father, Mrs Lowe? Where exactly up north is he?'

The question clearly irritated her. 'Manchester, I believe.' More questioning while she poured and handed them coffee elicited that Thomas Lowe was a business consultant. Though separated they weren't divorced and he still paid her a substantial amount of money each month. Sarah made a mental note to put out feelers with Manchester cops. 'Obviously I want to help, inspector, but does this have anything to do with Evie?'

It was the first time she'd mentioned the baby by name. 'Maybe nothing. But the more background we discover, the more ideas it may give us.'

'What progress *have* you made?' Jerk shrug.

'We're working on a number of lines of inquiry.'

'So none then?'

'What was your reaction when Karen told you she was pregnant?'

She perched on another stool. 'I'd so hoped it would bring us together. I said she could move back in, but she wasn't interested. I haven't even seen the baby. It's so sad.' *Not set eyes on Evie? Poor bloody woman.*

Sarah held fire a minute or so while the woman composed herself. 'Is Karen your only child, Mrs Lowe?'

Jerk shrug. 'Yes. We wanted more. I lost several. We were told not to try again.'

'I'm sorry.' There was genuine sympathy in Sarah's voice.

'Yes. Well . . . we had Karen.'

Sarah wondered if her judgement had been premature as well as harsh. Deborah Lowe appeared to have erected a shiny façade round a lonely existence. Superficially it was as stainless as her sinks. But it was fragile, as intangible as the air freshener.

'Just a few points before we go, Mrs Lowe. Do you know who Evie's father is?' It had to be put but she knew what the answer would be.

'You have to be joking. As if she'd tell me.'

'So you're not aware of any boyfriends?'

'Inspector. We barely talk.'

'Are you aware of anyone who'd want to harm Karen?'

'Harm Karen? Why ever would anyone want to do that? I thought you were hunting some sort of paedophile, some monster who snatched Evie off the street?'

She seemed shocked, definitely taken aback. Sarah trotted out the same old keeping an open mind spiel then handed Mrs Lowe her card. 'If you think of anything that might help, anything at all, give me a call. Any time night or day.'

It was as she was showing them out that Mrs Lowe mentioned a name. She was bending down to pick up a loose thread from the tiles. 'Karen would have been better off sticking to Michael.'

Sarah and Harries exchanged the latest in a series of bemused glances. 'I beg your pardon?' *Who the hell's Michael?*

'He's a nice boy. They met at school, went out for ages. He was a year or two older. Didn't Karen mention him?'

'No, Mrs Lowe.' Gritted teeth. 'She didn't.'

'Oh. Well, I don't suppose it's important then.'

SEVENTEEN

'**W**as she for real?' Harries checked the driving mirror as they pulled away from the kerb. The forlorn figure of Deborah Lowe stood in the doorway waggling half-hearted fingers.

'She's certainly sad.' Sarah tapped a postcode into the Sat Nav – Michael Slater's: the boyfriend erstwhile or otherwise that Karen had failed to mention. Mrs Lowe had eventually recalled his street address in Edgbaston.

'Mad more like,' he muttered.

'Probably just inadequate.' They'd drop by on the way back to HQ. There was an off-chance Slater would be at home.

'Is that another word for nutter?'

'That's a bit harsh, isn't it?' She cut a glance at his profile. 'She's lost her husband, good as lost her daughter.'

'Drove them clean away more like. Did you see what she did with those mugs?'

She ignored the ridicule, began to enjoy the banter. Exchanging ideas after an interview was essential and Harries certainly wasn't holding back. 'I don't suppose it was always like that,' Sarah said. 'She probably started married life as a happy housewife with a loving husband, expecting a house full of kids, a couple of Labradors and they'd all live happily after.' Sensing his glance on her, she wondered if he'd take the bait.

Slight pause, then: 'If I wasn't a lowly DC and a bloke, I'd say that was well sexist.'

She masked a smile. 'Yeah, but we're all different. If I was stuck at home with a Henry and a pack of J-cloths, I'd go up the wall.' She was scrolling through phone messages, checking nothing urgent had come in.

'Cleaning it, no doubt.'

She rolled her eyes. 'It's still enough for some women:

looking after a house, bringing up a family, making a marriage
work.'

'And you reckon that's what Deborah Lowe wanted?'

'Most likely.' She sniffed. 'And look what she ended up
with.'

'She got the house.'

'You're all heart, aren't you, Harries?' They were on the
Hagley Road, she was keeping an eye out for a shop that sold
sandwiches, water, anything to staunch hunger pangs.

'Not much heart in evidence back there.'

'Mmm.' But she knew what he meant. The place had been
more clinical than clean, sterile as much as stainless.

'The cushions looked like they'd bite if anyone sat on them.
And where were the books? The pictures, the photographs?
There wasn't a single snap in there. Not even of her only grand-
child.' He was certainly warming to the theme. 'And I don't
know about you, I couldn't take her seriously. All that twitching
round? She was like a penguin on speed. And I thought coffee
was bad for migraines.'

Post office, off-licence, betting shop, anything but. 'Oh,
come on. I doubt she realizes she's doing it half the time.'

'Want to know how often?'

Quick glance back. 'You weren't . . . ?'

'On average, every . . .'

'You were.' She shook her head. So that explained the
mystery note taking.

'The only warmth and colour in the house was on that tea
towel. I Love You, Mum. How does that work? She said Karen
barely talked to her.'

'Karen wouldn't have given it to her.' Launderette, fish and
chip shop, kebab house.

'Who then?'

'Bet you a pound to a penny she bought it for herself. That
way she could always pretend. But you know what they say?
Money can't buy you love.'

'Good name for a song that.' His smile faded. 'Actually,
that is what you call sad. Poor bloody woman.'

'Stop!' The barked order had nothing to with spotting a
sandwich bar. 'Back up. Now.'

'What is it, ma'am?' Then Harries saw it, too.

A newspaper billboard. Big and bold in black and white.

BABY SNATCHER LEAVES NOTE

Her palms were moist, heart rate up. It *had* to be a mistake. There'd been no note in with the photographs. Her mobile rang as she reached for the door handle.

'Quinn. What the fuck's going on? I want you in my office. Now.'

Back in the car two minutes later, the *Birmingham News* quivered in Sarah's hands as she rifled pages searching for the story. Harries peered over her shoulder. 'So why aren't they leading with it, boss?'

'Came in too late, perhaps,' Sarah murmured, still scanning the paper.

'Try stop press.'

I'd love to, she thought. He was spot on about its positioning. It was just a paragraph. Reading, she pursed her lips, reckoned it would get the full works in the next edition.

> The kidnapper in the Birmingham baby case has made contact with TV journalist, Caroline King. Ms King has confirmed that a note left on her car windscreen early today is from the kidnapper who snatched Evie Lowe in broad daylight from a street in Small Heath three days ago. Ms King refused to divulge the note's contents. It's believed she's now handed the communiqué to West Midlands police.

'I fucking don't,' Sarah snapped. There were only eight lines, but she'd read between them. The paper hadn't led on the story because it hadn't gleaned enough yet from King. They'd probably picked up the gist from one of her reports, but it was her exclusive, and she hadn't shared it. With anyone.

'Don't what?'

'Believe she's handed it over. It's why she was so keen to speak to me. Not.' Sarah rubbed her temples. There'd been a mistake all right. But not by the billboard writer. The cock-up was all hers. 'So keen she didn't even try my mobile.'

Harries started the engine. 'If Baker wants to know what's going on, we'd best hit the road.'

She nodded. 'Tell you what I want to know?'

'No need boss. I do, too.'

What the hell did the kidnapper say in the note?

EIGHTEEN

'*A sk the mother.*' Frowning, Sarah threw Detective Chief Superintendent Baker's words back at him. On the desk between them lay a copy of the kidnapper's message. The original and the lock of baby hair were with forensics. Establishing if the hair was Evie's was a priority. There was an outside chance they were dealing with a hoaxer. Christ, Sarah thought, she wouldn't put it past King to have planted the bloody thing herself. Either way, she'd been wrong about the reporter handing over the goodies. She'd shown up at the station bearing gifts for the boss. Sarah curled a lip: King probably had Greek blood in her veins.

'Ask the mother what?' She sounded even more incredulous this time. 'What's the kidnapper getting at?'

'You tell me, Quinn. Like you should've told me King was sniffing round. If you'd taken her call, this wouldn't have happened.' He flapped a hand at the photocopy. 'It's privileged information, we'd never have let it get out.' Its content – all three words – were now known to anyone with a TV or PC, and they'd be splashed all over the print media any time soon. Rubbing hands down his jowls, he muttered, 'Talk about damage limitation.' Baker had talked little else since she'd entered his office. That, and slamming stable doors after bolting horses.

It was one of the reasons Shona Bruce and John Hunt were on standby at the hospital ready to speak to Karen Lowe as soon as they got the green light from a medico. The other was to provide protection for the girl. 'Ask the mother' was open to all manner of interpretation. It took only one nutter, some deranged vigilante to see it as a slur, an accusation. Sarah narrowed her eyes, asked herself again if it was possible Karen was culpable in any way? She certainly had some explaining to do. And so did the police: the entire media circus was clamouring for interviews now. The note's existence wasn't the only angle they'd picked up from King. Her reports also carried a description of the baby's photograph received by Sarah that morning. God knew how King had got on to that. God, and whoever on the squad had leaked it. Sarah sighed. There was no place on the team for an informant, there'd have to be an inquiry.

Baker shoved back the chair, started circling the desk. It was habitual, like a big cat marking its territory. 'Why didn't you speak to her? She claims she made repeated attempts to contact you, Quinn. You could've nipped this thing in the bud. She came over as pretty amenable to me.'

Sarah pictured a little finger and Baker wrapped round it. She'd already been over the sequence of events with him, he just wasn't listening. King had known exactly what she was doing, or not doing. She could've phoned Sarah's mobile, she could have come to the station earlier. The reporter knew that as soon as the police were aware of the development, no way would she be allowed to run the item.

'Well, say something, woman. This is a bloody fiasco.'

'I'm not the only cop on the case,' she snapped back. 'She could just as easily—'

'No. But you're the only one supposed to liaise with the media. Not avoid them like a leper with AIDS.'

She took a deep breath. 'Even if I'd taken the call, she would've found a way round it.'

'Maybe.' He stood in front of her, hands in pockets, so close she caught coffee breath and Eau Savage. 'But you made it easier for her. And I suspect she knew you would. You don't exactly hide the antagonism. What is it with you two, Quinn?'

Folding her hands in her lap, she said, 'I've told you before, nothing.' Certainly nothing she was prepared to share with Mr Sensitivity Baker.

'And I've told you before.' He pointed a stubby finger. 'If bad blood between you and that woman jeopardize this case . . .' He let it hang fire.

Fire being the operative word, Sarah reckoned.

'We'll have to speak to her now, Quinn.' Her and every other hack in town.

She arched an eyebrow. 'When you say, "we"?'

'You.'

'Like I haven't already tried?' Several calls had gone straight to King's voice mail; the news desk at the Mailbox didn't have a location for her. Yeah right.

'Y'know what they say, Quinn? If at first . . .'

'Baker was probably in a foul mood 'cos of Todd Mellor much as anything you said, boss.' Even Harries didn't sound convinced. Gripping the wheel with one hand, he rolled back a shirtsleeve, then repeated the process with the other. His forearms were smooth, lightly-tanned and well-toned. Sarah glanced away, wondered idly if he shaved them. She'd just delivered a not quite blow-by-blow account of her spat with Baker, but her DC was certainly up to speed on its highlights. They were en route to Michael Slater's place in Edgbaston, the earlier visit to Karen Lowe's only known boyfriend having been aborted. The press could wait a while, Sarah had scheduled a news conference for later in the day. *Can't wait.*

The roads were chocker with Saturday shopper traffic, the air heavy with fumes and boy was it baking. Or maybe she was still steamed up. The conversation with Harries wasn't taking a junior officer into her confidence. No way was that a habit to get into. She wanted another opinion on how she'd handled King. Not that she'd admit it but she felt faint stirrings of unease as to whether she'd taken the right tack.

'Don't you think, boss? It'd be Mellor bugging Baker?'

She thought Harries was avoiding the question. Pressing an ice cold bottle of water to her forehead, she said, 'I'm sure Mellor going AWOL didn't help.' Harries had dropped by the incident room to pick up the latest while waiting for her to emerge from Baker's den. Apparently, the flat in Aston had been deserted, neighbours hadn't seen the guy for days though that was nothing new. Soon as a warrant was issued, a search team would take the place apart. Every cop in the UK was now on the lookout for Mellor and his pic had also been circulated to ports and airports.

'Isn't Baker's bark meant to be worse than his bite?'

His bark had been pretty toxic, Sarah recalled. And she was sure now that Harries was maintaining a diplomatic silence on the King question. That was the third time he'd skirted the issue.

Sighing, she wound down the window. It wasn't often she

went through self-doubt. Lack of confidence was no good to a cop. On the other hand, maybe she had a blind spot when it came to King? No matter. It wasn't fair expecting Harries to get involved.

'If you want my opinion, boss?' Concentrating on a tricky right turn, he paused a while, eyes squinting in the sun. 'I think you might have a blind spot when it comes to Caroline King.'

'Thanks a bunch.'

Well, she had asked.

NINETEEN

'I tried asking. I gave you every opportunity, DI Quinn.' Caroline King legs crossed, sat decorously in Sarah's office. The reporter had been told to hang round after the news conference. *What a bundle of no comment laughs that had been.* Sarah hadn't kept King waiting long, half an hour or so, sweating it out as it was known in the trade. She'd whiled the time in the incident room, catching up on incoming reports and tracking down Michael Slater's whereabouts. He'd not been at home when she and Harries called, but a neighbour told them where he worked. She'd arranged a meet for tomorrow, no point questioning him over the phone. As for sweating, King looked both cool and composed. Even her perfume had cucumber undertones. 'You can't say I didn't try.'

'Of course you did.' Sarah smiled pleasantly, held the reporter's gaze. She'd no intention of going into the call issue, it was a lose-lose situation. Playing a pen through her fingers, she studied King's face. The silence wasn't quite complete, she was banking on it becoming increasingly uncomfortable.

The reporter recrossed her legs, brushed imaginary fluff from her skirt. 'So what's this all about?' The casual delivery was at odds with the fidgeting.

'Tell me, Ms King.' Sarah lounged back in the swivel chair. 'What's the going rate?'

'Going rate?'

'Fifty quid? A hundred? How much does it cost to keep a cop in your back pocket?'

'He wouldn't fit, inspector.' She raised a knowing eyebrow. 'Unless, of course, he was bent.'

She turned her mouth down. 'So the informant's male?'

'I use the term loosely.'

'All your terms are used loosely. I'd say they were seriously slack.'

King's smile was tight though. 'You're entitled to your opinion, inspector. As you know, I never reveal my sources, police mole or not.' She reached for her bag, started rising to her feet. 'If that's all . . .'

'Stay where you are. Please.' Sarah paused briefly before walking round and perching on the edge of her desk. 'Did you consider – even for a minute or two – how much potential damage you could do releasing information about the kidnapper's note?'

'I did indeed, inspector.' Bright, breezy tone. 'It's why I made every effort to consult you.'

'That's bollocks. You and I both know that. You're also well aware I'd have told you not to use it.'

'Well you didn't, did you?' Her eyes darkened. 'And what makes you think you have God's given right to say what I can or can't report?' Slight pause. 'Or has your judgement become infallible all of a sudden?' Dangerous ground.

Sarah wasn't tempted to tread it. 'Even you must know certain information has to be withheld. Christ, Caroline, this could jeopardize the inquiry.' That was a rare slip – she'd not used the reporter's first name for years.

'There's a baby snatcher on the loose.' She flung an arm towards the window. 'People out there are scared. They have a right to know what's happening.'

Could she really not see it? Of course she could, she was being disingenuous. 'A right to know? And what about responsibility? The kidnapper's note might be a dramatic new line to you, but I deal in reality, people's lives. And you're endangering them.'

'Bullshit. Don't try guilt-tripping me 'cos it won't work. I'm doing my job here. And in case you've forgotten, the kidnapper left the note on *my* car. My acting on it means he or she may make contact again. Has that crossed your mind at all?'

Hadn't it just? Sarah rose, emulated Baker's pacing. 'Have you the slightest idea how many messages we'll probably get now? They'll arrive in every post, and it's unlikely any will be genuine.' Copycats, loonies, hoaxers – they invariably got in on the act.

'You can't know that.' King tried stifling a yawn.

'And what about Karen Lowe? Have you thought what effect the exposure's having on her? Knowing everyone's seen the note. Knowing how most people put two and two together and come up with anything but four. The girl's a complete mess.' Not strictly true. She'd been allowed home from hospital. Jess and a police minder were with her.

King swirled round to make eye contact. 'Let me talk to her then.'

'What?' She almost laughed. 'I can't believe you said that.'

'I mean it. Let me talk to her.' She reached an arm towards Sarah, maybe thought better of it. 'Let me interview her like I asked. In depth.'

'You?' Sarah sneered. 'Your lurid exclusive as good as questions whether she had a hand in her baby's kidnap.'

'Let me put the record straight then. Give Karen the chance to tell her side of the story.'

God. The woman was a one-track terrier. 'What part of the word no don't you get?'

She shrugged, studied her nails. 'And would your answer change if I told you how I found out about the photograph?'

'You mean who leaked it?'

'That's one way of putting it.'

'So what happened to the honest hack a minute ago who'd never reveal her sources?'

'Forget that.' She flapped a hand. 'Will you let me talk to her?'

'Let me get this straight.' Sarah folded her arms, tapped a foot. 'You're offering me the name of a police officer who's giving you privileged information if I give you access to Karen Lowe?'

'Exclusive access.'

'Silly me.' She tutted. 'Of course.'

Eyes wide, she beamed. 'You will?'

Sarah shook her head in disbelief, disgust. 'You'd really be prepared to see someone lose their job so you can further your career?'

She sniffed. 'Might.'

'Don't put yourself out for me, Ms King. I'll find out where the leak's coming from. I don't need your help.' Her fists were tight balls. 'I think you'd better leave now.' Not that the reporter could provoke her any further. She watched King gather her belongings and saunter to the door.

Turning, the reporter tilted her head. 'You didn't really think I'd tell you, did you? I just wanted to see if you'd go for it.'

'Get out.' *Before I go for you.*

'Is that another no?'

Sarah turned her back, heard the door open.

'Let's hope it won't be another cause for regret, inspector. Ciao.'

TWENTY

Saturday night. And definitely not at the movies. Sarah needed shut-eye more than a social life. Though the evening was young, the sky an almost royal blue, the long days, disrupted sleep, increasing stress were catching up. Glancing in the driving mirror, she registered tired lines and dark circles round dull eyes. Thankfully, a comparatively early bed beckoned: action would be confined to a hot bath and cold wine. Switching off – if she could – would hopefully recharge batteries running on near empty. She'd already banished the King question to the back burner, more than enough mental energy had been wasted on that woman. Besides, Baker was taking up much of her current thinking.

Sighing, Sarah turned the ignition and pulled the Audi out of the station car park. The boss had been a pain in the butt at the late brief. One of his more polite nicknames was Bruiser, and boy, had he lived up to it: bolshie, bloody-minded, argumentative, and that was the upside. Sarah grimaced. Doubtless the chief's stroppy attitude was down to an inquiry that despite new leads lacked results. Three days in, and the bottom line was they still had a missing baby not on their hands. The posters Sarah was driving past were both an unnecessary reminder and silent reproof.

Broad Street's bright lights, naked flesh and crowded bars were a reminder too, that there was life outside the job. Lately hers seemed to consist of wine in the fridge and *Friends* on the box. Adam was on some stag do in Newcastle. Not that she always felt close to him when they were in the same room. They barely exchanged words these days let alone body fluids. She tapped the wheel. Maybe it was time to move on . . .

And where had Todd Mellor moved on? He was out there somewhere. A search team would enter his Aston flat first thing. But was Mellor the real McCoy or the messenger boy? The squad jury was still out. Sarah reckoned the guy would have to be a retard to show up at the station like that.

So why did she sense a break could be imminent? Not all the pieces were there, but were there enough for a picture to emerge? The kidnapper making contact had to be the best lead. Forensic fingers crossed, tests on the note, the photographs and the lock of hair were ongoing. Karen Lowe might provide input on the meaning of the message though DC Shona Bruce's questioning hadn't elicited anything so far. Then there was the interview with Michael Slater, plus the calls coming into the incident room. As she always said: *It only takes one.* The only downside was Dora Marple who hadn't survived her injuries. There was still no evidence linking the old woman to the inquiry. Either way, any secrets would go with her to the grave.

Even so, quite a few pieces were there, just not in the right place. Feeling more positive than she had in a while, Sarah parked the motor, grabbed her briefcase from the passenger seat. Yeah. Bugger Baker.

Strolling to the apartment, she caught a few bars of *Summertime* blaring out from a passing convertible. Humming along, she was still smiling when she let herself in, flipped the light switch and froze. 'What the . . . ?'

Another piece – definitely in the wrong place.

Moving only her eyes, Sarah struggled to take in the macabre tableau. The doll was propped against the hall wall. Life-size and uncannily lifelike, its chubby arms were spread out, ankles not quite crossed. One blue glass eye stared back; the other was partially closed as if caught mid-wink. Shuddering, Sarah ran her gaze down the shiny flesh-toned torso. The doll was naked except for a nappy. No. It was just some sort of white cloth loosely wrapped round the hips. She frowned. Was the set up supposed to be some sort of sick representation? A child on a cross?

Of course not. The realization made her gasp. She'd seen this before. The pose was identical to baby Evie's in the photograph that morning. Stiffening, she held her breath, sluggish thoughts now racing. Had the kidnapper been here? Was he here still? Eyes creased, she pricked her ears, straining to detect the slightest movement, the faintest sound, other than her wildly beating heart. Slipping off her shoes, she felt the adrenalin fizz as she inched her way along the parquet floor, then in to every room, scanning and searching.

Five minutes later, back in the hall, she breathed a heavy sigh. Not of relief. Regret. What she wouldn't give to take the bastard down.

But no such luck.

Whoever it was had long gone. But how the hell did they get in? She retraced her steps to the entrance, examined the frame, the metal plate. No splintering, no scratches. And the door had been locked. Only she and Adam had keys plus a set she kept at work and another set with the woman in the apartment below.

Her glance fell on the doll again. She approached, crouched at its side. The pose couldn't be a coincidence. Apart from Karen Lowe, the photographs had only been seen by police officers. This had to be the kidnapper's handiwork, surely? And then she spotted the note propped against a vase on the console table. Words cut from a newspaper and pasted onto a small piece of paper. Four this time, not three:

Ask the mother, Sarah

Sarah. So what else was he saying. I know who you are? I know where you live?

Big deal. She tightened her mouth. *Come get me, baby.*

Forensics might shed some light. Rising, she headed for the phone, it rang before she reached it.

'DI Quinn? Paul Wood, incident room. The baby. We've had a call . . .'

It was all he needed to say. His voice told her.

Heart sinking, she closed her eyes. 'Where is she?'

TWENTY-ONE

T he narrow towpath rutted with cycle tracks ran parallel to Blake Street and Small Heath park. Sarah ducked under the police tape, heading for two uniformed officers guarding the bridge fifty metres or so in the distance. The near stagnant water on her right was dark, dank, foul smelling; occasional oil patches glinted lilac and pink. No brightly lit bistros and classy restaurants lined the canal here. Straggly nettle verges were littered with rusting cans, empty chip wrappers, used condoms.

A tear glistening on the younger constable's cheek warned what lay ahead, but nothing could have prepared Sarah. Could have prepared anyone. Touching his shoulder gently, she sidled past slowly, delaying the moment. Praying there'd been a mistake. Knowing there hadn't.

It was darker under the bridge. Auxiliary lighting not quite set up. She ran her torch over the grimy brickwork, the swags of cobweb curtains; here and there dusty grey weeds sprouted among faded graffito, in the far corner a desiccated dog turd. The moment couldn't be put off. Biting her lip, she lowered the beam, gasped as light flickered across the baby's body. She gave an involuntary cry of anguish. Shock. Pity. Pain. And searing fury.

Evie lay on her back on the hard cold earth. Her arms were at her side, the beautiful blue eyes Sarah would never see alive, were closed as if in sleep. Evie wore only a nappy. Dirty. Disposable. Sarah clenched her fists. It was a travesty. A life ended before it had barely begun. How could anyone do this? Moving closer, she knelt on the ground, grit and stones piercing her skin. She ached to lift the baby, cover her near nakedness. It was way too late to offer comfort. A small pink teddy bear lay just out of reach, a bare patch on one of the ears where tiny fingers had stroked away the fur. The bear was on its back too, a grotesque parody of the baby's death pose. Sarah longed to press the toy into Evie's hands, longed to breathe life into this innocent, sinned against little girl. And for an instant, she wanted to kill whoever had snuffed it out.

'The doc's just coming, ma'am.' Soft-spoken, hesitant, subdued.

Back still turned, she nodded. She couldn't trust her voice not to break, didn't want the young constable to see her grief. She'd never cried at a crime scene before. Like she'd never fainted at a post-mortem or thrown up at the stench of rotting flesh. It was one of the reasons she was known as the Ice Queen. But this was different. She fumbled in a pocket for a tissue. Didn't have one. Dashed away the tears with the heels of her hands.

'Sarah? OK if I take a look?' A man's voice echoed eerily in the archway. She recognized pathologist Richard Patten's Geordie accent.

'Of course.' Curt, composed. Rising, she brushed grit from her knees, emerged into the towpath's relatively fresh air. Space under the bridge was confined, claustrophobic, stank of vomit and cat piss. Over Patten's shoulder, she spotted Baker in the far distance, his coat flapping as he scurried towards them. Most of the key players, she noted, were already in situ. The FSI guys were kitted up, the lighting rig good to go. She was mildly surprised; she'd heard no one arrive and there was none of the usual banter now.

Patten handed her a linen hankie warm from his pocket. 'Your lip's bleeding, Sarah.'

She licked her mouth, tasted blood. 'Thanks.' She was grateful too, that Patten had got the call-out. Pathologists weren't all known for their people skills. Patten must've been first in the queue. He was tall, lean, late thirties, a dark fringe flopped over even darker – and intelligent – eyes. He was dressed down as usual: faded denims, white tee, creased leather jacket. She didn't care how casual his wardrobe was; he was one of the sharpest operators around. And they were going to need him.

'Nothing struck me, Richard.' She'd seen none of the usual signs of violence. There'd been no bruising, no obviously broken bones, bite marks, burns. She swallowed, sure now she'd be fine if she kept it brief, businesslike. 'She looks . . .' There was a catch in her voice, she dropped her head. *She looks like a little doll. Like the doll in the apartment.* She felt his hand on her shoulder, recalled touching the young constable in the same way. Healing hands. She wished.

'It's OK, Sarah.' Gentle, simpatico. 'I'll see for myself. You stay here.'

She couldn't. Her skin was clammy with cold sweat, her scalp tingled, her gut churned with wave after wave of nausea. She had to run, had to put some distance from the squalid stinking horror of it all. The last thing they needed was a contaminated crime scene.

'Nice one, Quinn.'

Bent double, breathing deep, Sarah was aware of Baker standing over her, shaking his head. Puking into a canal was not cool. But if he said one word, took one more pop . . .

'Here you go.' A plastic bottle appeared in her periphery vision. It was only half-full and the water tepid. Who cared? She rinsed her mouth, ran the back of her hand over her lips. It came away with damp red streaks. Baker sniffed. 'We've all been there, y'know.'

'Thanks.' She offered the bottle back.

'Hang on to it. It's going to be a long night.' The old boy had done her more than one favour. His bulk, she now realized, had shielded her from the prying eyes of a search team making its single-filed way along the towpath. 'Do we know who found her, Quinn?'

'A jogger.' Paul Wood had kept her briefed as she drove to the scene. 'She almost tripped over the body apparently. Harries is talking to her now.' She waved a hand towards a line of parked police vehicles.

He sighed. 'Makes a change from a man walking his dog.' *Don't boss, don't. No cracks, not now.* 'Anyone else around?' he asked.

'Not as far as we know.' The site wasn't exactly a local beauty spot, and there were no nearby houses or shops. They were checking on canal traffic with the water people. 'Kids were likely hanging round in the park earlier.' Swings and roundabouts weren't the draw. Youths congregated to shoot-up and swig copious amounts of gut rot. 'We'll get on to it.'

Baker nodded, glanced towards the action. 'Has Patten come up with anything yet?'

She followed his gaze. The bridge was fully lit now. Dark silhouettes cast stark shadows under the bricked archway. It put her in mind of a dumb show, prayed fervently that dumb was the last thing it would be. Crime scenes held secrets, crucial evidence, it was the experts' job to get them to speak.

'He'll be a while, I should think.' The pathologist was hunched over the body, light reflected off his steel case; a police photographer was shooting stills. They'd video it too, every surface, every corner, every crevice. She shuddered. No image would be as sharp or indelible as the one imprinted on her mind's eye.

'Jeez, chief. How could anyone . . . ?'

He lifted a palm. 'Not just how, Quinn. You know that.'

Who? Why? When? He was right. She didn't need the lecture. Belatedly, she told him about discovering the doll in her apartment, how it replicated Evie's pose in the photograph. How it was similar to the way the baby's body had been laid out. No point sharing her feeling a break was on its way. Instinct? Complete tosh.

'What's your thinking on the doll, Quinn?'

I know who you are. I know where you live. She shrugged. 'I thought it was a personal message, a warning to me.' But the murdering bastard had already carried out the threat. On a target as soft as it gets.

'Still could be,' Baker said. 'He's been inside your home, invaded your space. Forensics been round?'

'Probably still there.' They'd been told to pick up the key from her neighbour.

'You'll get the locks changed?'

'Course. What do you take me for?' She wouldn't. She was tempted to leave the bloody door open, make it easier for the guy. The old boy wasn't taken in by her quick-fire response.

'I mean it, Quinn.' He pointed a stubby finger. 'Don't try anything stupid.'

Why not? He was surely taking the cops for a bunch of fools. 'Come on, boss. You know me.'

'Do I?' He held her gaze, his was steadier. Truth be told, she was beginning to doubt she knew herself any more. 'We're not just hunting a kidnapper, Quinn.' The pause was unnecessary. She knew what he was getting at. Scowling, he shook his head. 'Christ, I'd have given anything for it not to come this.'

You and me both.

'Anyway, I can't put it off any more.' He'd echoed her earlier sentiment, she nodded her fellow feeling. Maybe he did have a beating heart inside that hulking chest. 'No need to hold my hand, inspector.' *Thank God for small mercies.* She'd seen more than her fair share. 'You can hang on here for the boy wonder.' *Harries? Why?* 'Now the baby's dead –' Baker turned to leave – 'someone'll have to tell the mother.'

Briefly she closed her eyes. Guess who?

'Where? When?' Caroline King swung her legs out of warm crumpled sheets, cursing her spinning head. The line was bad, the voice hushed, breathless, but the message was clear. The Lowe baby was dead. The cops were at the scene. Grabbing a pen from the bedside table, she jotted a few words on her wrist.

'Does the mother know?' Frowning, she strained to hear. 'Say again.' Loads of static. 'Sod it.' Damn line was dead, too now.

Wincing at the pain in her temples, she glanced at the time. Midnight. Too late for a house call? Not necessarily, but she was in no state to drive. Last thing she needed was to lose her licence. And a story this big needed a brain in gear.

TWENTY-TWO

'I'm not sure she even took it in.' Arms folded, Sarah leaned against the Audi parked outside Karen Lowe's block of flats. Harries' motor was up the road. They'd driven separately so each could go their own way after breaking the news. Neither seemed in a hurry to leave, to be alone with uneasy thoughts. It took a while to get over delivering a death knock. As for the recipient, it could take a lifetime.

The street was deserted but for a couple of lurching drunks murdering 'Danny Boy' and a brindled dog picking over the remains of an abandoned curry. Sarah could smell both animal and vegetable from here, thank God she no longer felt queasy. Harries had yet to respond.

'So what's your take on Karen's reaction, David?'

'Sorry, boss. I was just . . .' Wrestling with some of those thoughts. She repeated her observation.

'Yeah, you're probably right.' He turned his mouth down. 'The medication she's on won't have helped,' adding quickly, 'to take in the baby's death, I mean.'

Sarah flapped a hand. Explanation unnecessary. Tranquilizers and sleeping tablets would certainly blunt the edges. No chemical cosh in the world could take away the pain completely, or for long. 'Hopefully she'll get a few hours' sleep. We'll need to question her tomorrow.'

They both glanced up at the flat window. Curtains were drawn, amber lighting subdued, a figure crossed in silhouette. Jess Parry's. Sarah found it difficult to imagine the scene playing out in there.

'Did you get anything from the woman who found the body?'

He sniffed. 'She won't be jogging there any time soon.'

'Does she use the route a lot?' And notice anyone/anything they needed to know.

'A fair bit. I ran through the usual but –' empty palms – 'nothing useful. She'd help if she could, I'm sure. She seemed real public-spirited. Not like some.' Who look the other way, don't want to get involved.

Sarah watched the dog mooch past, cock its leg against a lamp post.

'Do you think Karen's holding back, inspector?' Inspector. Ma'am. Boss. She wished he'd stick with one or the other. The question was presumably because he'd picked up rumblings from some members of the squad – including Baker – that Karen knew more than she was saying. The wording on the kidnapper's note had a lot to answer for, and Karen's lack of comment didn't help.

'I think she's barely holding on at the moment, David.' Sarah massaged her neck, trying to smooth a knot of tension. 'Fact is, I just don't know. She looked grief-stricken, shell-shocked, completely out of it, everything you'd expect.' Slumped on the settee, she'd stared aimlessly into space, pain etched on her features. She'd barely reacted when Sarah took her cold hands into her own. 'But you don't need me to tell you . . . Hollywood isn't the only place to find actors, people lie all the time. And not just to the police.'

He nodded. 'I didn't expect her not to cry though. And she didn't say a word, did she? Didn't even ask how Evie died.' Asphyxiation was the pathologist's initial finding. Baker had phoned the information in just as Sarah was leaving the crime scene. Patten had spotted faint red pin pricks on the baby's eyelids: petechial haemorrhaging. Early signs were that Evie had been smothered.

Head down, Harries toed the pavement. 'I'm sure you're right though, boss. She's probably not taken it in yet.'

Unless she'd known all along and the news hadn't come as a shock.

Sarah fished car keys from a pocket. 'Only one good thing about tonight . . .'

'What's that?'

'The story's not broken yet, the press hasn't been sniffing round.'

TWENTY-THREE

Sarah stared at her reflection. She was in the bathroom supposedly getting ready for bed and sleep she suspected wouldn't come. Examining her face closely, she was surprised it showed no sign of stress, no inner turmoil. Surely no one witnessing that pitiful scene could remain untouched? The scarring, she knew, was mental not physical. Lifting her arms, she released the long blonde hair from its tight bun. The tension was still in her neck, she circled her head slowly two or three times.

Again, she studied her reflection: the eyes appeared less tired than before, the skin smooth, unblemished. *Like Evie's.* The flashback was involuntary. Sarah clutched the sink. The support wasn't enough.

What's wrong with me? She was accustomed to being alone, an only child, both parents dead, few friends outside the firm. But this urge for some sort of human contact was overwhelming.

She needed to talk, needed someone to hold her, needed someone to make it better. Chiding herself for the weakness she recognized too, how real the need was. Apart from the unprecedented vomiting earlier, she'd maintained her usual cool professional composure throughout, even when telling Karen her baby was dead. She'd offered the girl a little comfort, now she ached for it herself.

Adam picked up on the fourth ring. 'Hi there, lady. Can't you sleep either?' There was a smile in his voice.

'We've found her, Adam.' Barely a pause. He knew. Lying on the couch now she gazed through the window, a stiff scotch in the other hand.

'I can be with you in a few hours.'

'No. Don't do that.' It was enough he'd offered. 'I'll be fine. I just wanted to hear your—'

'I know, lady. I know.' Knew too, she needed to do the talking.

'We're waiting on the post-mortem, but the early signs point to asphyxiation.' She mentioned the petechial haemorrhaging then: 'I saw her, Adam.' She closed her eyes, still saw her, lying in that rank almost final resting place. 'There wasn't a mark on her body.' She heard rustling. Was he loosening a tie? Shifting position in bed?

'How's . . . Karen . . . is it?'

'She's at home. I was there earlier. Family liaison's with her now. A uniform posted outside.' She took a sip, rolled the spirit round her mouth. 'You know, it's strange, Adam . . .' The thought was taking shape even as she voiced it. 'Karen's been convinced from the start Evie was dead. Telling her tonight, it was as if she knew, like we were merely confirming it.'

'And did she? Know? Do you think?'

'She couldn't have, could she?' Because if she had . . . The notion needed thinking through but not now. Changing the subject she told him about her uninvited guest, his unwanted gift. Deliberately made light of it.

'Shoot, Sarah. Get the damn lock changed.'

'Sure.' Agreement was easier than arguing. He'd only fuss. As it happened, the forensic team had left details of an approved locksmith. Their note also said the apartment was clean. They meant forensically, given her aversion to all things domestic.

'You say there was barely a mark on the baby's body?'
He'd obviously been mulling it over. Something in his tone
made her sit up mentally.

'Go on.'

'I'm no expert . . .' No, but as a lawyer he specialized in
child cases. 'But I do know asphyxiation can be difficult to
detect and more important from your point of view to prove.'

Ridiculous. 'But the haemorrhaging . . .'

'I'm talking homicidal smothering.' She took a few more
sips, listening. He told her suffocating someone usually left
corroborative medical evidence: bruising, bleeding, lacerations,
even finger or nail marks. 'But if a pillow or cushion's applied
skilfully enough it won't necessarily leave any signs of
violence.'

'Sure, but what about . . . ?'

'The petechiae on its own doesn't prove she was murdered.
It can be present in other causes. Sudden Infant Death
Syndrome for instance. She could have died naturally, even
accidentally.'

'For God's sake, Adam!' She was on her feet now. 'The baby
was kidnapped.'

'Don't shoot the messenger, lady. I'm just saying . . .' She
heard a sigh. 'A good defence lawyer could argue death wasn't
deliberate.'

TWENTY-FOUR

S unlight streamed through the flimsy curtains. Sarah rolled
over onto her back, stared at the ceiling. How do you
get rid of cobwebs that high? Must be a colony of spiders
up there. She sighed, glanced at the clock. Nearly 7 a.m. She'd
had five hours sleep. Not much but at least it was deep and
relatively dream-free. Did she regret the rash decision to call
Adam? No. Yes. Maybe. It had certainly provided food for
thought. Even if she'd nearly choked on it. The idea of a
kidnapper getting away with murder was enough to make her
chuck in the metaphorical badge. It'd be interesting to hear
Richard Patten's thinking on it though.

She flung off the sheet, padded through to the kitchen. It wasn't her natural habitat, she left cooking to people who could and had the knack. She'd not expect a chef to walk a crime scene. Anyone could run to tea and toast though. While the kettle boiled, she showered and dressed, choosing a favourite taupe linen skirt suit. Look good, feel good was her old PE teacher's mantra. Not that it was infallible.

The phone rang just as she took the first bite. 7.15. It had to be work.

'Not eating in bed, are we?' Caroline King. Seething, Sarah scowled. If the reporter was aiming for amiable levity, she'd missed by a mile.

'Don't call me at home.'

'Sorry. I can't get through to the press office.'

As if. 'Someone'll be in – try again.'

'No time to faff around. You've found the baby, haven't you?' Sarah stiffened, asked where she'd got the information. 'Yes or no, inspector? It isn't hard.'

Breakfast had lost its appeal. 'I'm making no comment at this stage.' Nothing was being released until a news conference later in the day. 'I'll say again: where did you get that information?'

'Sorry. Can't comment on that.' The bloody woman was taking the piss. 'Is it true?'

Sarah sauntered to the bin, ditched the toast. 'You must be running out by now.'

The reporter's voice faltered for the first time. 'Running out?'

'That chequebook of yours. Can't have many left.'

'What makes you think I pay? Mind that implies the tip's sound. Take it as a yes, shall I?'

Take it and shove it. 'As per, you'll take it any way you want. I'm making no comment. Good morning . . .'

'Don't hang up. Tell me: are you taking Karen Lowe in for questioning?'

'Ms King.' She broke the connection. *Right.* Lips tight, she hit a fast-dial number. 'Frank?' Police press officer. 'DI Quinn. I've got a short statement for immediate release . . .' King's story wouldn't stay exclusive for long.

'I think we need to bring Karen Lowe in.' Quite a greeting, even for Baker.

Sarah raised an eyebrow. *And good morning to you, too, sir.* They'd turned up at HQ in tandem, weren't even in the building yet. And despite sunny skies and rising mercury, the morning was turning out anything but good. The heat was clearly getting to the chief. Not the meteorological kind. Sarah had anticipated he'd want pressure put on Karen Lowe but not this early. Walking in step – physically – they crossed the tarmac car park. 'Before you go fetch her, can you take the brief, Quinn? I've got a meeting. ACC Long.' Assistant Chief Constable, Operations.

'Sure, chief. But Karen Lowe? I'm not convinced she knows anything.'

Baker had shed the customary dark suit for a light linen number. It was doing nothing for his outlook. Staring grimly ahead, he said. 'No? Well someone is. What did the note say? "Ask the mother." Let's do it.'

She mentioned Adam's theory, suggested they wait for the post-mortem. He flapped a hand: was he even listening? 'OK, chief, but surely we should question Todd Mellor before speaking to Karen?' Once they'd tracked him down. The guy was still AWOL.

'Good point. You can start by asking if she knows where he is.'

What? She glanced at his profile. 'She's not even heard of him.'

'Hasn't she? And the blessed Karen never lies? You know that, do you, Quinn?'

Baker had one on him: a bee-ridden bonnet. And the buzz was getting louder. She lowered her voice hoping the subdued volume would rub off on the boss. 'I don't know that. Sir. No.'

Breaking stride, he turned, face flushed. 'It's not the only thing you don't know, Quinn.' Not flinching was a challenge. 'Get her in. Show her Mellor's mugshot.'

Standing her ground literally, she said, 'Karen Lowe was sick with grief when I last saw her. I doubt she's even up for questioning yet. I think we should leave it a while.'

'For the baby, time's already run out.' His eyes darkened. 'Christ. You were there last night, weren't you?'

Below the belt. Was the baby's image behind Baker's belligerence? Or was it his meeting with Tony Long? 'Yes, but Karen—'

'Wouldn't be the first mother to have a hand in killing her kid. So quit pussyfooting round.'

'Kill?' Her eyes widened. She harboured suspicions about Karen but they didn't go that far.

'Accessories, Quinn? They're not just bits of bling, y'know.'

Patronizing bastard. 'I don't think—'

'It's a well known fact women can go a bit funny after having a baby.'

'What! I don't believe I heard that.' Sexist, ignorant prat.

'A monkey's I do not give.' God, he was finger-jabbing again. 'I want her in. Inspector.'

'Are you asking or telling?'

'Neither. I'm ordering.' Brushing past her, he swept into the building.

Sarah glanced up, for the first time noticed faces at the open windows. It had been quite a floor show.

TWENTY-FIVE

The squad was unnaturally quiet, postures affectedly casual. Sounds of church bells drifted in vying with the local mosque's call to prayer. Faithful followers? Sarah took a deep breath, girded metaphorical loins. Officers who hadn't witnessed the stand-off had clearly been enlightened by those who had. John Hunt looked particularly as if butter wouldn't melt jammed in an armpit. She wouldn't be surprised if he or another of her fans had started a book on how long Baker would keep her on as deputy SIO. The boss could run a farm with the scapegoats he'd amassed over the years.

Striding to the front she greeted everyone with a brisk, 'Morning all.' Thirty or so pairs of eyes watched closely as she faced the team. They were probably looking for bruise marks. Tough. She'd already decided to act as if Baker had just presented her with a floral tribute. Even if she did feel like telling him where to stick the stems.

And it was an act. She was incandescent. The boss's dressing down was only partly to blame. Standing centre stage, she paused a few seconds, ran her gaze over the squad, then: 'You

all know we're no longer searching for Evie. We're hunting
her killer.'

Officers were still silent. But no longer with suppressed
embarrassment or Schadenfreude. Most had studied the crime
scene photographs blu-tacked that morning to what was now
a murder board. She noted a number of tight fists, clenched
jaws. She let the silence hang a while longer.

'I can't imagine a more callous crime or more cowardly
criminal. But let's get this straight . . . I don't know who the
killer is. I have an open mind.' The tacit corollary being: *unlike
some*. She paused. No one mentioned Karen Lowe's name –
even those who probably sided with Baker. 'The inquiry's got
a long way to go yet.' She took a file from her briefcase. 'I
take it you're all up to speed?' Every officer was expected to
keep on top of developments, overnight reports. 'Good. Let's
crack on then.'

She assigned detectives to trawl Small Heath park for potential witnesses, another officer to chase the Waterways people.
A specialist police team – POLSA – was already working the
towpath. 'And divers will drag that stretch of the canal this
morning. I need officers on the streets talking to passers-by,
stopping motorists.' She nodded as hands went up. 'Not you,
Harries. We have a date with Karen's ex or otherwise in an
hour or so.'

'What about the APB on Mellor, inspector?' Shona Bruce's
Edinburgh lilt.

'It's not going anywhere.'

'Unlike Mellor.' A clown at the back threw in the first even
vague approach at a funny all morning.

'Yeah, well let's hope we get lucky.' Sarah glanced at her
watch. 'The search of his flat starts any time soon.'

'Reckon Mellor had anything to do with the incident in
your apartment, ma'am?' DC Dean Lavery. Forensics had filed
an initial report, confirming the non-findings their note to her
outlined.

'I don't know. Whoever it was we need to trace them fast.'
Two detectives were already in Brindley Place, knocking doors,
talking to neighbours.

'I could do with more bodies, ma'am.' Office manager Paul
Wood, beefy arms crossed, was propping up a side wall. 'Calls
are coming in thick and fast.' The hotline was exactly that.

'No problem, Woodie. Let me know how many you need.'
There'd be no let-up now the news had broken.

'What about the media, boss?' Harries looked as if he could
do with a shave. Overslept, maybe?

Crews and reporters were milling outside the front of the
building. She'd clocked them driving in. 'I'll give them a
statement.' Pending a full blown news conference as and
when she was ready.

'They're hassling for interviews.' Lavery.

'So let them hassle.' She didn't care for the guy's shrug.
'You have a problem with that, constable?'

He raised both palms. 'Not me, ma'am.'

She deliberated for a few seconds. It was a distraction
from the main event, but: 'While we're on the subject . . . I'm
sick of getting calls at home from a reporter who's obviously
being kept in the loop. When I find out who's feeding
her the information, they'll be off the case and out of a job.
It's jeopardizing the inquiry. Clear?' Like it was a given.
'Good.' She started gathering papers. 'There's only one
priority.' Finding the killer. 'Any questions before we get
on with it?'

Glances were exchanged but no one spoke.

'Next brief at six then.' She was halfway to the door when
Lavery voiced the question on everyone's lips.

'What about Karen Lowe, ma'am?'

'Ah yes.' She smiled, like he'd reminded her. 'Detective
Chief Superintendent Baker thinks Ms Lowe needs a breath
of fresh air and a change of scenery. He's sure an hour or two
at HQ would do her the world of good. DS Hunt would you
be kind enough to bring her in? I'd like to see her in my office
at 12.30, OK?'

It was an impromptu affair on the steps of HQ. Sarah's aim
was to get the press off her back as much as anything. Knew
it would be temporary. Surrounded by a barrage of cameras
and mics, she read a brief statement outlining the discovery
of the baby's body. Wound up with a witness appeal, then:
'There'll be a news conference later. We'll ring round with a
time. Thanks a lot everyone.' As if.

'Where exactly was the body found . . . ?'

'What's the cause of . . . ?'

'How did she . . . ?'

'What leads . . . ?'

She raised a hand. 'I can't comment further. I'd like to . . .' Like hell. 'But there's an inquiry to run.'

Not too painful. The pressure of work plea paid off. Allowing herself a slight smile, she slipped through the revolving doors. It didn't last.

Caroline King was at the front desk, chatting to a sergeant. She broke off when she spotted Sarah, strode over. 'Inspector, can I have a word?'

'How did you get in?'

Lip curved, she tilted her head back at the desk. 'I was reporting a crime.'

'Course you were.' It was about the only way she'd have gained access.

'A word?'

'I've issued a statement.' She turned to leave.

'It's me who's got something to say.' Sarah couldn't read the glint in her eye.

'Go ahead.'

'Not here.'

'Forget it.'

'Suit yourself. But remember what happened last time you didn't hear me out.'

'Canteen?' She needed coffee anyway.

The breakfast rush had eased but eau de bacon fat hung in the air. Caroline King headed for a table near an open window, beginning to wish she'd pushed for Quinn's office as a location for this tête à tête. As Sarah approached ferrying drinks, the reporter gave her sleeve a surreptitious sniff. 'Nice place you've got here, inspector.'

'You're not here to admire the décor.'

'That's lucky. Cheers.' The thick white mug came away from her lips with a scarlet rim. 'Are you sure this is coffee?' She gave a wry smile, knowing it would take more than a show of mateyness to connect with Quinn.

'You had something to say?'

Probably a touch late for niceties then. 'First, tell me this: is Karen Lowe being brought in for questioning?'

'Change the record.'

'I need to know.' It would help her angle the story: Karen Lowe as victim or villain?

'I don't believe this.' Sarah shook her head. 'She's only just learned her baby's dead. Have you any idea what she's going through?'

The reporter sipped her coffee, taking stock. Quinn was in holier than thou mood.

'I can barely imagine, inspector, but talking it through with someone like me could help.'

'Since when did you qualify as a therapist?'

Since when were you made God? 'Believe me.' Caroline pushed the mug to one side. 'People find it helpful to talk to reporters at times like this.'

'Don't tell me – let me guess.' Wide smile. 'It's cathartic?'

OK, no more Mr Nice Guy. 'Nobody tells you anything, DI Quinn. You know everything all already.'

'If that's it . . .' Scraping back the chair.

'Will you listen for once? I've been in this business a long time. I know what I'm talking about. People get a sort of comfort, seeing their story on television or in the papers. It validates the experience.'

'For how long, Ms King?'

'Does that matter? If it helps – even for a while – it has to be worth it.'

'And it's worth what to you?'

'Your point being?'

'I suppose – very occasionally – what you're saying is true. But don't try and make out you're helping people. You're only doing it to further your career. End of. Quite frankly, it makes me want to throw up.' She reached for her briefcase.

'Pass the sick bag.'

Stiffening, she creased her eyes. 'What did you say?'

'Nothing. Back off, will you?' Caroline frowned; what was wrong with the bloody woman? 'Look . . .'

'I'm out of here.'

'Are you bringing her in or what? I need a steer. Even if it's off the record.'

'This is on the record, OK?' Palms on the tabletop, she leaned forward. 'Detective Inspector Sarah Quinn said she had absolutely nothing to say. You can quote me on that. Verbatim.'

TWENTY-SIX

Sarah and Harries were running a few minutes late. It was just after ten when they parked outside the Edgbaston home that Michael Slater shared with his parents. The squat pebble-dash semi like others on the small council estate had been personalized over the years. It was anyone's guess what the Georgian wall lights, mullioned windows and twin bay trees standing sentry said about the Slaters.

The short journey had passed in virtual silence. Sarah jotting notes, Harries concentrating on the road. He spoke as she knocked the door. 'Ma'am, I just want you to know.' The formal address: he'd read her body language. 'I think DCS Baker's wrong. I'm with you on the Karen Lowe question.'

'Thanks.' Smiling, she cut him a glance. 'I appreciate it.'

A door opened, but not the Slaters'. A woman emerged from the next house, cigarette dangling from slack lips. Slouched in the doorway, she folded flabby arms over pendulous breasts. 'No one's in, duck. They go to church Sundays.' She said it like it was a perversion.

'That's OK, Mrs . . . ?'

'I can pass on a message if you like. Tell 'em who called? Usually help if I can.'

I bet you do. 'It's fine, thanks.' She hammered the door again knowing Michael had timed the visit to coincide with his parents' absence. On the phone, he'd sounded more scared of incurring their wrath than of being questioned by the police.

'I told you – there's no one in. What you want anyway? I'm on Neighbourhood Watch, I am.'

Neighbourhood Witch maybe. 'Why don't you . . . ?' The woman would never know. The door opened and a teenager peered out, one hand still on the latch the other clutching a towel round his waist.

'That you, Mikey? Everything OK?'

'Fine thanks, Mrs Carver. Just a couple of visitors.'

'Long's I know.' Squinty-eyed, she took a final drag, flicked the butt at the hedge and sidled back inside.

'Are you inviting us in then?' Sarah said. 'Or are we doing this on the doorstep?'

'Sorry. I lost track of time. I was . . .' And train of thought.

'In the bath?' Harries gave him a verbal hand.

'Yes. No. I was taking a shower. Upstairs. In the bathroom.' His blush deepened with every word. 'Come through. Come through.' He ushered them into a small cramped room on the right; it took a while for Sarah's eyes to adjust to the gloom. Dark heavy furniture didn't help, neither did the tapestry wall hangings and brocade curtains. It was like stepping back into the 1950s. The youth, hair still dripping, looked expectantly at Sarah then Harries.

She indicated the makeshift toga. 'Maybe put some clothes on?'

'What?' He looked almost startled. 'Oh yeah. Course. Have a seat. Can I get you a tea or something?'

'Michael. Just go get dressed, OK?'

The towel caught on the edge of a table as he left. He froze stark naked for a couple of seconds before dashing out.

Lip curved, she shook her head. 'Pick it up for him, David. He's going to find the next few minutes difficult enough without that lying there.'

Draping the towel on a chair, he said, 'Seems young for his age, doesn't he? Well-mannered, polite, not arrogant or cocky like a lot of kids these days.'

'I wouldn't know. He had his back to me.' The deadpan delivery took Harries a while to cotton on to, then: 'DI Quinn!' Wide-eyed, he feigned shock. She was strolling round taking in more of the room's contents: a bag of knitting shoved behind the settee, board games neatly stacked on a shelf, cross-stitched samplers all over the place. 'Is it me or is there a theme here?'

Harries read a few aloud. 'The Lord's My Shepherd. Praise the Lord. Our Father. Nah.' He grinned. 'Must be you, boss.'

'Shall we go through to the kitchen?' Michael Slater dressed in denims and open-neck white shirt hovered uncertainly in the doorway. His short hair was damp, but probably dried dark blond, pale blue eyes were fringed with dark lashes. He was attractive and – as they'd seen – had a good body. His skin glowed, unless he was still blushing. 'I can make us a drink.'

'Sure,' Sarah said. 'Why not?' Hopefully the routine task would help him chill. He sure needed to. The room was stuffy, poky: pea green walls, black and white tiles, cream Venetian blinds. Dusty palm crosses were fixed to an ancient fridge by alphabet magnets. Sarah ran through name checks while he filled the kettle then waited until he faced them. 'Tell us about Karen, Michael.' Open-ended, easy starter.

'I don't really know much.' He turned his mouth down. 'We were friends. She said she didn't want to see me any more. And now we're not friends.'

'You can do better than that, Michael.' Pulling out a stool, she gestured Harries to do the same. The message was clear: we're not going any time soon. Harries underlined it with pen poised over notebook.

'We met at school, went out a few times.' He took three mugs from a cup tree. 'She was a nice girl. I was sorry when she said it was over. But it's nearly two years ago now, I've moved on.'

All those past tenses. 'Define "few", Michael.'

Throwing tea bags into the mugs, he said, 'I'm not sure.'

Sighing. 'Twice? Ten? Fifty.'

'Does it matter?'

Sarah tapped her fingers slowly on the table. 'Does the local vicar preach a long sermon, Michael?'

'Look, we went out off and on for about eighteen months. We went to the pictures a bit, mostly we'd go to a pub or a wine bar.' He had that rabbit in the headlights look again. 'Not that we got drunk or anything.'

Under-age drinking was the last thing on Sarah's mind. 'Did you bring her back here, Michael?'

'No. It was never that serious.'

'Why did she end the relationship?'

'It wasn't a *relationship*. We were just good friends.'

'How good?'

Flash of truculence. 'What are you saying?'

'Friends can have *relationships*, Michael.'

'Yes. But we never . . .' He gazed down at his hands.

'Never what, Michael?'

'You know what.' Hint of defiance? 'We didn't do it.' *Why so coy?*

Sarah arched an eyebrow. 'Have sex, you mean?'

'No. Yes. I mean never made love.'

'Why not?'

Clenched jaw. 'Not everyone goes round jumping into bed, you know.

Don't they? 'Did you want to, Michael?'

'No,' he shouted. Shuffling his feet, he jammed hands in pockets.

'Why? Karen's a good-looking girl, you're an attractive young man. It's only natural. No one would blame you.'

'Well we didn't.' Petulant. 'I know what you're trying to say.'

'What's that, Michael?'

'That I'm the baby's father.'

Incredulous. Offended. 'Did I say that, DC Harries?'

'No, ma'am.'

'Are you?

'No way. Karen and I never . . .'

'Had sex – I heard.' She flapped a hand. 'Did you try it on and she didn't want it? Is that why she gave you the elbow, Michael?'

His knuckles were taut, white. 'No. I did not "try it on" as you put it.'

'Are you seeing anyone now, Michael?' She wasn't even sure why she'd asked.

He looked confused. 'What's that got to do with it?'

'Are you?'

'I don't see it's any of your business but no, I'm not.'

'So why did she end it?' A tap dripped. An electric wall clock ticked. He jumped a mile when the kettle switched itself off. 'Leave it, Michael. Answer the question.'

'If you must know, I got the impression she was seeing someone else.'

'Who?'

'She never said, denied it when I asked.'

'So why did you think she was seeing someone?'

'Little things. She'd call off dates, turn up late. Just seemed to change somehow.'

'How did that make you feel?'

Tight mouth. 'I told you: cut up.'

'Angry?' Enough to hurt her.

'No! I was sad. I . . . liked Karen a lot.'

'And now?'

'I'm cool.'

Anything but, Sarah reckoned. The shirt had damp patches and a line of sweat glistened over his top lip. Didn't mean he was guilty but, boy, was he gauche.

'We've found the baby. Did you know that?'

'Really?' His eyes lit up. 'That's brilliant.'

'Dead.'

The colour drained from his face. 'Dear God.' He slumped against the sink, expressions changing as he went through some sort of internal dialogue, then: 'How did she die?'

'We don't know yet.'

'Please God she didn't suffer.'

Sarah frowned. 'Did you meet Evie, Michael?'

'No. But she was just . . . an innocent child.'

'Exactly.'

The interview lasted a further ten minutes. She tried drawing him out on other people Karen knew, if she'd mentioned rows with anyone, whether she ever saw her father. They took details of his movements on the day Evie was abducted and how he'd spent the previous night. However unlikely Michael Slater was the baby's father let alone her killer, the alibis would be checked. Sarah jumped down from the stool. 'OK, that's all for now. If you think of anything else, give me a call.'

He studied her card, slipped it in a pocket. At the front door, he hesitated before letting them out. 'Inspector? Do my parents have to know about this?'

She gave a tight smile. 'Not if you're telling the truth.'

'So is he?' Harries started the motor. 'Telling the truth, boss?'

Sarah glanced back at the house. Still deathly pale, Slater was watching from a downstairs window, the woman next door waved exuberantly from hers as she adjusted the net curtain. It would be a miracle if the Slaters didn't hear about their son's little local difficulty.

'What's your thinking, David?' There was no mileage colouring his views, she wanted to know if they differed from hers.

'I wouldn't be surprised if he's lying.' Checking the mirror, he waited for a cyclist to pass before pulling out. 'Either that or he's gay.'

She snorted. 'How does that work?'

'Come on, boss. He's what nineteen, twenty? Good-looking. All parts in working order. He hung round with a girl like Karen Lowe for eighteen months. What full-blooded male wouldn't give her one?'

'Are you saying Karen's easy?' She glanced at his profile. He sniffed. 'I don't think it'd be hard.'

'Pun intended, David? Come to think of it –' she curved a lip '– maybe that's his problem.'

'Impotent?' He'd caught her drift. 'I don't think so. He didn't have his back to me, boss.'

'What turned him on then?'

'Visions of you in a police uniform?'

'A crack like that could get you a written warning, constable.' He raised a placatory hand. 'Sorry, I didn't—'

'*Joke*, David.'

'Could've fooled me, boss.'

'You could be right though, David. Maybe he is gay, and that's why she went out with him. A relationship like that could be useful.'

'Useful?'

'To divert attention from the real thing? An illicit affair? Maybe she needed to protect someone – a married man, teacher, priest, someone like that.' Sighing, she gazed through the window.

'Course, Slater might just be celibate, boss. He's not got anyone on the go now, has he?'

She turned her mouth down. 'Couldn't even bring himself to use the word sex, could he?'

'Weirdo.'

'You just can't get your head round any bloke not wanting it 24/7?'

'Something wrong with that, boss?'

Masking a smile, she checked the phone for messages, put a call in to the incident room. 'OK . . . say Michael Slater and Karen did get it together, why would he lie unless he thinks he's the baby's father?'

'Christ, boss. Some youths round here worry more about buying a pit bull than fathering a kid.'

'Yes. But you said yourself, Michael Slater's not like a lot of youths.'

'You think he has something to with the crime?'

'Don't know.' She shrugged. 'But I think he's got something to hide.'

TWENTY-SEVEN

'I've got nothing to hide, Mr Baker.' Todd Mellor sat opposite the DCS in Interview Room Two. Mellor had turned up at the front desk just gone eleven – unannounced, unaccompanied and unfazed by the national hunt. While every cop in the country had been keeping an eye open for his sorry ass, Mellor claimed he'd been at a mate's place in Handsworth knocking back cheap booze: the body weight of an elephant if the stink of alcohol was anything to go by.

Baker shifted in the seat, wished to God the room had a window.

'I came soon as I knew, Mr Baker.' A smiling Mellor lounged back, ankles crossed, thumbs tucked in jeans' waistband. Care in the world he hadn't got. He'd no idea, allegedly, that the cops were after him until he caught his mug on the TV news. Baker was seriously underwhelmed: Mellor had had ample time to come up with a story. If not an anthology.

'Tell me about the last time you paid us a visit, Mr Mellor.' The detective placed laced fingers on the metal table.

'Eh?' Bleary grey eyes creased as he raked his stubble.

'The envelope you pushed through the door?'

'Oh that.' Like it was junk post. 'I was doing someone a favour.'

Course he was. 'The tooth fairy? Mary Poppins? The Pope?'

'No need to take that attitude, Mr Baker.' Self-righteous bristling. 'I found it on the pavement just down the road. I thought I'd do the decent thing, pop it in for you, like.'

Course he did. 'And I suppose you'd no idea what was in it?'

'Not a clue.' Blithe smile. Either he was still bladdered or taking the piss.

Baker nudged DC Dean Lavery who opened a file and slid a copy of the baby's photograph across the table.

'Ring any bells, Mr Mellor?' Baker asked.

His smile faded when he registered the image. 'Oh, no.

You're not pinning that on me.' The chair caught on the lino as he scraped it back.

'Pinning what, Mr Mellor?'

'That.' He jabbed his thumb at the print. 'It's nothing to do with me.'

'It was in your possession.' Baker felt the faintest stir of doubt. But then the guy would say that, wouldn't he?

'I told you—'

'Tell me again. Where and when exactly did you find it? *Lying* there?'

He was sober enough to pick up the implication. 'I'm telling the truth.'

'When did you take it?'

'What?' Dense? Devious?

'The picture, what do you think?' Baker sighed theatrically.

'I didn't.' His bottom lip protruded.

'Like taking pictures of children though, don't you?' Rising, he circled the table. 'Quite the happy snapper, aren't we?'

'I know what you're getting at, but—'

'Karen Lowe. How did you meet her?'

'I've never set eyes on her in my life.'

'What's she ever done to you?' Leaning into Mellor's space, he flinched at the smell: stale beer laced with rank body odour.

'Nothing! How could she? I don't know her, never met her.'

Baker reached for the photograph. 'Beautiful, isn't she? The baby, I mean.'

Mellor shrugged.

'We found her body last night.'

'God rest her soul.' Eyes closed, he crossed himself.

'Did you kill her, Mr Mellor?'

'Are you mad? I'd hardly be sitting here talking to you if I had anything to do with it.'

Baker held Mellor's gaze. 'That's exactly where you'd be, sunshine.'

Eyes narrowed, he shook his head. 'You're trying to set me up, aren't you?'

'Now why would I want to do that?'

Scrawny arms folded across his chest, he tightened his mouth.

'Well?' Baker prompted.
'I'm saying nothing.'

Baker sank his teeth into an egg baguette, mayo oozed from
the edges. Sarah was reading the transcript of Mellor's interview. She'd been summoned to the sanctum the minute she
set foot in the building.

'He's getting lawyered up,' Baker said.

She glanced at him, frowning. 'Reckon he needs a brief,
boss?'

'Needs a bath, I know that. IR2's being fumigated.'

She rolled her eyes. Any case against Mellor looked pretty
thin to her. Waving the statement, she said, 'This is so lame
– he's probably telling the truth.'

'He's all we've got at the moment.' Baker brushed crumbs
off his shirt front. 'Won't do any harm, letting him sweat.'

Last thing he needed, surely. 'Was he at this mate's place?'

'You said it.' He aimed the baguette at her to underline his
point. 'A mate's not going to drop him in it.'

'But he corroborates Mellor's whereabouts?'

One-shouldered shrug. 'For what it's worth.'

She stared but Baker wasn't making eye contact. She felt
faintly uneasy. The pressure was on for a collar, but not at
any price: it had to fit. 'What about the bedsit? Anything
incriminating?'

Baker shrugged. 'Bit of dope.' Not exactly bodies under the
floorboards. 'They've not finished the search yet.'

'I take it Mellor didn't see who dropped the envelope?'
Stupid question. It'd be on record if he had.

'Do me a favour, Quinn.' Scathing.

'And he denies all knowledge of Karen Lowe?'

'Like he'll admit it? What does she say?'

'I've not asked yet.' The girl should be on the way in now.

'Well, get a sodding move on.' She was at the door when
he spoke again. 'Actually, Quinn –' wiping his hands with a
paper napkin – 'the post-mortem's at 12.30. Can you cover
it?'

'And see Karen Lowe at the same time? I don't think so.'
She ran a finger above her lip. 'Egg on your face, boss.' Hoped
it was the only kind.

TWENTY-EIGHT

'Front desk here, DI Quinn.' A woman's voice on the phone. 'A Mr Lowe to see you?'

'Mr?' *Must be rushed off their grey cells down there.* 'I think you'll find it's a miss.' Smiling wryly, Sarah glanced at her watch: 12.15. Karen could kick her heels for a few minutes.

'I think not, inspector. His name's Thomas Lowe and he'd like a word.'

Thomas Lowe? *Bingo.* 'Is there an interview room free?'

A sneak preview through IR3's spyhole revealed the woman's confidence was well-founded. Thomas Lowe was definitely all man, alpha male at that: tanned, lean and seriously fit. She smoothed her hair. When she entered, he glanced up, a tentative smile showed even white teeth.

'DI Quinn?' Standing, he towered over her. 'I'm Tom Lowe. I came as soon as I heard. I'd like to help if I can.' The voice was pleasant, more Eton than Aston, but warm and engaging. It was what he said that triggered an alarm bell in Sarah's head.

'You heard what, exactly, Mr Lowe?'

'About the abduction? One of your people got in touch. Said there was a big search on? That you were keen to talk to me?'

And another bell tolled. 'You've heard no news today?' *Or recently?*

He turned his mouth down. 'Should I have?'

Clearly he didn't know. She tilted her head at the chair. 'Please, Mr Lowe.' *Sit down, while I work out how best to break it to you that your granddaughter's dead.* It wasn't necessary.

'You've found her?' He must've intuited it in her voice.

'Yes. Last night. I'm so sorry.' He lowered himself into the chair as she told him they'd launched a murder inquiry. He bit his lip, struggled for composure. She sat on the edge of the desk observing as the businessman stared at a blank wall. He had a strong jawline, high cheekbones and deep-set blue eyes. Thick black hair curled over a white collar, his dove grey suit was well-cut. He looked the epitome of cool elegance – on the surface.

'Would you like a few minutes on your own, Mr Lowe?'

Glancing at Sarah, he made an effort to focus. 'No. I'll be OK.' He ran a finger under his eye then cleared his throat. 'How did she die, inspector?'

Slight hesitation. 'We're not sure yet.'

'Don't worry. I won't break down or anything.'

'It's not that, Mr Lowe. The cause of death hasn't been confirmed.' *And I don't know you from Adam.*

'Was it . . . ?' He looked down at his hands. 'Was she . . . ?'

They were questions most victims' relatives couldn't quite bring themselves to ask. Sarah shook her head. 'No. She wasn't assaulted. There were no signs of violence. Evie looked as if she was asleep.'

Eyes closed, he turned his head. Again, she gave him time, wanted to know where he'd go with it.

'I'd have come sooner if I'd known.'

And do what? 'The story got a lot of media coverage, Mr Lowe.' Not critical, curious.

He shrugged. 'I never look at TV and don't read papers. Most of the rubbish you don't want to know, the rest you can't believe.'

Too much information. Or displacement small talk?

She crossed her ankles, leaned her palms on the desk. 'So the first you knew about Evie's abduction was when?'

'Late last night. As I said, one of your people rang.' Frowning he added a wary, 'Why?'

'Just clarification, Mr Lowe.' Groping in the dark, hoping to shed light. Most interviews were like that. Having to connect instantly with complete strangers, sift fact from fiction, truth from lie, distinguish deception from distraction. She'd no reason to suspect Thomas Lowe of anything other than running out on his family. It didn't mean his innocence was beyond question. And she suspected he was canny enough to know that.

'Clarification?' He arched an eyebrow. 'Can I make this clear, inspector? I appreciate you have a difficult job to do. And I know it involves delving into intimate details of people's personal and private lives. If it means you'll get on and catch the killer, you have my full cooperation and I promise not to take offence. Deal?'

Smart arse. Control freak? She felt like telling him to piss off. At the same time at least it meant cutting to the chase. 'Fair enough.'

'Fire away.'

'Have you been in contact with Karen recently?'

'Have you spoken to my wife?' She nodded. Hoped he wasn't going to answer every question with another. 'Then I'm surprised you need ask.'

'I know you separated several years ago. From your daughter, too?'

'Do you have children, DI Quinn?' *Puh-leese. Not that line.* 'You maybe won't understand this.' *Yep. Same old same old.* 'I loved Karen. We were very close. I held her when she was born, heard her first words, watched her first steps, taught her to read.' An unwitting smile played at his lips. 'Once I knew Deborah and I couldn't have more children she became – if possible – even more precious. Everything I did, I did for her.'

Sounded pretty self-serving to Sarah. 'So what went wrong?'

'My wife didn't like it, she resented the relationship, wanted to keep Karen to herself. Didn't even like her to have friends. She wouldn't let her go anywhere, do anything. It was sad really.'

Sarah pursed her lips, recalled her sympathy for the woman. 'She loved her too.'

'It wasn't healthy.'

'Maybe your wife needed attention.'

'Like I didn't try? She wouldn't let me near her. Then she started distancing me from Karen.' He rose, walked round the room. 'I was spending more time away from home by then, building up the business. It was easy for Deborah to plant insidious seeds in Karen's head. And she did. She showered her with presents, bribed her with gifts, and eventually it worked.'

'Worked?'

'I couldn't take it any more. I felt like an unwelcome presence in my own home.'

'So you left?'

He turned, facing her. 'It didn't happen overnight, inspector. It built up over months.'

'But not to see her again? Your only child?'

'I did try early on. But it was too painful. In the end it was easier not to see her at all than go through the agony of part-ings and recriminations.'

'Easier for who?'

'For Karen!' He broke eye contact. 'OK, for me too. I'm not proud of it. But I've always provided for them. They're my flesh and blood. I know my duties.' Bristling, he retook his seat.

'And Evie? Have you spent time with her?'

'Sadly not. I left it too late. I had this crazy idea that Evie would help heal the breach. That becoming a mother would soften Karen's feelings towards me, that she'd let me in to her world again.'

'Did you try talking to her?'

'I never quite got round to it.'

She suspected tears glittering in his eyes were for himself as much as the baby he'd never seen. He'd probably never opened up like this in his life, but she wasn't a therapist. And apart from background, it wasn't going anywhere. If he'd had no recent contact with Karen he couldn't bring anything new to the inquiry table. She thanked him for his time, asked for numbers where he could be reached.

Handing her a card, he said, 'If you see Karen, tell her I asked after her.'

'You could tell her yourself. She's probably in the building now.'

'She won't see me, inspector. I know that.' At the door he turned. 'Are you close to an arrest?'

She shook her head.

'But you have leads?'

'Several.'

His eyes lit up. 'What about a reward? Whatever amount you think best? I'll happily put up.'

'I don't think that's necessary, Mr Lowe.'

'If you think again . . . the offer's on the table.'

TWENTY-NINE

Sarah found Karen Lowe in her office slumped alongside Jess Parry. The space stank of cheap perfume that did nothing to disguise the stale tobacco fumes coming off Karen. Sarah walked to the window, opened it wide, took in a couple of deep breaths. Turning, she perched on the sill. 'I've just seen your father.'

Sullen silence.

Sarah sighed. The girl did herself no favours. She found it hard to believe Karen might have colluded in her baby's kidnap and felt the ordeal of being questioned so soon after Evie's death was asking a lot. But Karen should think herself lucky Baker wasn't in the chair. The old boy didn't do pulled punches. Sarah was happier conducting the interview herself and had opted to carry it out here rather than an interview room to make it less of an ordeal for Karen – it didn't make it any easier for Sarah. She knew she was playing for time because – rare admission – she was unsure how to open the questioning.

'Did you not hear me, Karen?'

'Sorry, did you say something?'

Wind-up mode, then. Sarah smiled. 'He was telling me a little about your childhood.'

The girl opened her mouth to speak, thought better of it. Instead picked at a loose thread on her jeans then leaned down to re-tie already tight laces in Nike trainers; a grey hoodie completed the new look. Sarah wondered why she'd swapped the usual shift dresses for the uniform of the street. If it was an attempt to deflect the public's pointed fingers and whispered asides, she doubted it would work. Thanks to the media, Karen's face was instantly recognizable, even without the customary make-up. Shame she hadn't eschewed the scowl too.

'He suggested the early years at home were happy.'

'Really.' Biting a thumbnail.

'That you and he were close.'

'Can't remember.'

'When was the last time you saw him?'

'Can't remember.'

The indifference bordered on insolence. Her defensiveness was probably a coping mechanism but it made communication with Karen difficult, let alone connection.

Sarah let it go. 'He asked after you.'

'Look, what is this?' Snarling. Eyes flashing. 'I'm not here to talk about him. You want to question me about Evie. That's why you brought me in, isn't it? Why the fuck don't you get on with it?'

Jess shifted in her seat, clearly uneasy with the acrimonious exchange. Sarah walked to the desk, picked up the phone. 'DC Harries. My office please.'

'What's that about?' Karen asked.

'I want another officer present.' She sat down, reached for a slim file.

'I can't believe I'm hearing this. You think I had something to do with it, don't you?' Karen leaned across the desk, her face inches from Sarah's. Shrugging off Jess's restraining arm, she yelled, 'Well, don't you? Answer me you stuck-up bitch.'

'Sit down.' Firm, calm. Sarah felt her pulse take a hike. Karen flopped back on the chair, spittle in the corners of her mouth. Sarah shoved a box of tissues across the desk. 'I don't know who killed your baby, Karen. It's my job to find out. And I'll do whatever it takes.'

A tap at the door, Harries popped his head round. 'DI Quinn. Miss Lowe.' It was Jess's cue to leave.

'Where you going, Jess?' Plaintive.

'I'll just be downstairs.'

'Why can't she stay? I want her with me.'

'That's not possible.'

'Are you charging me?'

'You're not under arrest. But if you want a lawyer . . .'

'No, sooner I leave this shithole the better.'

Sarah placed a copy of the kidnapper's note in front of Karen: *Ask the mother*. 'Why did he write that?'

Arms folded. 'How the hell should I know?'

'The implication is you know something about the kidnap.'

Rapid foot tapping. 'Well, I don't. End of.'

Sarah leaned forward. 'I have to ask, Karen. Were you involved in any way with Evie's abduction?'

'What sort of stupid question's that?' Tossing hair over her shoulder.

The only theory Baker had come up with that made even the vaguest sense was that Karen and an accomplice had planned to sell the baby, split the proceeds. Little wonder Sarah was hesitating. It was a hell of a suggestion to make.

Playing a pen between her fingers, she said, 'There are people out there who'll go to any lengths to get a child, pay any amount of money.'

Her eyes narrowed. 'You don't think?' Almost a whisper. The incredulity morphed in a heartbeat into blind rage. Launching herself out of the chair, she took a swing at Sarah. Harries grabbed the girl's arm, gently lowered her back in the seat. 'Evie's dead for Christ's sake. Can't you understand? I'd never have harmed her. Not in a million years.'

Probably not. Deliberately, or directly. Sarah laid Todd Mellor's photograph next to the note. 'Do you know this man?'

'No.'

'Look at it please, Karen.'

She glanced at the picture, sighing. 'No.' Then picked it up, studied it properly. 'Is he a suspect?'

Sarah shook her head.

'Who is it then?'

'Why did you break up with Michael Slater?'

The change of tack barely threw her. 'I didn't. He chucked me.'

'He says you met someone else, moved on.'

'Yeah, well. He's talking through his bum.'

'Did you have sex?'

'What do you think?'

'What I think isn't important. Is he Evie's father?'

'Who knows?'

'We can arrange a paternity test, Miss Lowe.' Obviously Harries was getting brassed off with the girl's attitude as well. He continued in a reasonable, level tone, 'I can't understand why you're being like this. I'd have thought you'd want to move heaven and earth to help us find Evie's killer.'

'Finding the killer isn't going to bring her back.' She sank into the chair, defences broken, fight gone. 'All I know is she's dead.' Eyes brimming with tears. 'And I've got nothing left to live for.'

THIRTY

'Cheers.' Sarah raised her glass, downed a mouthful of Sauvignon. She and Harries had nipped out for a swift one. A debrief in the Queen's Head was as good a place as any, and they'd earned a break. 'Boy I needed that.' Sank another mouthful.

'Hard going, isn't she?' Harries made inroads into half a Guinness.

'Karen Lowe's her own worst enemy.' Sarah grimaced, recalled recent events. 'Or maybe not.' Glancing round she half-expected to see more cops in the pub, though thinking on, it was half-two, late for lunch, even the working kind. The pub was the squad's local, all low ceilings, subdued lights, dark wood panelling, dimpled brass. The landlord had a collection of copper kettles. Could've been his idea of a joke.

'Someone's certainly got it in for her.' Harries dipped a chip in a mound of mayonnaise on the side.

'Probably not Todd Mellor though. D'you think she recognized him?' Sarah didn't; she'd spotted no reaction from Karen. She was eyeing Harries' egg and chips now. Why did she always want what someone else ordered? Her cheese sandwich had lost its appeal.

'No, but she'll certainly know him again. Gave that mugshot a right going over, didn't she?'

Either way, Sarah reckoned Mellor would have to be released. The search had uncovered nothing further at the bedsit. If they were going to detain the guy, they needed evidence. Not Baker's personal conviction.

'Well done, by the way, David. Finding the right button to push.' Credit where credit was due. Karen had more or less dropped the bolshie act after Harries' mild censure. The rest of the interview had passed without incident or – more's the pity – enlightenment.

'Thanks, boss. Shame she didn't come up with anything new though. Think she's holding back?'

'I did.' Sarah sighed. 'And now I'm not sure. We might need to bring her in again. Why would she though, David?'

'Survival instinct? If she knows who the kidnapper is she's probably scared he'll go after her if she opens her mouth.'

'Not sure she holds life that dear at the moment. What was it she said? With Evie dead she's got nothing to live for?' Sarah shoved the plate to one side. 'If she has got information, I can't see why she doesn't give it up. Publish and damn – rather than be damned.'

'Unless she was going for the sympathy vote?'

A file landed with a thwack on the table. 'Read that, Quinn.' Baker's face was sterner than she'd seen it, his mouth a tight line.

'Can I get you anything, sir?' Harries was half out of his chair.

'Some of us are working, lad.' Put in his place, Harries sat back. Not that Baker noticed. His glare was fixed exclusively on Sarah.

'That's out of line, sir.' Calmly, she reached for the file, damned if she was going to grovel, she rarely took time out for a bite. As for Baker's bark, she was pretty sure it was down to where he'd just come from. Attending post-mortems on adults was arduous enough, seeing a baby's body on the slab was the emotional pits.

'It's out of this sodding world, Quinn.' He watched as she skimmed the report. Richard Patten's initial findings reflected Adam's thinking on the phone the night before. Closer examination had revealed no signs of violence, excessive or not. The pathologist had gone further, suggesting the red pin pricks could have been caused by a rough blanket or clothing, even someone unwittingly holding the baby too tightly. Hand on hip, toe-tapping, Baker said, 'We're treating as murder what Patten reckons could be accidental death. Even natural causes. Makes us look a bunch of clowns.'

'Natural causes?' Harries frowned.

Baker flapped a hand. 'Fever. Cot death. Christ knows.' Baker was still staring at Sarah. 'The markings aren't enough to prove she was smothered. There could be any number of explanations, all a damn sight less sinister.'

'It's not like she died in her own bed, sir,' Sarah said. Unlike Baker, she'd had more time to consider possibilities. And

unlike Baker, the findings' impact on police image wasn't
something she'd lose sleep over. 'No one in their right mind's
going to dump her like that if they weren't responsible for her
death.'

'You said it, Quinn: in their right mind. There's a hell of a
difference between killing, and concealing a body. As it stands
we've no evidence either way, medical or forensic.'

'So we find it.' She'd had enough of Baker's bluster. He
was yelling like it was her fault.

'Pass the eggs.' He scowled. 'I'm not your sodding granny,
Quinn.'

She rolled her eyes. 'OK, so it's not a straightforward death,
but—'

'No, DI Quinn.' His tone was more telling than the words.
'And it's not a straightforward inquiry.'

She narrowed her eyes. 'What are you saying?'

He gave a casual shrug. 'It needs careful handling.'

'Are you taking me off the inquiry?'

'I'm saying careful handling. It's sloppy at the moment,
Quinn. On top of everything else, every lead, every line's being
leaked to the media. Some cop playing kiss and sell?'

'I'll trace whoever it is.' Tight-lipped.

'Just like that? Like you'll find the name gift-wrapped and
tied up in neat little bows? Get real, Quinn.'

'He's a bastard, Adam.' Sunday evening, Sarah twirled the
stem of a wine glass in her fingers, her long legs wrapped
round a high stool in the kitchen. Though her hair was down,
the lights low and Steve Wonder was providing a soothing
soundtrack, she was still uptight.

'Not literally, but I know what you mean.' Adam winked,
topped up her drink. His tan looked good against the tight
white T-shirt. He'd been in the apartment when she got back,
peeping out from a huge bunch of her favourite sunflowers.
He'd clearly hoped the surprise visit would cheer her up, but
she'd had more than her fair share of unexpected arrivals that
day. Watching as he effortlessly prepared supper – grilled
chicken and green salad – she'd delivered a blow by blow
account of her encounter with Baker. Adam had made all the
right noises but she suspected by now he wanted to move on.

She couldn't let it go, picked desultorily at a bowl of olives as he stacked the dishwasher. 'He didn't have to come to the pub like that. I had the mobile. But he was itching for a fight, wanted to see the look on my face.' As for undermining her authority in front of Harries . . .

'Come on, lady, he's a control freak, you know that. At least he didn't take you off the case.'

'He may as well have.' He'd made it abundantly clear he'd be taking a firmer hold of the reins, and that included taking on her media liaison role. She'd been sidelined at that afternoon's news conference, watching from the metaphorical benches as Baker conducted proceedings. He'd given the press meagre pickings, refusing to be drawn on any aspect of the case other than the pressing need for witnesses. 'Obviously he doesn't think I'm up to it.' And God, it rankled.

'Bullshit. You know that.' He draped a cloth over the drainer then shifted his stool closer. But was it? She gave a token smile. The inquiry was going nowhere, her confidence was at rock bottom, Evie was dead and as Karen Lowe had said, nothing was going to bring her back. Tears pricked her eyes, anger as much as angst.

'Come on, lady.' He stroked her arm. 'Stop feeling sorry for yourself. You know what kind of bloke Baker is. Don't let him get to you. Let's have an early night.' Grinning, he waggled a Marx brothers' eyebrow. 'Let me take you away from all this.'

The offer was tempting, the transient release of sex appealing. She lifted her gaze, realized she'd barely glanced at Adam all night. His good looks weren't the only thing she took for granted. 'Sorry, honey. Thanks for being here. You go ahead.'

He pecked her cheek, turned at the door. 'Five minutes, or I come get you.'

Why couldn't she switch off? Maybe a nightcap would help. She slipped off the stool, headed for the sitting room and the Armagnac. The door was open and a flickering light cast shadows across the ceiling. It took her a second to work out Adam had left the TV on. She hit the overhead light switch and glanced round for the remote but a voice stopped her in her tracks.

Caroline King was on screen. It was the late news. Sarah listened incredulously to the report. She'd missed the top line but it couldn't be any worse than what she was hearing.

The reporter had obviously caught wind of the pathologist's findings. No, not caught wind, the information had been carefully fed. All faux concern and fake conviction King was spouting theories like there was no tomorrow. What sort of line was, *smotherly love?* As for: *was Evie killed by a caress?* Where the hell was she getting this stuff? Sarah balled her fists, lowered herself on to the settee. Judicious journalistic catch-alls were scattered throughout the story, key phrases like 'it's believed, reports suggest, I understand'. The news-speak blurred the boundaries of fact and fiction, accuracy and fairy tale. The piece ended with a carefully worded pay-off: *West Midlands police refuse to confirm that teenage mother Karen Lowe is currently being questioned in connection with her baby's death.*

What? 'You stupid bloody woman.' The whispered words had come unbidden. They were aimed at the reporter, but Sarah was aware they could as easily describe herself.

Hundreds of thousands of viewers watched the same bulletin. Like Sarah most then switched off and went to bed. The kidnapper didn't; the subsequent fury was too great even to consider sleep. After an hour spent pacing and muttering, the kidnapper could no longer fight the urge to get out of the house. At this stage the idea was half-formed, hazy images floated at the edges of the mind, faded in and out of focus. Driving aimlessly brought the fuzzy impressions into sharp relief, stiffened resolve. It was the only way, it had to be done. The compulsion was overwhelming.

THIRTY-ONE

'A neighbour raised the alarm, inspector. The mother got up to go to the loo and looked in on the baby. The cot was still warm.'

It wasn't cold in her bedroom but sitting on the edge of the bed, Sarah shivered. The phone not the clock had woken her. DS Paul Wood.

'Have you called Baker?' There was a silence. Woodie

probably hadn't heard the chief's latest directive: everything had to go through him. 'Give him a bell now and don't tell him you rang me first.'

She glanced at the clock: 4.55 a.m. By 5.10, she was showered and changed. Adam hadn't stirred.

Driving quickly along near empty roads, Sarah ran through the scant information Wood had supplied on the phone and the huge number of questions it raised.

A six-month-old baby taken from her cot. The mother and baby alone in the house. The mother had seen or heard nothing. It was pure chance that the discovery had been made so quickly. The father was on a course in Coventry but should be travelling back now. The mother had run screaming to neighbours and was still there waiting for the husband and her own parents to arrive.

Sarah knew nothing about the family. As with any inquiry, filling in detail and background was one of the first tasks. But on two points, she was already near certain: that the baby had been taken by the person who'd snatched Evie, and that – despite the pathologist's ambivalent findings – Evie's death had been deliberate. She smacked the wheel with the palm of her hand.

She'd no evidence let alone proof, but one factor was beyond doubt. With a family liaison officer for company, Karen Lowe was blameless in this instance. And surely Patten would have to revise his findings now? Neither thought, though they vindicated her beliefs, brought any pleasure.

How could they when the kidnapper was holding a second baby? And then a picture of the first flashed in her mind's eye. Evie under that filthy stinking bridge. *No one in their right mind would leave a baby like that?* And if that same person now had another baby to dispose of? Was it conceivable they'd return to the same dumping ground?

She shook her head but Evie's image and what she knew were irrational thoughts remained. Sod it. How long would a detour take? She rang the incident room. 'Woodie? Can you get hold of DC Harries? Tell him to meet me at Blake Street.'

Sarah was hard pushed to explain the impulse that had driven her to take a look at the bridge. As Baker put it, later that morning: You bloody fool. What if the killer had still been there?

But it wasn't the killer she found. She saw the baby almost immediately. A tiny, near-naked body lay in the same position and spot that Evie had been left barely two days earlier. Edging cautiously closer, Sarah played a torch across dark walls glistening green with lichen and damp. She was afraid not for herself but what she'd do if the kidnapper was lurking in the shadows. Nothing human was there. Only herself and a baby whose name she didn't yet know.

Thoughts racing, quickened heartbeat slowing, she took the phone from her pocket. Training kicked in, she had to call in a crime team, contact Baker, alert the incident room. *But not just yet.* She needed a moment. Just a moment. Kneeling, she closed her eyes. Head down, hands covering her face, bitter silent tears trickled through her fingers at the futility of another senseless crime and her inability to catch the killer. No one could hear. No one could see. And even if they could, this time she didn't care. The scene would stay with her forever. A few seconds to get her thoughts together wasn't a lot to ask. A soft footfall alerted her. Spinning round, she saw Harries standing a few feet away. 'How long have you been there?' Her voice cracked, sounded harsh.

He raised both hands. 'Just arrived ma'am.' She saw in his eyes it was a lie to save her face. He probably wanted to comfort her but that would mean revealing he'd witnessed her tears. Rising, she brushed dust from her trousers.

'Everything OK, ma'am?' Tentative. The concern well-meant but badly-timed.

'No, everything's not OK. Everything's a bloody mess. We need the full team again.' Forensics, photographers, POLSA. 'I want Patten out too.' He questioned her with a look. 'There are marks on her, David.' Tiny red pin pricks around the eyes. 'I'm sure they're the same. I knew what to look for.'

This time.

It was just after 6 a.m. when Sarah arrived at HQ. Baker had called her back. She went to the Ladies first, washed her hands, splashed cold water on her face. On the way in, she'd driven past some of the thirty or so officers he'd deployed to the crime scene. The bridge and surrounding streets would now be chocker with police vehicles and activity. It was lucky she wasn't banking on thanks from the DCS, she'd have been out of pocket. Though the inquiry's early steer was down to her intuitive thinking, he'd sneered about not wanting any more Mystic bloody Megging then bollocked her about the folly of going alone into potentially dangerous situations. The real reason he'd called her in soon became clear. He'd changed his mind about the media; he wanted her to hold the morning news conference. Before that, he wanted her to break the news to the baby's parents. She'd agreed without protest. No mileage anyway. As senior officer it was his prerogative.

Thanks for the buck, boss.

How do you tell someone their child's dead? Sarah dreaded it, always had, always would. Whatever's said, however it's expressed, nothing will ever be the same again.

A few short words amounted to a life sentence.

Stuck in heavy traffic on Hurst Street, for once she didn't curse. It only served to put off the inevitable but the delay, however brief, was welcome. Given her experiences as a cop, she firmly believed a child's death was the one tragedy it was impossible to recover from completely. Was it worse, she wondered, to be told your child had died at the hands of a murderer? Was the pain less if a child's death was down to accident or illness? She doubted it. The end result was the same. A life cruelly cut short. And the legacy for those left behind? An eternal cycle of if onlys, what ifs and whys.

Waiting on a green light, she tapped the wheel, glanced at the street life: people walking to work, kids dawdling to school, others hitting the shops. Everyone took it for granted until it was snatched away. As the line of traffic moved again, she sighed. The black thoughts weren't going anywhere. Even the sun beating down from an unbroken blue sky wasn't enough to lift her spirits. Delivering a death message never got easier. It was different every time and reactions always impossible to predict. She cast her mind back to Karen Lowe. The girl had appeared relieved, almost seemed to expect it. There'd been grief too of course, but had life already hardened her? She'd acquired independence early from a family life she seemed to despise. She'd grown away but not grown up.

And Sarah knew that all this mental meandering wasn't helping one iota.

The harsh reality was that she was about to arrive at the home of complete strangers and her knock on the door would wreck the rest of their lives.

Harry and Charlotte Kemp were in their early forties, Harriet their only child. Mr Kemp was a senior lecturer at the Food College, his wife had given up teaching when Harriet was born. She'd had problems conceiving, was happy to be a full-time mum. Both now waited in the sitting room with Charlotte's parents. Mr Kemp, who'd only recently been told the child was missing, had arrived home a couple of hours ago. An FSI team was upstairs still examining the baby's bedroom. The rest of the property had been checked.

All this Sarah learned from a uniformed officer on the doorstep of a neat thirties villa in Handsworth Wood. PC Linda Ash, a fresh-faced brunette, had been one of the first attending officers. She'd not heard the baby was dead, she'd stayed at the house out of concern for the mother.

Keeping her voice down, she said, 'Mrs Kemp's not well, ma'am. High blood pressure or something. Her mother's called the doctor. I thought it might be him now.'

Sarah considered for a few seconds then said she'd hold back from seeing the couple until the GP arrived. Linda's face lost its colour, she'd picked up the implication. 'Come through to the kitchen, ma'am. I'll make coffee.'

The room was bright and cheerful with lots of warm pine and red gingham: curtain, cloths, even crocks on a dresser. The dark red shade could've been overpowering but was counter-balanced by light streaming through a huge picture window. Sarah's glance took in a high chair in the corner, a huge yellow teddy bear in the seat, arm raised in a wave. Baby bottles gleamed from one of the work surfaces, a unit held Peter Rabbit pottery, a line of bibs dried on a radiator. Brightly coloured magnets spelt the baby's name on the fridge. Sarah's heart sank as she pictured the family laughing happily round the table. Yesterday. Arms folded, she leaned against a wall, watched Ash spoon coffee into a mug.

'She's blaming herself I think, ma'am.'

'Most mothers do.'

'Yeah, but with it being so hot she's been keeping a few windows open. The forensic guys are pretty sure entry was through one of the French windows at the back.' Stirring boiling water in, she said, 'Mrs Kemp can't recall closing it, let alone locking it.'

Poor bloody woman. Head down, Sarah toed the tiles.

The young officer asked softly, 'Where did you find the baby, ma'am?'

She told her briefly, then: 'It's likely the same kidnapper who snatched Evie Lowe.'

'God knows what it'll do to them.' Her eyes brimmed with tears. 'They waited years before having a baby and now this.'

Tell me about it. Sarah nodded, face impassive.

'To lose her like that. How'll they ever—'

'Enough already.' She raised a hand.

'Sorry. You still have to break it to them, don't you?' She handed Sarah her drink. 'I'd better get back to the family. Shall I bring the doctor straight through to you?'

'Sure. Thanks, Linda.'

'Y'know ma'am, I can't see why the media calls this every mother's nightmare.' She paused, hand on door. 'People wake from nightmares, don't they?'

Charlotte Kemp collapsed on hearing the news. The GP who'd been treating her for hypertension called an ambulance. An irregular heartbeat was causing concern. A paramedic stabilized the condition en route to hospital. Mrs Kemp was now undergoing tests. Before leaving, the GP told Sarah an ECG would establish the type of arrhythmia and treatment given accordingly. He didn't think it was life threatening. Sarah felt a part of Charlotte Kemp had died already.

THIRTY-TWO

If the story had been big before, it was massive now and the news conference was bringing out the sharpest operators. During the short delay while a press officer rustled up a bigger room, Sarah watched from her office window as some of the pack arrived, witnessed the backslapping bonhomie, the banter and easy smiles of what she dismissed as the old hack network. Grimacing she turned her back, knew the camaraderie was fiction, like most of the reporting.

Opening a file, she started tackling the backlog of paperwork currently bowing her desk. For once, the endless admin was an almost appealing alternative. She'd barely picked up a pen when the press office rang. 'Ready ma'am?'

'Bring it on.' *It can't be that bad.*

The room was crammed with cameras, mics, cables, the atmosphere charged from the word go. Sarah suspected the pack had sniffed blood and she was the sacrificial lamb. The second she finished issuing the facts, the accusations started flying around.

'Why didn't the police issue a public warning?'

'Wasn't it a mistake . . . ?'

'Are you considering your position . . . ?'

And the hits kept coming. Loaded questions from reporters who probably had the answers written already. The press officer to her right kept his head down, shuffling papers. Outwardly composed, Sarah sat motionless, running an insouciant gaze over the ranks. Under the table her knees trembled slightly and she knew her pulse was racing. It was partly the pressure but the early start and lack of food weren't helping. Hopefully she didn't look as knackered as she felt.

She felt marginally worse spotting Caroline King's small neat figure on the back row. The reporter was her usual well-groomed self: tailored red suit, pointed red talons. Her unusually low profile was more unsettling than the questions still being raised.

'Will the killer strike again?'

'How did you feel when . . . ?'

'What steps are you . . . ?'

Sarah's dogged silence finally got through. When the questions petered out, she spoke. 'I've told you what I can.' Admittedly not much: the discovery of a second baby's body, an appeal for witnesses at relevant times and locations. 'I'm not getting into feverish speculation. Any help you can give will be much appreciated. I'm happy to do one-to-one interviews after this. But I'd ask everyone to keep it brief. No one

needs reminding how urgent it is that the killer or killers are
brought to justice.' The official line to the media was that the
police had an open mind on numbers. In reality squad opinion
was split. Sarah had heard via Baker of rumblings at the early
brief about whether a copycat was responsible for Harriet
Kemp's death.

'But you're not, are you?' The drawled question came from
a reporter on one of the nationals. Tall, thin, sallow complexion.
John? Jake? Sarah couldn't recall offhand, but knew they'd
crossed words in the past. 'It's not even half a story.' He
stroked a sparse brown moustache. 'We need the baby's name,
address, a pic or two.'

'I've already explained why that's not going to happen.'
The Kemps were adamant about details not being released.
Sarah wished it was otherwise. She'd tried persuading Harry
Kemp to supply a photograph, even take part in a media
appeal. Coverage could force a reluctant witness into the
open or even a response from the killer. But Charlotte Kemp's
condition, though no longer a cause for concern, had been
brought on by stress. Doctors had warned against additional
pressure.

'It's supposed to be a two-way thing, y'know, love.' *Is it,
petal?* Sarah pursed her lips. 'You want us to warn folk there's
a maniac out there, but you're not giving us the wherewithal.'

Wherewithal? Folk? She hoped the guy's prose was pithier.
'As I said, Mr . . . ?'

'Yeah. Yeah.' He flapped a hand. 'You've told us what you
can. What about the notes the kidnapper sent? Can we have
a butcher's?' Cocky grin. 'As a little quid pro quo?'

Latin. He probably wasn't from the *Sun,* then. 'No. You can't.'

'Fair enough.' The alacrity meant he knew he was pushing
his luck. 'How about confirming a report that before you found
the second baby, Karen Lowe was in for questioning?' She
remembered his nickname now. First time she heard it as Talk.
Then realised it was Torque, as in Torquemada.

'Not everything you see on the news is gospel.' She cut a
glance at Caroline. *Is it, Ms King?*

'Look, love.' He scratched the side of his face. 'If you want
effective coverage we have to have a still of the baby. A shot
of the parents at least.'

'What part of "you can't" don't you get? The mother's

in . . . ill for one thing.' Shit. She'd almost given it away. Had her recovery been quick enough?

'What about the father?' Persistent git. At least he'd not picked it up. 'Surely he wants to help?'

'He's made it quite clear. At this stage the family don't want publicity. I have to respect that.'

'What about respect for yourself, love?' he sneered. 'Two dead babies. No one in the frame.' He got up, started walking out. 'Not a record to be proud of, is it?'

It was a hell of a parting shot. Whatever she came out with, she was damned. As far as Torque and his cronies were concerned the police had cocked-up. With a bottom line that ran: two babies abducted, two lives lost. *Maybe they were right.*

Standing, she gathered her files. 'We'll do the interviews outside.' She needed the air. Heading out, she noticed an empty seat at the back. Wondered why Caroline King had slipped away early. She narrowed her eyes. Dismissed the thought. No. Even King wouldn't stoop that low.

Caroline King's subdued back row silence was uncharacteristic. It was nothing to do with deferring to colleagues and certainly not Sarah Quinn, she was still smarting from a verbal battering at breakfast time. Angie Baxter, the editor who'd led last night's bulletin with the Karen Lowe story, had launched the onslaught on the phone. Even now, Caroline couldn't let the injustice of it go. Already well briefed, she only needed to keep half an ear on the news conference, so while Quinn droned on at the front, she reran the exchange in her head.

The police press office has been on threatening all kinds of action.

What you talking about, Angie?

No, darling, what were you talking about?

I don't know what you mean.

Neither do the cops, Caroline. They say Karen Lowe was never in custody. They want to know where you got the information.

They can piss off.

Maybe so. But you do answer to me. They reckon the piece was a pile of crap. Complete tosh. That's she's not been near the station.

They would, wouldn't they? They don't like being made to look stupid.

Me neither, Caroline. If the story doesn't stand up . . .

Caroline knew the story was sound. She'd not only seen Karen leave the station, she'd managed to slip the girl a card and whisper a few words before the minders poked their oars in. Karen hadn't got back, but hope lies eternal and all that. And sod Baxter. If her own editor was going to side with the plod . . . She'd hung up at that point, let the bloody woman think they'd been cut off.

Glancing up now, she glared at another bloody woman. Caroline had no doubt Quinn had dropped her in the mire. For a start, the police press office was full of failed cops or useless ex-hacks. She couldn't see any of them having either the nous or the clout to call the editor direct. For another, Quinn had made it clear more than once she had scores to settle with the reporter. Caroline would lay heavy odds that the complaint came straight from the horse's mouth: Sarah-no-comment-Quinn.

The reporter smoothed her hair, crossed her legs, reckoned Quinn must've had a rough night. Either that or she'd run out of blusher. She curved a lip. No. The cop's skin had lost its gloss, she looked tired and drawn. But then she'd have had an early shout. The reporter's heads-up call had been much later and incomplete. That was the only reason she was here. Not that Quinn was giving anything anyway.

What part of 'you can't', don't you get? Supercilious bitch. Even Torque was getting the bum's rush. *The mother's in . . . ill for one thing.*

Nice one. Quinn was definitely knackered, losing it. Caroline grabbed her bag from the floor, snuck out on tiptoe. The reporter had already paid upfront for the family's details but until Quinn's slip she'd not been aware Charlotte Kemp was in hospital. Establishing which would be a piece of piss. At most, half a dozen calls. She eased her phone from a pocket. Even before reaching the Merc, she hit pay dirt.

THIRTY-THREE

'How sure are we Harry Kemp's clean?'

Baker, haunch perched precariously on a desk, stroked his chins. The rasp was audible even from where Sarah leaned against the back wall. The early shout must've meant he'd missed out on a shave. Midday now and he'd called available detectives to an ad hoc brief. It was a smallish gathering: the bulk of the squad either working Small Heath or Handsworth Wood. Sarah's slightly late arrival was down to the string of interviews she'd just given on the front steps of the building.

DC Dean Lavery gave a jaunty thumb's up. 'Hundred and ten, guv. Kemp's clean as a whistle.' Lavery wasn't long back from the general hospital where he'd been despatched to talk to the dead baby's father. Crap job but someone had to do it. Sad fact is more children are harmed by so-called loved ones than strangers. Harry Kemp fitted the doting dad profile to a tee, but it could be a façade. A cop had to go beyond that, uncover any hairline cracks that might exist.

Mind, Lavery was the last officer Sarah would send on a task that needed kid gloves. Apart from mediocre interview skills, he had the sensitivity of a dead slug, but with two major ongoing inquiries, Operation Bluebird was stretched and then some. They weren't quite on a wing and a prayer, but Baker had requested reinforcements.

'You've checked his movements, lad?' Baker waved a copy of Lavery's report. Whatever other failings, the DC always kept on top of the paperwork; big brownie points in pen pushing. Sarah skimmed a copy now. Kemp said he'd arrived at Coventry Uni at eight the previous evening. He'd been due to start a four-day management refresher course this morning. He'd opted to stay on campus even though he could easily have commuted. *Bad choice. My God, he'd regret that now.* The police had phoned his mobile at 05.30. He'd been woken by the call and left for home immediately.

'Mostly, guv,' Lavery said. 'They seem to pan out OK.'

Sarah's raised eyebrow was primed for one of Baker's blasts. For the first time she noticed Harries in the far corner; his expression suggested he knew what was coming too.

'Mostly? OK? That's sloppy and slack in my book. You talk to everyone. We need his movements confirmed and the time-line. And don't forget to check his phone records.'

'You got it, guv.' Amiable. But Sarah clocked a tic in the jaw that suggested he resented the reprimand.

Baker must be desperate though. She pictured him in a field clutching at straws in a dense fog. What was he thinking? That Harry Kemp had some sort of love nest on the side and had lied about being tucked up in bed? It sounded damn thin to her. Mind, she'd seen Kemp when he heard the news. The guy looked as if he'd been shot.

The entire squad had been stunned by the abduction of a second baby. It shook what was a frail theory anyway, that Evie Lowe had been specifically targeted. Charlotte's death upped the odds no end towards a random attacker. Sarah narrowed her eyes. Or had Evie's killer flipped? Murdered again, this time without reason, let alone motive? Did he or she know the Kemps or was it possible Harriet had been abducted simply because she was accessible, available, in the right place at the wrong time?

An open window. A sleeping baby. A deadly combination. *God forbid.* If either scenario was true, who could say it would end there?

'Who's been checking links?' Baker nodded as a couple of hands went up. It was among the first tasks in any inquiry where there was more than one victim. Have the people come into contact in any way before the crime? However slim, are there existing connections? It could be anything from having the same doctor to shopping at the same Sainsbury.

'Nothing yet, guv.' DS Derek Holt spoke for the three detectives working the seam. So far the only thing the Kemps and Karen Lowe had in common was the abduction and death of their babies. The Kemps were in their forties, professionals, homeowners living in a des res suburb; Karen a teenage single mother living on benefits in an inner-city council flat.

'Keep on digging,' Baker said. 'There's got to be something.'

'Not if it's a copy cat, guv.' Paul Wood was one of the officers who'd mooted the suggestion at the early brief. The notion in that school of thought went along the lines of an individual exploiting the Evie Lowe killing to execute a grudge against the Kemps. Sarah wasn't convinced: it would have to be a bloody big grudge.

Baker nodded, bottom lip jutting out. 'You've met the parents, Quinn – any thoughts?'

What a question. 'They seemed decent enough, but I was only with them a few minutes.' As far as she knew there could be an extended family of skeletons lurking in the wardrobe.

'Point taken. Either way, we run full background checks. Derek, I want you and your team talking to everyone who knows the Kemps: family, friends, colleagues, neighbours. Check with criminal records, social services, banks, building societies, the lot. If you need more bodies, let me know. What about informants? Anything come up? Anything worth pursuing?'

Most police officers have tame snouts on the fringes of the criminal world. Sarah listened to feedback from the floor, the story was similar from several detectives: contacts would help if they could but had nothing concrete on offer.

'Someone out there knows something.' Baker dragged his fingers down both cheeks. 'We'll have to go back, set up roadside checks, knock doors again, ask more questions. Surely someone's got to remember something?'

No one demurred. Everyone was aware that despite what the telly would have viewers believe, most police work was plodding painstaking routine.

DC Lavery raised a forefinger. 'What about a reconstruction, guv? Get Karen Lowe or a lookalike to take part? Maybe prompt a memory or two.' He said it as if it was a groundbreaking idea, sat there waiting for a pat on the back.

'It's in hand thanks, lad.' It was more pat on the head. Baker and Sarah had already considered it, decided to stage one on Thursday, a week to the day since Evie's abduction.

'Is it worth approaching *Crimewatch*?' Harries asked.

Sarah rolled her eyes. Baker registered the gesture. 'Problem, Quinn?'

'We're cops. Why can't we just get on with it rather than relying on a breakthrough on some TV show?'

Baker cocked his head at Harries inviting a response.

'An approach doesn't stop us "getting on with it", ma'am. And who said anything about "rely"?'

She felt herself blush. Despite the polite tone, the admonishment was one step from insolent. 'Well, that's lucky, constable. Because there've been two killings in five days. The next edition's not for three weeks so we really can't afford to wait for Kirsty Young's cavalry.'

She was aware her voice had risen, felt the heat as her face probably reddened. The room was pin-drop silent.

Harries held her gaze steady then his even voice asked, 'Perhaps you have a better idea, ma'am?'

'Grow up the pair of you,' Baker snapped. 'We'll do it if needs be. Just pray it doesn't come to it.'

Sarah unclenched her fists, wiped damp palms on her dress. Her reaction had been well over-the-top. She knew the real target of her anger was the media en masse and Caroline King in particular. Harries had been her whipping boy, but the DC had a right hook of his own.

'There has to be something we're missing.' Baker, hands in pockets, wandered across to the whiteboards, stood with his back to the squad. 'What the hell is it?' He ran his gaze over black and white stills of the terrain, street maps dotted with coloured markers and photographs of two tiny victims. Glancing round, Sarah noticed every officer scrutinizing the boss; everyone seeking leadership, inspiration, results. The pressure, intense before, was mounting almost by the minute. She felt it too, and the greatest burden was self-imposed. For the first time in her career she was scared. Scared of failure. Scared of not being able to prevent the unspeakable happening again.

'You wanted to speak to me?' A youngish voice, female, soft, slightly breathless. Caroline King frowned, didn't recognize it, could barely hear it and as she was in her motor on the Aston Expressway shouldn't be taking the call anyway. 'Who is this?' A tad testy.

'You mentioned compensation. What's that all about then?'

Gotcha. Caroline gave a radiant smile. Karen Lowe had taken the bait. In this sue-you society, the word compensation was an open sesame, and one the reporter had whispered earlier to the girl along with police bullying and intimidation. Telling Karen she was a journo wouldn't have gained Caroline an entrée, but hinting at a damages pay out worked magic when it came to opening doors.

'Karen!' She was in full gush mode, tone injected with warm bonhomie. 'Thank you so much for getting back to me.'

'I haven't got long so get a move on.'

Cheeky sod. 'Where are you?' Caroline glanced in the mirror, the last thing she needed was to be pulled over by the cops.

'At home.'

'Alone?'

'No.'

'Is someone in the room with you?' Earwigging?

'Look, what's this about? Are you saying I've got grounds for a complaint or what?'

'Absolutely.' Total poppycock. But if it enabled the reporter to engineer a meet, well: ends, means and all that. 'But think about it, Karen. If the police are there now, it's not something we can discuss in detail on the phone.' And once she had a foot in the door, there were other aces up her sleeve to sweet talk Karen into opening up. *Christ, Caro, cut the clichés.*

''K. You can come round.'

'No can do. Your minder won't let me in. Cops don't like solicitors.' She hadn't actually said she was a lawyer so it was less white lie more grey area.

'No, but I can. You coming or what?'

THIRTY-FOUR

'What?' Open-mouthed. 'Are you sure?' On the phone to forensics, Sarah grappled simultaneously with the wrapping around a prawn mayo sandwich. She'd been chasing the lab for days and the earlier spat with Harries had acted as even more of a spur to get concrete results. Apart from the pit stop in the canteen, she'd put the call in as soon as she sat at her desk. The way she saw it, forensic evidence had a damn sight more credibility than the dubious benefits of TV coverage. Even so, it was difficult to get her head round what she'd just heard. Wasn't fish supposed to be brain food? *Good call.* She popped a prawn in her mouth.

'I can't give you a cast iron guarantee, Sarah. Believe it or not the notes weren't signed.' Phil Sewell. Everybody's favourite funny man. Not. The lab boss bore a passing resemblance to Hugh Grant, fancied himself rotten and took condescension to a new low.

'I appreciate that, Phil.' She forced a smile into her voice. 'I'm really surprised, that's all.' And picked out another prawn.

Who wouldn't be? Sewell's theory was that the notes, believed to be from the kidnapper, probably emanated from two writers. Well, cut and paste merchants. He felt whoever had tucked the note under Caroline King's windscreen wiper wasn't responsible for the one placed in Sarah's apartment.

'All I'm saying, Sarah, is that the only common factor is the newspaper they came from.' God. He even sounded like a drama queen.

'And they were cut from the *Sun,* right?'

'Yes. I've sourced the issues, can tell you which headlines and articles. But I'd have expected the paper they were stuck on and the glue that was used would be the same. The fact they're not doesn't *prove* they were composed by different people but it does point that way.'

'Points but no proof,' she murmured. *And definitely no prizes.* She was almost talking to herself.

'I've already said that.' *Yeah yeah.* She curled a lip. He was probably stroking a superior eyebrow. 'All I know is that when I've come across this sort of thing in the past, the stuff used is invariably identical. Think about it.' Like she wasn't? 'How many people have several different writing pads and glues in the house? Or bother going out to get them?'

Her fingers tapped the desk. On balance he was probably right. What he'd said was true enough but not good enough. Not good-in-a-court-of-law-enough anyway. Sitting back, she gazed through the window where jet trails formed a perfect cross against a pale blue sky. 'What about the lock of hair, Phil? Anything on that, yet?'

'I think I might have mentioned it, don't you?' She pulled

a face at the phone. 'I take it you're aware by now how long these things take?' She knew his next line, mimed it in synch. 'It's not *CSI* here, dear.' Mr Sarky Git was right again. Even fast-tracked they were looking at a fortnight before the finishing post.

'A girl can wish, Phil.' She'd not let Sewell wind her up; pain in the butt or not, he was at the top of his game. 'So, summing up on the notes . . . there's either one smart cookie in the frame.' Sharp enough to use different materials to misdirect the cops. 'Or we've got two letter writers on our hands.'

'I'd go for the latter. Given how well the inquiry's going – shame they're not in your hands.'

'Why don't you piss off?' This time she was talking to herself. Much as she'd like to tell him where to go, he'd already hung up.

'Why doesn't who piss off?' Harries hovered in the doorway, lips twitching.

'Knock next time, eh?'

'It was open, ma'am.' His smile broadened as he stepped inside. 'Those phone skills, boss. Where'd you pick them up?'

She softened her mouth. 'It was Sewell over at the labs. I think he must go to the same charisma classes as Baker.' *Shit.* 'You didn't hear me say that, OK?'

He made a play of cupping his ear. 'Pardon?'

She rolled her eyes. 'Do you want to wait while I finish this?' They'd be heading out to Small Heath shortly, following up a couple of calls that had come in to the incident room. 'You might want to read it too.'

'Sure.' He looked over her shoulder as she typed an email to Baker précising Sewell's thinking. When she hit send, he gave a low whistle, strolled back to take a seat. 'If it *is* two writers, yours would have to be from a copycat. Someone who'd heard the original on the news.'

She took a bite of sandwich. 'Yes, but . . . ?' She narrowed her eyes.

'What?'

'They'd know the wording that way, but how would they know it was cut from the *Sun*?'

'Coincidence. Lucky guess.'

She shook her head. 'Did Caroline King's report carry the name of the paper, a close-up of the note?'

'I don't think so. Actually I'm not sure.'

'It needs checking.'

'I'll get on to it, boss.' He nodded at the desk. 'Are you finishing lunch before we go?

She smiled. 'Yeah. Why not?'

'So, did Sewell upset you as well?'

'As well?' She paused, sandwich halfway to mouth. 'Why'd you say that?'

'I know you didn't tell me to piss off, but you didn't exactly go a bundle on my *Crimewatch* idea.'

'Yeah, sorry about that.' On reflection her crack about the cavalry had been a touch below the belt. 'I'm sure you were trying to be constructive.'

He waited until she swallowed, then: 'I hear a but in there.'

'I'm not a fan of programmes like that. Actors playing villains. Cops playing to the gallery. The only real people are the victims. The distinctions get a bit blurred somehow.'

He turned his mouth down. 'It's had quite a few successes, boss.'

'They're not going to trumpet the failures, are they? And how many people has it scared stiff? All that "don't have nightmares" bollocks makes me sick.'

'You've really got a down on the media. What've they done to you, boss?' It was a gentle tease that went with the glint in his eye.

She knew he was joking but there was an old saying about true words and jests.

'Nothing. I'm sure they're OK in the right place, at the right time.' *But when they're not?* In her mind's eye she saw a street in London, an officer covered in blood. Heard the shot again, a single scream. *Stop it, don't go there.*

'You OK, boss?'

Grimacing, she ditched the rest of lunch in the bin, grabbed some water, then walked to the window and perched on the sill. His concerned gaze was still on her face. He was emotionally intelligent, almost certainly sussed her hostility to the press had a personal edge. Pre-empting any probing on that score, she steered the conversation back to the professional conflict. 'Don't get me wrong, David. I know they can be useful but their priorities are different to ours. We catch criminals. They

catch the next bulletin. We chase detection figures, they chase
viewing figures.' She gave a thin smile. 'I swear some of them
make it up as they go along.'

'That's a bit sweeping, isn't it?' He ran a hand through his
hair.

She shrugged. 'I'm not saying they're all sharks. I've come
across some sharp operators out there. On the other hand,
I've read stories after press conferences and couldn't believe
the reporters had been in the same room as me.' She slipped
off the sill, wandered back to the desk, started gathering papers.
'They probably get their heads together afterwards and work
out what angle to take. If enough of them say the same thing,
well, there's safety in numbers.'

'That's pretty harsh, boss. They can do a lot of good exposing
scandals and cover-ups, highlighting injustice, corruption, even
just passing on info.'

Lip curved, she glanced up. 'You sound like a public service
announcement, David.'

'Yeah, but fair's fair. You know what I mean.'

'Then it's a shame the stupid and unscrupulous give the rest
a bad name.'

He held her gaze. 'You could say the same about the
police.'

'I think you'll find the press already do. Anyway, are you
coming, or what? It's time to hit the road.' She was rummaging
in her briefcase. Where the hell were the car keys?

He was on his feet, heading for the door. 'If you're looking
for your keys, boss, I saw them on your desk.'

'Clever dick.'

THIRTY-FIVE

'She's not the sharpest knife in the police canteen.' It
wasn't the wittiest line she'd ever come up with but
Caroline King was mentally rubbing her elegant little
hands in glee. After a false start, she was surprised how well
it was going. Not so much a case of feet under the table as
tucked up on Karen Lowe's lurid pink settee. The Barbie décor

alone meant the women would never be best friends, but for the moment they shared a mutual foe.

'Quinn's a hard-nosed cow.' Karen ran a hand over her mouth.

Caroline tilted a bottle towards the girl. 'Top up?'

'Cheers.'

She smiled. The plonk had been worth every penny. Though the session had been hard-going initially. Even on the doorstep, Caroline had realized her glossy appearance, in marked contrast to Karen's, could work against her. So she'd majored on aspects easier to alter. The long vowels got short shrift immediately as she calculated how best to play the girl. Mirroring body language was good and subtly adopting speech patterns and accent helped, but connecting emotionally was the real skill. Fake that and you were in. Caroline had lost a child too, she'd confided to Karen. The doctors had done everything they could, of course, but . . . It was the trump card in a pack of lies that had led to this cosy little head to heart.

'Y'know, Karen, Quinn wouldn't let me anywhere near you. I begged her to let me have a chat with you, offer my help. She made out there was no way you wanted to talk to me.'

'She didn't even ask.' The girl flicked a lank strand of hair from her face. 'Never even mentioned it.'

Running a scarlet nail round the rim of her glass, Caroline cast the odd covert glance at her quarry who was huddled into a corner of the settee, hugging a pink fur cushion. When not sucking furiously on a cigarette, Karen's lips were set in a scowl, she was clearly mulling over what she'd heard and patently not appreciating Quinn's stance.

'Yes.' Caroline sighed, circled a slim ankle. 'I thought you'd turned me down. That you didn't want anything to do with me 'cos I'm a reporter.'

'I'd no idea you were after me.' She was picking loose strands of the fake fur, laying them on the arm of the chair.

'It's why I mentioned compensation when we crossed paths the other day. I reckoned it just might persuade you to let me in. I'm really sorry about that. I hated not being straight with you.' She hung her head in what might be shame. 'Goes against the grain.'

''S' OK.' A waved hand brushed off the apology. 'No sweat.' Plenty of smoke though.

Caroline had explained early on that a claim against the
police was a no-no. And that she had a better proposition. She
took a sip of wine. 'I'm surprised the minder didn't mention
it.' Jess something. Perry? Parry? She couldn't remember the
name, only that the woman could be a problem. 'When are
you expecting her back?'

'I'm not. I needed my own space, know what I mean?'
Karen had apparently told the family liaison officer to leave.
That she felt like a prisoner in her own home.

'I can well believe it.' Sage nod. 'Eyes and ears of the
police, aren't they?'

The girl's face dropped. 'I liked her. She was—'

'Oh, I'm sure she was good to you, Karen. They're well
trained and all that, but when push comes to shove, we
all know what side they're on. I came here once before and
she wouldn't let me in. But that would've been Quinn's
say-so.'

'Quinn's a cow,' Karen snarled. 'She should've at least told
me you wanted an interview.' She stubbed out the butt in a
packed ashtray.

The reporter remained silent for a while. Pacing was
important, the next stage in the strategy vital. Karen was no
intellectual, but neither was she anyone's fool. Caroline
leaned forward, put the glass on a low table.

'What really bothers me . . .' She paused, lips pursed, then
shook her head. 'Never mind. Forget I said anything.' The
mystique had the desired affect.

'No, go on. Tell me.'

'It's just . . .' She narrowed her eyes as if considering
whether to divulge what was on her mind. Didn't want to
overdo the dissembling though, she wanted the girl thinking
she'd dragged it out of her. 'No, I can't.'

'Please.' Karen touched the reporter's sleeve. 'Go on.'

She took a deep breath. 'OK. I told Sarah Quinn I wanted
to do an in-depth interview with you. That it would be seen
by millions of viewers. And that it could help lead them to
the kidnapper.'

'Like a proper film? On the telly?'

She gave a rueful nod, watched as Karen mentally digested
the missed opportunity of fleeting fame. The *coup de grâce*
was imminent. She hesitated. *Was it fair?* Surprisingly, she

felt a twinge of genuine sympathy for the girl. It didn't last long.

'See, Karen, with the proper publicity and exposure I think it might have helped us find Evie.' She paused to give the words full import. 'Before it was too late.'

Her gaze searched the reporter's face for not-so-hidden meaning. 'You're saying it might've saved her life?'

'I can't say that, Karen. Of course I can't.' She placed a gentle hand on the girl's arm. 'The sad thing is, we'll never know now, will we?'

'I can't forgive her for that, Caroline.' Eyes brimming. 'Y'know they actually had me in for questioning? And now another baby's dead. And the killer's still out there. I'd do anything to see the bastard behind bars. Show that bloody woman how wrong you can be.'

'Would you, Karen?'

'In a heartbeat.'

'In that case, I think I know what we could do. Tell me, how many pictures of Evie do you have?'

Karen had lots, seventy odd. Caroline had taken them back to the Marriott and spread them over the bed like a patchwork quilt. She'd needed a hot shower, told herself it was to get rid of the cigarette smoke clinging to her hair and skin. Now, wrapped in a fluffy white bathrobe, she cast an expert eye over the colourful montage, making mental notes on the shots with most potential.

Having spent several hours cooped up in Karen's flat, Caroline was revelling in her own company and what could be one of the biggest exclusives of her career. She sipped a gin and tonic. The time spent with the girl had been a good investment. Karen had signed a contract agreeing the story could be filmed. Caroline had taken the paperwork along just in case. It was in her bag now next to a chequebook.

A fat cheque nestled in Karen's purse. The girl had – in effect – handed back a blank one. She'd given Caroline *carte blanche* or, as stipulated in the contract, unlimited access and total editorial control over the story. Tomorrow Karen would open up her door and her heart to the cameras. Caroline had convinced the girl that extended coverage could lead to the killer's capture,

that the moving story could prompt someone harbouring the
criminal to come forward and that Karen's on-screen courage
would help and inspire others. The fact that the film would
be a lasting tribute to Evie had almost certainly clinched the
deal.

Caroline padded to the mini bar for a refill. With full glass
in hand, she sank into an armchair, picked up the phone. For
her the bargaining hadn't even begun. As a freelancer, she'd
yet to decide where to offer the material, let alone negotiate
her fee. Tapping her lip with a finger, she ran a mental
eeny-meeny-miny . . .

'Bob? Caro here.' Silken tones. 'How you doing?' Lifting
a leg, she admired its contours as she talked through what was
on offer with ITN editor Bob Grant. 'So what d'you think?
Is it good or is it shit hot?' TVs played in the background,
she heard the odd raised voice but it was Grant's she waited
for, and as pauses go, it was long.

'I don't know, Caro. It sounds more like a strand in a doco
to me. Not sure there's enough to sustain a special.' She
pictured Grant pushing trendy specs into his hairline, thumb
hooked in belt buckle as he stood in front of the newsroom's
bank of monitors.

'You're joking. It'll be brilliant, Bob. As for visuals, there's
Evie smiling, sleeping, sitting up. You name it, we've got
it.'

'Even so . . .'

Caroline was fuming. The more infuriated and frustrated
she felt, the more persuasive and placatory she sounded. 'It'll
be great telly. Trust me, Bob.' She injected more warmth into
her voice. 'You can trust me, you *know* that.' The appeal was
to baser instincts. They'd been lovers off and on for years,
Grant's recent marriage had made no appreciable difference
to their affair. Her words weren't a veiled threat. Unless he
read them that way.

'It's still a bit look-at-life-ish, honey.'

Tame? Twee? Cutesy? Bloody cheek. 'You're kidding, mate.
It's look at death, look at what it does, look at police pressure,
look at the hunt for a double killer. Christ, Bob, it's got everything. Exclusive coverage of a grieving mother while the cops
run round like dickheads.'

'That's the point, Caro. You're offering a follow-up feature.

Viewers want the latest developments. Two babies are dead
now.'

The Kemps were the proverbial ace up her sleeve. Though
not yet in the bag, she knew where they were. Crossing her
fingers, she mouthed a silent prayer, then: 'That's why I'm
offering you both. Exclusive coverage of the Kemps and
unlimited access to Karen Lowe. Hard news and human life
story. What more could you want, darling?'

'When's the earliest you can deliver?'

There was no time for finer feelings or conscience wrestling.
Caroline had to meet a deadline. She'd committed herself
to coming up with the goods. It wouldn't quite be professional suicide if she failed to deliver but her reputation would
take a hammering. It was more than that though. Caroline
wanted the Kemps' story for herself as much as supplying
it to Bob. The sensations were physical. Her palms were
moist, heartbeat quickened. It was the thrill of the chase,
without the chase. She knew where to locate the couple.
Her informant wasn't cheap, but the contract was exclusive.
The Kemps wouldn't be going anywhere in a hurry. Her
concern was that if she didn't get a move on another journalist might suss it too. As far as the competition was
concerned, she didn't anticipate a stitch-up, it was more a
tapestry she had in mind.

THIRTY-SIX

At about the time Caroline King was threading her
needles, Sarah Quinn was tying loose ends on the day's
paperwork. Not that the admin ever really stopped:
officer reports, witness statements, summary of incoming calls
to catch up on, and as Baker's deputy it fell to her to maintain
Operation Bluebird's daily log detailing decisions taken,
actions tasked, progress made, budget spent. The record would
be referred to whenever the case was reviewed. And as in any
major ongoing inquiry, it would be, probably several times.
The backtracking could establish if and when wrong steps

were taken and which paths should be retraced. In effect, it was a record of accountability. So the brass knew where to lay the blame.

Rolling back the swivel chair Sarah yawned, stretched her arms in the air, then crossed her hands on her head. Coming up to eight o'clock and she'd had enough. Her stomach had been grumbling for at least an hour. Grimacing she recalled there'd be no Adam tonight fixing supper. They'd snatched a few words earlier on the phone: there was a big case on in Aylesbury; he probably wouldn't get back until the weekend. She blew her cheeks out on a sigh. An empty apartment held little appeal, there was too much on her mind, she needed taking out of herself. If Harries hadn't tapped on the door, she'd never have asked. That's what she told herself anyway.

'I'm heading off now, boss. Anything I need to know for tomorrow?'

'What are you doing tonight?' Impulse. The invite was out before she really thought about it.

'Who? Me?'

'No, Hannibal Lecter.' *Must have food on the brain.* 'I'm starving. I could murder a balti.'

'Er . . . yeah . . . no . . . sure . . . can I just make a phone call?'

She flapped a hand. 'No worries if you're tied up.'

'No. It's not that. It's just . . .'

No eye contact and the hint of a blush. Either he had some-thing/someone on or he was fazed by the boss asking him out. Mind, it was a touch out of the blue. She masked a smile. 'It's only a bite to eat, David.' She wasn't looking to exchange body fluids.

Half an hour later they were making inroads on Peshwari naans in the Cinnamon Tree. The restaurant in the balti triangle was a favourite of Sarah's. The food was top notch, its décor an acquired taste. Garish murals of snow-capped mountains and lime green carpets weren't easy on the eye. Focussing on the massive fish tank recessed into one of the walls wasn't quite so taxing, or looking at Harries who was glancing at his plate, smiling.

'Something on your mind, David?'

'I was thinking about the last time we grabbed a bite.' The

candlelight glinted in his eyes. 'That late lunch in the Queen's Head? Baker beating a path to the table?'

She snorted. 'I shouldn't worry. He's not into curry. The old boy only likes spice in his aftershave.' *Cut it out, Sarah.*

'He was in an ace mood at tonight's brief, wasn't he?'

The delivery was so dry for a second she thought he was serious. But nobody could be that wrong. 'Yeah, right.'

'Except nothing was. He didn't have a good word for anyone.'

'Miss Quinn. You're looking ever more lovely, if I may so.' The owner Rajeev Choudry had appeared at her elbow. It was no hardship. Tall, dark, model looks; he was one of the most beautiful men she knew. He always wore tailored black trousers and white Nehru shirts, but wasn't a guy you'd mistake for a waiter.

'Thank you, Raj. Flattery will get you everywhere.' She flashed a smile, ran through the introductions.

He nodded at Harries, barely took his gaze off Sarah. 'We haven't seen you for a while. The bad men are keeping you busy, I suppose?'

'You suppose right, Raj.'

'This baby business, it's a terrible thing.' He swept his fringe from heavily-lashed eyes. 'The young mother . . . Karen, is it? She's eaten here a few times.'

Sarah's hand stilled as she reached for water. 'You know her?'

'I didn't know who she was until I saw her face in the papers.'

'When was she here last, Mr Choudry?' Harries chipped in.

'It was a while back. She was pregnant.' He held his arms in a wide circle in front of his waist. 'She made a joke about not having the dishes too hot in case the baby came early.' His smile faded.

'Any idea who she was with, Raj?'

'She came a few times, but never with the same man.'

'Recall any names?' She took his empty palms as a no. 'Would you recognize any of the men again?'

'Maybe.'

'If you see . . . ?'

'You'll be the first to know. And I'll ask around the staff. Enjoy.' Head bowed, he made way for their approaching waiter.

Dishes served, appetites kicked in and they ate in silence for a while. She made a mental note to get a DC over to the restaurant first thing. He or she could flash pics of Michael Slater and Todd Mellor on the off chance.

'Getting back to Baker.' Harries was using the naan as a scoop. 'Reckon he was having a bad day or what?'

'Baker?' She'd lost the trail.

'Yeah, at the brief. It was bollocking central in there. Talk about foul mood.'

A mouthful of lamb gave her time to consider. Baker's performance that night had been poor, but taking a pop would be unprofessional. 'It comes down to management style, David. He varies it all the time. It's meant to keep the squad on their toes.'

'Can't see there's much mileage in it.' He took a swig of lager. 'Pisses people off when they're working their balls . . . sorry . . . fingers to the bone to get a result.'

She agreed. All stick and no carrot was counter productive, but Baker wasn't here to defend himself and she was well aware that the closer to the top, the tougher and lonelier the job got. And she saw an element of duff eggs in the wrong basket.

'Baker had it in his head Todd Mellor was in the frame. He wasn't happy letting the guy walk.' Mellor had been released that afternoon shouting his mouth off about a police state and threatening to flog his story to the papers. 'Karen Lowe looks to be in the clear too. Baker's feeling the pressure, big time, David.'

'And we're not? So what are you saying? We bang a few suckers up in the cells just to keep the chief in a good mood?' Head down, he was engrossed in both eating and the heat of his righteous indignation.

She curved a lip, rather liked the fact he seemed to have forgotten she was his DI.

'No, I'm saying it's important not to get fixated. Do that and you risk closing your mind to other options.'

'He's got enough years under the belt to know that surely?'

'So who's perfect? Cut him some slack.'

The conversation moved on to other topics: films, books, bands. She found him good company, relaxed, easy going. The place was filling up, it was time to go. Harries glanced round while they waited for the bill, nodded at Raj as he passed the table. 'D'you come here often then, boss?'

She laughed out loud. Knew he'd asked because she was on first name terms with the owner. 'That's a rubbish chat-up line, David.'

Smiling, he held her gaze. 'And if I came out with a better one . . . ?

THIRTY-SEVEN

Caroline King had rehearsed the all-important opening line many times.

'Mr and Mrs Kemp, I know what you're going through and I'm so very, very sorry.'

The tears had played a crucial role, though Caroline's convincing performance had sealed the deal. She'd lied of course. Not to gain entrance to the hospital. Doctors don't wear white coats these days, but her short-sleeved white jacket had helped open doors. She'd teamed it with a winning smile and authoritative air. She'd also dispensed with most of the slap and tied back the distinctive bob. The medical case she carried had been acquired years ago and kept in the boot for just such emergencies. Once inside, she thanked God for BUPA and private rooms and headed for the Kemps. It was then that the truth became the hospital's latest casualty. The couple had obligingly mistaken her for a medic. A misapprehension she was happy to allow but careful not to confirm. The confusion had enabled her to enter the small side room, close the door and deliver the well practised line.

Clearly confused, their gazes had searched her face. Charlotte Kemp lay propped up on pillows. Her husband sat in a chair at the side of the bed. She'd hoped one of them would pick up the dialogue but neither spoke. She prompted with: 'I know how tragic it is when a baby dies.'

'Thank you, doctor.' Harry Kemp placed a hand over his wife's. 'You must see it a great deal in your job.'

'No, what I'm saying is . . . I've lost a baby too . . . her life barely begun.' Caroline's voice broke and she staggered slightly as tears fell. She was so convincing she almost believed it herself even though her only brush with motherhood was an early abortion five years back.

Nonplussed, Harry Kemp rose. 'Have a seat, doctor. Can I get you some water?'

'Thank you, no.' She allowed him to steer her towards the chair, then moist-eyed she looked gravely at each in turn. 'Please forgive me for intruding on your personal grief. I didn't want to come here at all.' The couple exchanged bewildered glances. Harry Kemp opened his mouth, but Caroline raised a hand. 'Please. Let me speak. If I don't set the record straight now, I'll never forgive myself.'

'Look, doctor . . .' He ran his fingers through thinning mousy hair. Poor guy was too confused to continue and too polite to get stroppy. She almost felt sorry for him.

'I'm not a doctor. I'm a reporter.' She dropped her head. 'My editor sent me. He said if I didn't talk to you I'd be out of a job.'

Kemp tightened his lips. 'That's tough. But there's no way my wife and I want to be in the papers. So if you don't mind . . .' He pointed to the door.

'Of course. I understand. I told him exactly that. It's just . . . he said if I didn't get down here, get an interview, I'd never work again. And, well, there's only me and Sally at home now.'

'Sally?' he asked.

'My other daughter. There's just the two of us since Bob . . .' Thank God they didn't ask for more, just the allusion to an additional personal tragedy was enough already.

'We're sorry for your loss,' Harry Kemp said. 'We still don't want publicity.'

She nodded, pulled a tissue from her pocket. 'God I hate this job sometimes. Believe you me, I wouldn't have come at all except I know how much it helped me to talk about Sarah.' She dabbed the tissue round her eyes.

'Sarah?'

'My daughter who died.' Caroline smiled wanly as if picturing the dearly departed loved one. It was a much older Sarah she had in mind, one who was very much alive and kicking.

'How do you mean, it helped?' Charlotte Kemp spoke for

the first time. Her complexion was a touch pale, but the face framed by chin-length blonde hair was pretty enough.

'It's difficult to put into words, Mrs Kemp.' She tried explaining it the way interviewees had in the past. 'Talking to reporters about Sarah somehow kept her memory alive. And I wanted other people to know her story. I didn't want her to be forgotten. Of course I've still got the video at home. I often get the tapes out to see her.'

'It was on TV?' Charlotte again.

'It was a big story at the time.'

'We've got pictures of Harriet.'

'I'd love to see her, Mrs Kemp.' She gave her warmest smile, sensing the mother would be the softer touch. 'D'you have any with you?'

They had.

'She's beautiful.' *Well, she's OK.* Caroline's voice brooked no argument but didn't gush.

'There's some lovely film of her too. Harry got the camera out every time she moved, didn't you love?'

DVD. Could this get any better?

'I took quite a bit on the mobile as well.'

It so could. As if reluctant, she handed back the baby's photograph. 'To think the monster who killed her is still walking around out there.' Rueful shake of the head. 'That's the only other reason I could bring myself to come and see you.'

'How does that work?' Harry Kemp said.

'I'm convinced some stories I've covered have contributed to putting people behind bars. I honestly believe that. Otherwise I'd have got out of this game long ago.' A quick glance at Kemp showed she still had work to do. 'Oh I know we're not perfect. A lot of reporters make things up as they go along. But not me. I want to help. And right now the police need all the help they can get.'

'What's your point?' Charlotte asked.

She hesitated, ostensibly considering whether to take them into her confidence. 'Look, I hate saying this but they've been working on the Evie Lowe abduction for days. They still have no idea who they're looking for. They've got no leads, no clues, no witnesses. Between you and me, they're desperate. In cases like this they depend on people coming forward. People who probably don't even realize they have important intelligence.'

'And?' Harry Kemp.

'The best way of getting results is with publicity.'

'You would say that wouldn't you?'

'But I know what I'm talking about, Mr Kemp. I've been involved in a lot of cases where TV coverage has helped catch criminals and ensure convictions. It's a great feeling to know I play a small part in it.' She paused only to rearrange her halo. 'But I understand your reluctance. No hard feelings.' She caught an exchange of glances between the couple, detected a definite wavering. A nudge should do it.

'Again, strictly between us –' she lowered her voice – 'what worries the police most is that the killer will strike again. That he's got a taste for it now and is out of control.'

'Look, Miss . . . ?

'King. But please call me Caroline, Harry.'

'OK, Caroline. When Charlotte's feeling a little stronger, maybe we can give you a call?'

Sod that. She'd miscalculated the size of the nudge. A hefty shove was needed. 'Of course.' No problem. Smiling, she reached for her case. 'I'll give you my card, Mrs Kemp. I'm sure it won't be too late.'

Another exchange of glances between husband and wife, then: 'Alright, we'll do it.'

Charlotte sipped some water. 'Come back tomorrow, around ten.'

I don't think so. That was her slot with Karen Lowe. 'Let's do it now.' Opening the case, she wielded a camera. 'And Mr Kemp could you let me have the pics on your phone?'

THIRTY-EIGHT

10.02. Police headquarters. The phone rang as Sarah was leaving her office.

'DI Quinn? Tom Lowe here. I was wondering if you'd had any thoughts on my offer?'

Offer? Frowning, she glanced at her watch. She was supposed to have hooked up with Harries in the car park at ten. 'Can I get back to you, Mr Lowe? I'm just on my way out.'

'The sooner the better, given there's a second baby dead.'

Like I need reminding. Bristling, she kept a civil tone. 'I'm well aware of that, Mr Lowe. We're doing everything we can. But I'm already late.' The Kemps had agreed to talk to her.

'According to the *Birmingham News* the inquiry's going nowhere. I'm prepared to give up to £5,000. I'd have thought that sort of figure would persuade someone to come forward.'

Every loony in loon-land. The idea hadn't been discounted but neither she nor Baker was convinced a reward would reap benefits. 'That's very generous, Mr Lowe. As I say, I'll call you later. We can talk it through then.'

'If you're busy, inspector, I'm happy to discuss it with a senior officer. Or I could go to the press. I'm sure the editor of the *News* would be interested in carrying the story.'

'That's your call, Mr Lowe.' Maybe he was on to it already, she was talking to the dialling tone.

Harries lowered his window, tapped the steering wheel. Something must have held her up. DI Quinn was rarely late. Sunlight glared through the windscreen, he pulled down the visor, motor already like a furnace. The young DC was feeling the heat in other ways. He loosened his tie, rolled back his sleeves. What had started as a harmless fling with a reporter, could threaten not only his job but also what he hoped might become more than the professional relationship he already shared with the boss.

It was early days, but he'd really enjoyed Sarah Quinn's company in the restaurant last night. He'd always found her physically attractive, and had caught glimpses of passionate emotions under that cool exterior, but had she felt a spark too? Or was he deluding himself? She'd laughed off his cheesy chat-up line, but hadn't told him to back off. He sighed. Knew the quandary he was in now made a tight corner look like the Gobi desert. If he'd told her early on about his one-night stand or two with a hack, it wouldn't be such an issue, but the fact he'd kept quiet made it a million times worse, made it seem as if he had something to hide.

Even if a more than business partnership with the boss was

a no-no, she'd automatically assume he was the source of the leak. The way the DI saw it, getting pally with any reporter was unprofessional. So what did he do? Tell her, or hope it never came out? And pray that Caroline King had been joking when she . . .

'Sorry about that, David.' Sarah slipped into the passenger seat. 'God, it's like a sauna in here. Aren't you hot?'

Sarah's pale grey cotton dress clung to her clammy skin. Maybe the air conditioning at the hospital was on the blink. The Kemps' private room was tropical and with four people taking up the space it felt claustrophobic. Sarah's low armchair was near the bed opposite Harry Kemp's, Mrs Kemp sat bolstered by a mound of pillows, Harries leaned against a clinical white wall taking notes. He'd already filled half a dozen pages: the couple's movements on the day Harriet was taken, a list of family, friends, colleagues.

Charlotte Kemp had a touch more colour than when Sarah saw her last, but that was thanks to mauve shadows under puffy bloodshot eyes. She'd bitten every fingernail to the quick and was now chewing at loose skin round her thumb. Sympathy cards lay in an untidy pile on the bedside cabinet as if she couldn't bear to see them displayed.

'Just a few more questions and we'll get out of your hair.' Sarah gave a tight smile. It wasn't returned. 'I'm wondering if either of you noticed anything odd in the last few days, anyone following you, acting suspiciously, someone hanging around the house perhaps?'

'Nothing like that, DI Quinn.' Mr Kemp glanced at his wife. 'We've talked it through already, done little else, couldn't come up with anything.' She saw now that his mussed hair was down to the almost continual finger-combing, wondered if it was a recent habit.

'Has anyone been to the property recently? Trades people? Charity workers? Callers of any kind?'

He bit his lip. 'None that we don't know and haven't used before. Surely you don't think . . . ?'

'We have to check, Mr Kemp. Names, addresses would be useful.' Harries jotted details of a window cleaner and a builder, they'd had a window fixed recently.

'Have there been any odd phone calls? You answer and

there's no one there or they hang up?' There was an appreciable sigh before Kemp said, no. 'What about social networking
sites? Are either of you on Facebook?'

'I am actually,' Charlotte said. 'I keep in touch with
colleagues at the school where I worked, a few ex-pupils. But
they're people I know and trust. None of them would hurt us
like this.'

Sarah nodded. 'A good deal of what we do is for elimination
purposes, Mrs Kemp. If we could have access to your account?'
Harries took down the email address and password.

'You really are desperate, aren't you?' Harry Kemp ran
both hands through his hair this time. 'There's a monster
stalking the streets and you're checking up on sixth-form
girls.'

'It's certainly not all we're doing, Mr Kemp. Rest assured,
a hundred plus officers are on the case working round the
clock.' She aimed a subtle time-to-go-nod at Harries. They'd
got enough to be getting on with and Kemp was getting arsey.
Not that she blamed him. The man was raw with grief and
obviously saw the questioning as rubbing salt in open wounds.
She grabbed her briefcase, pushed back the chair. 'One thing
before we go, Mr Kemp, have you thought again about a media
appeal? It could just tip the balance.'

He snorted. 'Tip the balance? I don't see much in the scales,
inspector.'

'Even so, I think it could help.'

'So do I. It's why we've done one already.'

Harries could barely keep up with Sarah's long-legged stride
across the hospital car park.

'How could they?' It was a hiss through clenched teeth. 'To
fall for a trap like that.' He'd never seen her like this: blind
fury was one way of describing it. She certainly seemed oblivious of his presence, storming ahead, muttering. Thank God
he hadn't mentioned his dalliance with the reporter.

'Yeah, but hold on, boss. Was it a trap?' He knew this was
a verbal minefield, trod carefully. 'They're educated people.
You heard them say there was no payment involved. It's not
as if she forced them.'

She stopped suddenly, swung round, eyes blazing. 'Caroline
King tricked them, Harries. She sneaked a camera into a hospital,

inveigled her way into their room, exploited their vulnerability, trampled on their feelings.'

'It was a witness appeal, ma'am. It wasn't as if she was holding a gun to their head. They could easily have said, no.'

'Whose fucking side are you on, Harries?'

A couple of passers-by cast curious glances their way. Harries paused and unlike her kept his voice down. 'I guess I'm on the victim's side, ma'am. And I can't see the problem. You wanted the Kemps to do a turn.'

'They've done that all right. Come on.' She headed towards the motor. He'd driven a couple of miles before she spoke again. 'Have you seen any TV today, David, or last night?'

He cut her a glance; clearly she was still thinking it over. 'No, ma'am.' And he wondered if her thoughts coincided with his: if Harry and Charlotte Kemp had made the news, the cops would have heard by now. Which begged the question: if Caroline King had exclusive footage of the grieving couple, why the hell hadn't she used it?

No news is good news? He grimaced. *Yeah, right.*

'This is good, Caro. Really good.'

The young man's keen-eyed focus was on a monitor, one of three on the console in front of them. Caroline had note pad and Mont Blanc to hand. A desk close by was strewn with half-drunk cups of coffee. Light in the edit room was subdued, making the pictures on screen seem brighter, more vibrant. They'd been viewing the rushes on tapes shot that day at Karen Lowe's flat, more than an hour's worth. Caroline had already logged picture sequences and earmarked the best interview clips. The rough cut was twice the six-minute duration she'd been given but that was a good sign, an indication the footage had impact. And picture editor Chris Cooke had just voiced the same thought.

'Cheers, Chris.' She cut him a glance. He was a taciturn piece of work, tall and long-limbed, laid-back to the point of languid. Even the smile was lazy, and rare. It played across his thin lips now. Caroline had chosen Cooke as carefully as she'd selected the pictures and words for that night's piece. Like the crew she'd worked with earlier, Cooke was the best: quick, decisive and with a creative edge. He loved working with pictures, told her often enough that one was worth a thousand of her bon mots. Cooke kept the chat down too and it suited Caroline. Not having to listen to an endless stream of newsroom gossip and gripes. When he did chip in it was usually worth hearing.

He wasn't just talking now, but for Cookie waxing lyrical. At best, picture editors were non-committal, at worst casual-couldn't-give-a-toss. Compliments were rare as pink unicorns.

'I mean it, Caro. This stuff's top mint.'

'Let's get on with it then.' She was gratified but not surprised. Aware she had some remarkable footage. It was why ITN was hanging on to it until the later bulletins. It was too good to squander on daytime. She was also acutely conscious of the fact she had just three hundred and sixty seconds to tell two life and death stories. Every second had to shout.

The intro was a no-brainer. They still had the Kemps to themselves, a hard news topping that wrote itself. It left four minutes forty-five seconds to condense and encapsulate the Karen Lowe material. Caroline tapped the pen against her teeth. It should be a piece of piss. She'd coached Karen well and the girl had been surprisingly quick to grasp what was required. They'd concentrated on her love for Evie and skated over less wholesome factors like absent fathers and family breakdown. If those aspects had been left out, Karen's bitterness towards the police had been built up. Caroline checked her notes and told Cooke to run the cop sequence again.

On screen, Karen looked lost, frail, bereft. Staring forlornly at a picture of Evie, her voice, though breaking, came through loud and clear on the speakers: 'I can't help thinking if the police had . . .' She'd forgotten her lines at that point, glanced off camera. Caroline heard her own voice giving the cue.

The next take was word perfect. 'I can't help thinking if DI Quinn had let me talk to the media Evie might still be here. I hope and pray that no more babies are taken –' she dashed the heel of her hand across a damp cheek at this point – 'before the police catch the killer.'

Caroline checked her notes, gave Cooke a timing. 'That's where I want to mix in pics of Evie and Harriet.' It was a shame in a way because the viewer wouldn't get to see Karen's tears but going back to the babies was the only way to end the piece. 'So what do you reckon, Chris? A Kleenex job or what?'

He shrugged, frowning. 'Why are you so keen to name that cop?'

'Was I?'

'No, I made it up. Come on, Caro. What's she done to you?'

'You could ask her the same question.'

'How come?'

'How much time have you got?'

'How much do you need?'

'Let's finish the piece. Let Bob see it. Then I'll buy you a long drink and give you the short version.'

THIRTY-NINE

'I want to hear her version before deciding whether to take action.' Staring ahead stern-faced, Sarah stirred brown sugar into a double espresso. Harries was making inroads into a pain au chocolat before it melted completely. They were at a pavement café off the main drag through Moseley. Sunlight glared off passing motors giving Sarah retina flash. She shook her head. She'd been dead wrong about Caroline King. The reporter had taken stooping to a new level. Still eating, Harries either hadn't heard or was keeping his head down. She glanced round at the other tables, saw two men in suits drinking wine, a group of women who looked as if they'd dropped by after the gym, an old guy with a ciggie in his mouth studying the *Racing Post*.

Lucky for some.

The detectives were killing ten minutes waiting for the Cinnamon Tree to open. Sarah had meant to task a DC at the early brief with taking in Person of Interest snaps to show the staff. She had copies in her briefcase. The job had slipped her mind. Probably because there were more pressing matters on it, including now the reporter.

'A witness appeal's fine. It's the underhand way she went about it. Entering the hospital without permission. Carrying a concealed camera. Concocting some sob story.' Her spoon tapping on the metal table provided punctuation. 'And she knew which room to go to. How?'

'Come to that, boss, how'd she even know they were in hospital?' He was gathering crumbs with a moist finger. 'We didn't release the info, did we?'

His query was casual. Too casual? Eyes narrowed, she cut him a glance. He'd struck a nerve. Deliberately? She was painfully aware she'd inadvertently given the fact away at the news conference. It was one of the reasons she'd lashed out earlier. But someone must have supplied detail. Wing, room number, floor. King couldn't have just wandered round a building that size and struck lucky. Was there a chance Harries was playing a game of double-bluff? 'I've no idea, David. Have you?'

'Not me, boss.' He lifted his head. 'Have to ask her.'

He'd be a damn good poker partner. Or she was getting paranoid. She shrugged. 'Yeah, well, it's not for want of trying.' She had a bunch of questions but the reporter wasn't even answering her phone. All the numbers were going to voicemail and King wasn't at the Mailbox or the Marriott. 'She's what you might call lying low.'

With the accent on lying.

'Yes, he's definitely been in with her.' Raj Choudry tapped one of the photographs lying side by side on the bar. Sarah and Harries exchanged glances. In the background, white cloths billowed as a couple of waiters laid tables. The subtle fragrance of spices was laced with the heady perfume from lilies crowding half a dozen huge glass vases.

'You're absolutely sure about that, Raj?' Sarah crossed her fingers at her side.

'No doubt. I have a good memory for faces.' He lifted his gaze to her. 'Especially pretty ones.'

Harries sniffed. 'Can you remember when it was, Mr Choudry?'

'Yes. It was the night I told you about. The time she made the joke about the baby coming early?'

Sarah did a rough calculation. If Karen had been heavily pregnant, the visit must have been around fourteen months back. So Michael Slater had been lying too. He said he'd not seen since Karen since they broke up a couple of years ago.

'And they've not been in since?' She stepped to one side as a waiter sidled past to reach something behind the bar.

'Not that I'm aware.'

'He was in a couple of weeks ago, Mr Choudry.' The waiter nodded at Slater's photograph. 'That night your wife was poorly.'

So smooth-talking Raj was spoken for. 'Was he with anyone?' Sarah asked.

'Yeah. Skinny girl. Long brown hair. Sour-faced.' The waiter gave a gap-toothed smile. 'Know what I mean?'

Almost certainly. Sarah pulled a newspaper out of her brief-case. Karen Lowe's picture was on the front page. 'This the one?'

'That's her. They were having a right ding-dong.' He winked. 'Know what I mean?'

'It doesn't prove anything, boss.' Harries had just parked the motor outside Slater's house in Edgbaston. Strike while they had an iron hot or not, was Sarah's thinking. On the way over, she'd put in a call to Baker to keep him up to speed, the chief was still in a review meeting, she'd left a message.

'It proves he was lying, David. If he lied about not seeing Karen . . . who's to say he's not lying through his teeth about everything else? Know what I mean?' They exchanged a thin smile. The waiter's every line had finished with the same four-word catchphrase. And the questioning had continued a while. Apparently Karen had stormed out of the restaurant, leaving a sheepish Slater to settle the bill. Releasing the seat belt, Sarah said, 'I loathe liars.'

'They go with the territory, don't they, boss?' He locked the motor, eyes squinting in the sun.

'So? I still hate them.' They made a difficult job almost impossible. It was a constant game of sorting truth from chaff. Cops end up doubting everything and everyone. Even them-selves sometimes.

No one answered Harries' first knock. 'Not likely to be in, is he? Didn't you say he works at Aldi?'

'Yeah, but his parents might be. If not, we'll shove a note through the door.' That might stir things up a little in the Slater household. She felt no compunction to keep mum any more about police interest in their son. His mendacity meant that courtesy had been forfeited. She was already scrabbling in her briefcase for a card when Harries hammered again.

'You after Mikey, then?' Wafting smoke signalled the re-emergence of the neighbour from hell. Sarah wondered if the ciggie was surgically attached.

'We might be,' she said. 'Do you know where he is?' *And what the frig is it to you?*

'It'll be 'bout that girl.' Sallow jowls quivered as she nodded sagely.

'What girl?' Sarah asked casually.

'You're the old bill, ain't you?' She waved the fag at Sarah. 'I seen you on the telly. So you ain't chasin' parking tickets.'

Tempted to shove the ciggie where the sun don't rise, Sarah tightened her mouth working on a response that didn't include the word 'off'.

Harries had one already. 'What girl's that, Mrs Carver?' And treated the woman to a warm smile. Sarah cast an askance glance. Her memory for names was good, but that was A*.

'Her whose babby's been killed. Karen, innit?' Despite the upward inflection, it was more statement than question.

'Sounds as if you know her?' Harries with another smile.

Mrs Carver held the fag aloft. 'I'd see her on the doorstep sparking up, so I'd come out and have a little chat, put the world to rights.' She took a deep drag then smiled showing tea-coloured teeth that needed correcting too. 'It'd be more 'n yer life's worth to light up in Irene Slater's place. Mind, we're a dying breed, ain't we?' The cackle at her own wit turned into a coughing fit.

Sarah felt like hastening her demise. Mrs Carver was typical of a certain kind of witness, usually elderly, often lonely, who enjoyed the unaccustomed attention and was in no hurry to relinquish it, or the information they held. If they did. Sarah's nod at Harries to continue the questioning was barely perceptible. Mrs Carver had clearly taken a shine to the young detective who'd not only remembered her name but was giving the impression her every pronouncement was a pearl. Unwittingly or not, the old bat had already landed Michael Slater further in the mire by catching him out in at least one more whopper. He'd never brought Karen home? Yeah right.

'Irene's Michael's mum? And she wouldn't let Karen smoke in the house? That right, Mrs C?'

Mrs C? Talk about charm offensive.

'Didn't know, did she?'

It was like pulling teeth with blancmange pliers. Sarah gritted hers.

'How come?' Harries prompted.

'It was all on the QT. While the cat's away, eh?' She flicked the butt into the long-suffering hedge. 'She don't like him having girlfriends. 'Mong other things.'

Sarah glanced round. A lilac-haired woman was shuffling past pushing a shopping trolley with wonky wheels. 'All right, Flo? How's it going?' The woman had to make do with a wave. Flo Carver had eyes only for the young bill. 'Come inside, ducks. Don't want every Tom, Dick and Harry earwigging, do we?'

Forty minutes it took. Forty minutes of desperately trying not to inhale too deeply. It wasn't just the aggressive smoking: Flo Carver had six maybe seven cats. How many had marked their territory was anyone's guess, but what with all the feline pee and fag smoke it was an olfactory ordeal. The old woman's sense of smell must be shot to shit. The detectives emerged with streaming eyes and clothes that needed dry cleaning.

They also had what could be the goods on Michael and possibly the low-down on the Slaters: Irene and Max were early sixties, retired, reclusive, Michael an only child. His late arrival had come as a shock, they hadn't wanted kids. Spare the rod and spoil the child? That was never going to happen. Apparently they kept him on a short leash and treated him accordingly. Like a dog if Mrs Carver was to be believed. All this she'd apparently picked up from Michael over the years. Mr and Mrs Slater didn't mix, thought themselves 'too posh for folk round here'. Since Mikey was a young lad, Flo Carver had taken pity on him, told him her door was always open. 'Like a second mum', was stretching it a bit, Sarah suspected, but the old woman spoke of Michael with genuine warmth. Many a time, Mrs Carver said, she'd been on the point of phoning social services. But he always had an excuse for the bruises and finger marks, begged her not to make trouble. As far as she knew Karen was Michael's first and only girlfriend. His parents had tried putting the kibosh on the relationship. But he'd rebelled probably for the first time, kept seeing her even though they'd threatened to chuck him out on his ear. Even a worm will turn was the way she described it. And the baby? Was it Michael's? That she didn't know. She'd not set eyes on Karen for over a year, hadn't known she was pregnant and Michael hadn't breathed a word. What about his parents? Would they have known? She'd hoped to God, not. If they had any idea he'd fathered a kid the wrong side of the blanket, his life wouldn't be worth living.

'Sounds like something out of the Victorian era.' Harries checked the driving mirror, took a left. 'What do you think, boss? Is Mrs C on the level?'

Sarah shrugged. Some of it sounded pretty self-serving and self-important. But she couldn't see any reason why the neighbour would fabricate the story. 'She could be grinding an axe, I suppose. Clearly she's got no time for the Slaters. What was it she called them?'

'Bible-bashing God-bothering, ignorant bastards.' He sniffed. 'Not all they bashed if half what she said was true.'

'Never know what goes on behind closed doors, do you?' She recalled the inside of the house, the religious samplers, the huge Bible, the dark heavy furnishings, thought how stark and forbidding the place must've been for a young boy. Flo Carver's home for all its faults and filth was probably a welcome bolt-hole.

'She seemed fond of Michael,' Harries said.

'Seemed pretty taken with you too.' She winked. 'Had her eating out of your hand.' The groan was synchronized. It wasn't a thought to hold. 'You're right though, David. She obviously has a lot of affection for him.' Would that include covering his back if she thought he'd done something wrong?

'I wonder if the feeling's mutual?'

It was a question they might put. Once they tracked him down. According to Mrs Carver, since the detectives' last house call, she'd not seen hide or hair of Michael or his parents.

FORTY

'He's not been into work this week either.' It was the late brief, a less than animated squad. Sarah had just wrapped up the current state of play on the Karen Lowe-Michael Slater connection. Baker in shirtsleeves and open collar had taken his customary perch on a desk at the front. He'd already précised Operation Bluebird, assigned actions and announced numbers would shortly be bolstered by a dozen officers seconded from stations across the city and a further six back-up civilian staff. Detectives were restless, shuffling about, they'd sat still for far too long.

'You're thinking he's done a runner, Quinn?'

'Hard to tell, chief. He's taken unscheduled time off before.' Though according to Slater's boss at Aldi he wouldn't get the chance again. When he did go back, someone else would be shelf stacking.

'And the parents?' Baker swigged water from a plastic bottle.

Sarah shrugged. 'Again, the neighbour says they're away quite a bit. They go on religious retreats apparently and they spend a fair bit of time in Cumbria. They own a fixed caravan up there. Could explain the apparent disappearance.'

'But you don't think so?' Despite the seeming indifference, he'd picked up her unease.

'It's the timing I don't like. Seems hell of a coincidence.'

'So what are you saying?'

'I wish I knew, chief.' She blew her cheeks out on a sigh. 'Fact is Michael Slater is the only man we *know* to have had a relationship with Karen Lowe. She could've had a string of lovers, but he *could* be Evie's father. They both deny it like there's no tomorrow and they both claim they're not seeing each other any more. Now that could be the truth, or it could be because Michael's parents would go down on him like a ton of bricks.'

'And he'd care because?' Baker's tone was derisory. Not surprising, a lot of youths cops came across would sell their granny for a fiver, dissing parents was the default mode. She relayed to the squad what she'd heard about Slater's background, upbringing, alleged abuse. Probably unconvinced, Baker waved a get-on-with-it hand.

'Either way Karen and Michael were spotted two weeks ago in a local restaurant having quote: a right ding-dong. Whichever way you look at it, they've been spinning a web of lies.'

'And?' His swinging leg suggested he was less than rapt.

'It's possible the parents found out, put two and two

together.' She hesitated. The mental scenarios she'd run seemed almost too far-fetched to put into words. Had Micha suddenly cracked? Decided he'd had enough of his parents' bullying? Was it possible he blamed them for what happened to Evie because if he'd not been forced to hide Karen's existence, he could've been there for her and the baby? Had he snapped and taken them out of the picture? Or was it vice versa? Flo Carver had dithered in the past over whether to call in social services. Had the Slaters' heavy-hand come down too hard and a thrashing gone too far?

Baker sniffed. 'So you reckon he's chopped them into little bits and buried them under the patio?'

A couple of squad members sniggered. Baker was taking the piss, but clearly giving it some thought too, was on a similar page.

'No patio, chief.' She said deadpan. 'Your guess is good as mine. They could be anywhere.'

'As could the lad.' Baker ran a hand over his face. 'Is there enough for a warrant?'

Three adults with supposedly sound minds, missing less than a week? She turned her mouth down. 'Can't see it, chief.'

'No nasty smells? Whingeing neighbours?' Tapping the side of his nose, he added unnecessarily, 'If you get my drift.'

She rolled her eyes. 'No.' And if there were it would take years before any stench breached Flo Carver's nasal passages. On the other hand, the woman might have her uses. 'Leave it with me, chief.' She glanced at Harries. The task she had in mind would suit Prince Charming down to the ground.

Baker got to his feet, wandered over to what was now a line of whiteboards. 'Big question is: where does this fit with the inquiry?' For the umpteenth time he gazed at a mishmash of pictures, street maps, markers, handwritten notes. Lines added in felt tip ran between some exhibits. He turned, sank hands in pockets. 'We've got two dead babies, Quinn.'

She held out empty palms. 'Still working on that, chief.' The Lowe-Slater connection was evident if not complete. But where did Harriet's abduction figure? She'd asked a couple of detectives to establish what, if anything, linked the Slaters and the Kemps.

Baker nodded. 'And Karen Lowe? She got anything to say for herself?'

Sweet FA at the moment. 'She's not at home either, chief.'

'Where've you been? I've been chasing you all day.' Sarah's voice was clipped. Just for a second, she'd been tempted not to answer the phone. Gone eight, she'd been halfway to her office door when it rang. Getting home had been more on her agenda.

'I'm here now, and all yours.' Caroline King had put in the call. It was known in the trade as back-covering. Bob Grant had viewed the package featuring Karen Lowe and insisted, as the reporter knew he would, that Sarah Quinn be given the right to respond. 'What can I do you for, inspector?' Her voice oozed jocular mateyness.

'It's more a case of what I can do *you* for.'

Caroline laughed. 'That's a joke, right?' Wished she could see the DI's face. Keeping her sweet was crucial.

'The Kemps. Illegal entry. Impersonating a doctor.' Caroline heard tapping: presumably Quinn's digital accompaniment. 'Concealed camera. Secret filming.'

'Hey, back up. They were happy to go on record.'

'And if they'd told you to get lost? I've no doubt you'd have sneaked a few shots anyway.'

Natch. 'You can't say that.'

'I just did.'

'OK.' She tried keeping the exchange light. 'So what now? Are the boys in blue coming round with batons and hand-cuffs?' *Kinky.* Actually that might not be a bad idea. Except the cops hadn't got a case: the legal grounds were too shaky. They both knew that. Caroline reckoned Quinn was kite flying.

'I'm issuing a warning, Ms King. Be under no illusion. Play another trick like that, and there'll be a formal complaint.'

Ooh, I'm quivering in my Manolos. 'You got it, inspector.'

'Where did *you* get it, Ms King?'

'Uh?' She knew exactly where the cop was coming from.

'You knew where to find them.'

'Come on, you gave it away at the news conference. I saw it in your face.'

'Yeah, sure. Room number. Blood group. Inside leg. Where do you get your information?'

'I say again, I can't reveal my sources.'

'Has the piece gone out yet?'

'They're using it tonight, I think.' Caroline glanced at her watch. In one hour forty-five minutes exactly.

'I'll watch with interest.'

'While I've got you on, inspector . . .' Wheedling.

Deep sigh. 'Make it snappy, OK?'

'Sure. Karen Lowe.' Nice, non-committal. Caroline could almost hear Quinn's eye-roll.

'Don't tell me you're still banging on about that?'

'Yeah. As I say it's important.' Particularly when in less than two hours a report containing emotive and damaging criticism of Quinn would be seen by God knew how many millions of viewers. Bob Grant was uneasy; he'd never yet been landed with a law suit. But the editor had only ordered Caroline to contact Sarah, not what words to use.

'Look, I've told you a million times. I've said all I'm going to say on the subject.'

'Is that a no comment?'

'It's a no further comment. Unless . . .'

Thank you and good night. Caroline cut the connection and punched the air. Soon she'd be in a bar downing a large gin. She'd just had the tonic.

Pensive Sarah replaced the receiver, perched on the edge of her desk, picturing Caroline King. Superficially, the reporter had changed little since their first meeting. On the few recent occasions they'd been face to face, Sarah had clocked the odd white hair nestling in the signature black bob, faint lines edging King's eyes. She ceded, though, the reporter was in good shape and didn't appear to have lost her edge.

For years now the two women had kept their distance, drawn together intermittently by their jobs, the same jobs that had brought them together. Both based in London back then, it was inevitable they'd work some of the same cases. At first they kept the relationship professional: crime fighter and crime writer; came across each other at crime scenes, news conferences, court rooms. They were young and ambitious in jobs where women were often regarded as decorative, dumb or dangerous. Now and then, they'd hook up socially over a drink. The risk was that chat about bloke-ism at work could spill over into details about the job itself.

For some time, Sarah blamed herself as much as Caroline for what happened. She rarely looked back and when she did could only visualize the scene as a series of jerking black and white silhouettes like a silent movie, except for Caroline's scream. The only slow motion sequence was Jack, dying. Jack Keene. Sarah's partner and lover.

'Shoot, Caro, I'm surprised there's not more bad blood between you.' Chris Cooke lounged in a leather armchair long legs sprawled under the table. The shade of Rioja in his glass matched the colour of the décor.

'It wasn't all down to me.' Caroline had kept her promise of a post-edit drink or three in the Press Club. It had taken Chris less than a couple of minutes to drop a particularly meaningless 'no comment' in the sound track. The package had received final approval and first plaudits. The reporter had just given Cooke edited highlights of her history with Sarah Quinn.

'But it may not have happened if you'd not been there.'

'It wouldn't have happened if the police had gone straight in instead of pissing around.'

'Has it never occurred to you they might've been hanging back to get what they needed for a conviction?'

'Oh, come on. They were hardly going to catch him in the act, were they?'

That, more or less, was exactly what the police had been hoping.

Once stirred, Sarah couldn't let the memories rest. Still perched on the edge of her desk she let the images flood back. Maybe facing it again would lay a ghost or two. The undercover operation had been meticulously planned. Its aim to apprehend a man who'd attacked and mutilated six women in London over a period of six months. The rapist targeted young blondes alone on the streets, the attacks confined to the Brixton area during the early hours. Predictably the press had dubbed him The Butcher of Brixton, the more sensational reports spelt out why. Unsurprisingly, women were terrified to go out. More than a decade ago now, few people would recall details; some police officers would never forget.

The police strategy was to use a decoy, a young detective constable. Sarah. She was to be wired, kept under constant surveillance and like the rest of the squad, armed.

Even now, she was adamant she'd not told Caroline King *when* the plan would be executed. It was enough that she'd mentioned it at all. She wouldn't have said a word except throughout the investigation the reporter had helped the police. It was vital that women were warned of the danger and aware of the risks. Caroline had kept the story alive, not just in the newspapers but on the front pages. She'd told Sarah she saw it as part of her job to help make sure the rapist was captured before adding more victims to a list already too long. It was this commitment on Caroline's part that led to Sarah's indiscretion.

With hindsight Sarah had told herself she should have realized the major part of the reporter's job was to secure a good story. But neither had she known then that Caroline was sleeping with a detective on the team, a detective who filled in the blanks.

No one knew for certain what or who had alerted the rapist. The very scale of Operation Stranger carried an inherent risk. On the night events happened so quickly, Sarah was barely aware a shot had been fired, let alone who it killed. She'd played her part perfectly, drawn the rapist out of the shadows, felt his hot breath on her neck. Then a sudden noise, a scream. She learned later that Caroline King had watched him pull a gun, was convinced Sarah would be shot. The fact he carried firearms was unknown. Prior attacks had borne only the ugly marks of knives and glass.

Jack had been closest, broke cover, drew fire. He'd lost his life, the rapist was serving his in maximum security, Sarah's had been damaged irrevocably. Her career could have been over. The big question at the inquiry was who'd leaked details to the press. Caroline King consistently refused to reveal her source, but swore it wasn't DC Quinn.

Sarah's immediate response had been to resign anyway. She'd revealed the existence of an undercover operation to a reporter. In getting the details, Caroline King had only been

doing her job, however despicable. It was only when she was
going through Jack's papers that it sank in how despicable.
Caroline had been sleeping with Jack. Sarah had lost her lover
– months before his death – to Caroline King. Sarah had ripped
up her resignation letter, she'd damn well not lose her liveli-
hood as well.

'You all right, Quinn? Look as if you've seen a ghost.'

She hadn't heard Baker come in. Glancing up, she gave a
tired smile. 'I'm fine, chief. Just thinking.'

'Glad to hear it.' He tapped his brow. 'I'm off home. See
you in the morning.'

'Hold on a tick.' She grabbed her briefcase and keys. 'I'll
come down with you.'

'You sure about this, Quinn?' He held the door, winked as
she walked past. 'People might talk?'

'Am I bothered?'

FORTY-ONE

The boss would go ballistic. Apeshit. Seated at a desk in
the incident room, Harries held his head in his hands.
He'd just put the phone down on a pissed and seriously
pissed off Caroline King. Would she even have mentioned the
Karen Lowe report if she hadn't had a drink? He doubted it.
The booze had loosened a spiteful tongue. She knew the story
was dynamite. And now he knew it too. He saw a green genie
lolling against a gin bottle giving him the bird.

Rising, he wandered to the window, checked the car park.
Looked as if DI Quinn had already left. Should he call her?
Nah. It had to be face-to-face. He ran fingers through already
mussed hair. Damn shame he'd rung Caroline, told her he didn't
want to see her again. Maybe his calling the shots had provoked
her even more. The speculation was academic. In little more
than an hour, a bulletin would go out savaging Sarah, damaging
her reputation. Talk about hatchet job. He couldn't see a way
of stopping the story's transmission, but he had to warn her.
At the very least she needed to watch it, hear what was said
so she could work out a reply. How to alert her without

jeopardizing his job? How to disclose something of which in theory he should know nothing?

He was working on that. Grabbing his jacket he dashed out, weaving a path through imaginary rocks and hard places.

'You said if anything came up boss?' Harries stood outside Sarah's apartment holding aloft a carrier bag with a tell-tale clink.

'Two bottles?' She pursed her lips. 'Are you celebrating?'

'I wasn't sure which you prefer. Red or white?'

'What if I said rose?'

'You could go half and half?' He cocked an eyebrow.

She was smiling but he was still on the doorstep. He knew she was waiting to hear where he was going with this. Much as he'd like it to be otherwise, theirs was a professional relationship that didn't include home visits, especially unannounced arrivals. With the stakes so high, he'd calculated the risk of an icy rebuff worth taking. He hoped any chill would be confined to the Chardonnay.

Her smile seemed warm enough. 'I know this is a cheek and I shouldn't be here. I just thought . . . you know . . . maybe we could . . . talk over the case? Tell me to get lost . . . if you like.'

'Get lost.' Her deadpan delivery was drier than the wine.

He looked down, about to apologize, mentally counting the cost of his miscalculation. When he glanced up she was trying not to laugh.

'You did say, "if I like".' She opened the door wider. 'Doesn't mean you have to go, though. Mind, it was worth it for the look on your face.'

'Did you like the look?' Whoops. Had he crossed another line?

She held his gaze then pointed to the bag. 'Come through. Let's have a drink.'

His bemused glance took in a kitchen that was messy bordering on chaotic. He masked a smile. The disarray figured, he guessed. The boss was so disciplined at work, she had to let her hair down somewhere. She had her back to him, pouring the wine. Shame her hair was still up. Though he'd never felt the need to imagine the state of the Quinn kitchen, he'd fantasized frequently how its owner might look were she a touch dishevelled.

'There you go.' She handed him a glass then leaned against the sink.

'Cheers. This is really good of you, boss.'

'I'd offer you a bite but my cuisine's more hoot than haute.'

He'd clocked a tin of alphabet spaghetti on one of the work surfaces. 'What were you going to do with that, eat it or read it?'

'Open it.'

'You can't be that hungry?' The wall clock showed 21.50. He couldn't leave it much longer. Then he spotted the TV. He'd thought initially it was a microwave: there was a bread basket on top filled with packs of pasta. 'I could throw a few things together for you.'

'Puh-lease. Don't tell me all you need is a stick of celery and a bit of mouldy Stilton and you can knock up lobster thermidor?'

'Nah.' He turned his mouth down. 'Can't stand sea food.'

She laughed.

'What have you got in the fridge?'

'Pass.'

'May I?'

'Be my guest.'

It was a huge Smeg, almost food-free. 'The contents of a fridge say a lot about a person you know, boss.'

'Is that right? And what are they telling you about me?'

Two bottles of champagne. Five Italian wines. A six-pack of Becks. 'That you entertain a lot?'

'Wrong.'

'That you should entertain a lot.'

'And that's it?'

'Hold on.' He turned round clutching an onion and a pack of tomatoes. 'Right. This is what I've deduced. That you are a woman who is about to sit down . . .' He waited until she took a stool, then added, 'But not before she's poured more wine.' She rolled her eyes, but entered into the spirit. 'While I toil away producing perfect pasta à la Quinn and we talk about the case.'

'Sounds like a plan.'

Twenty minutes at most, Harries reckoned. Caroline had said the piece was going out in the Close-up on Britain slot that invariably led the second half of the bulletin. He prepped a few veg then sauntered to the TV, reached for some penne. It would be too crass to switch the set on by accident. But could he make something of his earlier mistake?

'Do I detect a deliberate deception going on here, madam?' Would she go along with the light-hearted tease?

'What's that, Sherlock?'

'The TV appears to be masquerading as a microwave.'

'Yeah, course it is. Why would I do that?'

'You don't want anyone to know you're a telly addict? Hooked on the soaps?'

'I'm so hooked, I don't even know if the set works.'

'Only one way to find out.'

It worked. It worked like a dream. He'd anticipated switching it on and casually leaving it playing in the background. There was no need. The story was being trailed: a newsreader's disembodied voice over a picture of Karen Lowe holding Evie.

Mother of murdered baby blames police . . .

Sarah stared in disbelief at the screen.

'Here, boss, drink this.' Harries who'd had an idea what to expect had been shocked by the headline, dreaded to think what would be in the full report.

Sarah drank the wine without tasting it, barely aware she'd taken the glass. 'Blames the police for what, for Christ's sake?'

'I don't know.'

'What the hell's she going to come out with, David?'

'I don't know.'

Sarah walked to the door. 'Bring the bottle. We'll watch in the other room. I want to record it. In case I can't believe it the first time.'

It was worse than she'd feared.

The Kemps' contribution was benign compared with what followed. They came over as a desperately sad couple grieving for their baby and appealing for help to catch the killer. Karen Lowe came over as a desperately sad mother grieving for her baby and baying for blood: Sarah Quinn's.

She sat in shocked silence. Harries drained the bottle into her glass, handed it to her without speaking. Immersed in their separate thoughts, both jumped when the phone rang.

'Did you see it, Quinn?' The chief certainly had. 'You've been framed?' For a second she thought he'd flipped, then: 'Only instead of Harry Hill doing the honours we get Karen bloody Lowe dishing the dirt.'

'You could say that.'

'You did see it then. The crap that's just gone out?'

'Yes. I did.'

'And?'

She stroked her temple with a finger. 'It was one-sided to say the least.'

'One-sided?' The headache just got worse. 'One-sided! It was a pile of shite. I want you in my office first thing, Quinn. We need to work on a rebuttal. I'm demanding a right to reply and I'll push for equal air time.'

Right to reply. Caroline King's call earlier. Sarah briefly closed her eyes.

'They'll have no bloody choice,' Baker blustered. 'I can't understand why you weren't approached for a comment at least.'

No wonder the bitch had rung off in such a rush.

'I was. In a way.'

Slight pause. 'By?'

'Caroline King.'

'When?'

'Earlier today. I said no comment, but—'

'What!'

'If you'll just let me finish—'

'You'll be lucky if King hasn't finished you off, Quinn.'

'I thought I was commenting on something else. I'd no idea she'd interviewed Karen Lowe.'

'She wasn't calling to inquire about the state of your health. Why the hell didn't you ask what she wanted?'

'I did.'

'And?'

'She hung up.'

'And left you out to dry.' She opened her mouth to remonstrate, but Baker had moved on. 'Another thing, Quinn: how come she knew where the Kemps were?'

'I don't know.'

'Best find out sharpish. And while you're at it, work on a way of how you get out of this shit.'

With even less courtesy than he'd started, he rang off.

'Baker, huh?'

The voice reminded her Harries was still there. He'd kept a low profile while she was on the phone. He'd only have heard one side of the conversation but you didn't need to be a genius to fill in the blanks.

'Who else?' Sinking back into the settee, she sounded casual, unconcerned. There was a niggle at the back of her mind she was trying to pin down.

'Would you like another drink?' Harries' question pushed it further back.

'What?'

He raised the unopened bottle in reply.

'No. No thanks. Look I've got a few things to do and an early start in the morning, David.'

'Sure. Of course. Is there anything I can do before I go?'

She held his gaze, tried reading his expression. 'No, nothing.'

In one way or another, she thought, he'd already done enough.

Sarah lay awake into the night. She'd viewed the recording of King's report so many times she could play it word imperfect in her head. Perhaps she'd looked at it too much and was no longer seeing it properly. But something in the piece had planted that half seed of an idea in her head. She was pretty sure it must be something Karen Lowe had said. The rest of the item was predictable wallpaper pictures for King to voice over, numerous stills of the baby and footage of Karen. There were shots of her in a park, shots of her walking around the estate, shots of her at home leafing through large photo albums of Evie's too short life.

Concentrate. She was sure there was something there, something significant, something she had to pick up on. *Useless.* Around three a.m. she threw off the duvet, wandered into the kitchen, put water on to boil, dropped a chamomile tea bag into a mug. Leaning against the sink, she glanced round. The place was messier than normal with Harries' peelings and stalks littering the work surface. She smiled. The guy was good company, however unexpected. She had a feeling he fancied her and talking about the case had been an excuse to call round. Was she flattered? Sure. A little flirtation wouldn't hurt. It certainly wouldn't be going anywhere. Even if Adam wasn't on the scene, she wasn't on the market for a relation-ship at work. Once bitten . . .

She spotted a pan on the cooker, congealed onions and tomatoes swimming in a pool of oil in a pan. She curled a lip. It was just as well they hadn't eaten, her stomach was churning anyway now.

Then she froze, ears pricked. What was the noise? *Low voices?* She cocked her head, tried to pinpoint where they were coming from. Breath bated, she tiptoed to the door. *Bloody fool. The Pink Panther* was on the box. She'd left the sodding set on. Striding into the sitting room, she reached for the switch. Her hand stilled: the act reminded her of Harries again and sparked a different sequence of thoughts.

If he hadn't dropped by . . . If he hadn't started cooking . . . If he hadn't switched on the TV. Timing? Coincidence?

In bed later, with sleep still eluding her, she stopped thinking 'if' and started asking 'why?'

FORTY-TWO

'Why?'

'Why what exactly? Sir.'

'After she hung up – why didn't you call her back immediately. Find out why she was so keen to get a comment?'

Because I missed out on your dish of hindsight. Sir. Sarah had been in with Baker for forty-two minutes. She'd not expected it to drag on this long, knew it would last three minutes more at most. Something vital was about to come up. Not that she could see the future any better than the past, but because she'd arranged it with Harries. He'd ring at 9.45 on a pressing matter and she'd get to leave. Her suspicions about Harries were on hold, she'd keep a watching brief while allowing him the benefit of the doubt. Which was more than Baker was giving her. At the moment she wasn't so much on the carpet as admiring its underlay.

She knew he was ego-aggrandizing at her expense but in a

way he was right: she should have phoned King back after that call last night. She pursed her lips. The error ten years ago had been saying too much, yesterday it had been saying too little. She'd make up for it big time when she next saw King. Baker tapped his foot, still waiting for an answer.

'You're right. I should have called her. I should have known when she hung up so fast that she was up to something. I'm sorry, sir.'

'You'd best not be taking the piss, Quinn.' Fifteen minutes she spent listening to Baker's lecture on handling the media, mainly King. His ideas for the latter were inventive if not – for her, anyway – anatomically impossible. She glanced again at her mobile. If it didn't ring any minute she'd road test them on Harries.

'Anyway, Quinn, I had a word with her editor first thing. Guy called Bob Grant.'

'Oh?' Took his time getting round to that. 'Has he agreed to a retraction?'

'Not exactly.'

'An apology?'

'Not in so many words.'

Great prowess dealing with the press, chief. 'What then?'

'We'll be asked to contribute when they do a follow-up.'

'And that's it?'

'That your phone ringing?'

'9.45 I said. Not a minute more. Not a minute less.'

'Yeah, but, boss . . .' Harries was striding to keep up as Sarah headed down the corridor to the incident room.

'Do you have any idea what it's like to be cooped up in the same room as that man for more than an hour?' His Old Spice hadn't even started wearing off.

'Something important came up.'

'I know that. I told you it was vital you got me out of there the second—'

'No, I mean it, boss. We got a call.'

Something in his voice made her stop, turn. 'This had better be good.'

'A punter. Some bloke reckons he saw a woman on the waste ground carrying a baby, the same day Evie was abducted.'

'Why the hell hasn't he come forward before?'

'He wasn't aware of all the fuss.' Harries paused. 'Until he saw Karen Lowe's interview. Last night.'

No wonder he'd hesitated. It was quite a bombshell. Sarah's thoughts raced. The guy could be a prime witness. Had she made a bad call, not giving King access to Karen sooner? Had the reporter been right all along? She shook her head. *No way.*

'Has this bloke been on another planet?'

'He's . . . erm . . . well . . .'

'Stop pissing around Harries.'

'His name's Walter Clarke. He's in his late-seventies and he was calling from Lea Bank.'

She'd heard of the place. 'The rest home?'

He nodded.

'Brillliant.' She sighed.

'They're old. Not stupid, ma'am.'

She ignored the rebuke, asked another question. 'It's over Walsall way, isn't it?' They were walking again, heading for the motor this time.

'Yes. He used to live in Small Heath. One of those houses they knocked down in Blake Street? He likes getting back when he can give the staff a slip.'

'Wanders a lot, does he?'

'It doesn't mean his mind's not all there.'

She sniffed.

'What's the matter with you, ma'am?'

'I beg your pardon?'

He shook his head. 'Doesn't matter.'

Clearly it did.

They were pulling out of the car park when she next spoke. 'So what else did Mr Clarke have to say?'

'Not a lot. The old dragon who runs the place took the phone off him. Said if we wanted to speak to him we could go there. It was her phone bill he was clocking up.'

'Reckoned it was a waste of money, did she?'

His knuckles whitened round the wheel. 'We've got our first real break since this case began and you're belittling it before we even speak to the guy.'

She turned her head, gazed through the window.

'You just don't like it, do you?'

'I really wouldn't try telling me what I like or don't like, constable.'

'The fact the break came via the media. Would it be any easier if it wasn't Caroline's piece?'

'I'd so back off if I were you.'

'If I were you I'd be pleased not—'

'I've no intention of whooping with joy because a septuagenarian with a penchant for away days sees a woman with a baby. It doesn't mean I'm not interested. Don't assume I'm dismissing it. But there's a long way to go before a jury says guilty.'

Sarah found herself desperately wishing for a short cut through Walter Clarke's meanderings. He'd talked them through his school days, army days, high days and holidays. *Give me a break, Walter.* If there was any consolation for the inordinate amount of time this was taking it was being late for the showdown with Caroline King. She'd asked Dean Lavery to phone the reporter, invite her in for a little chat. He'd texted twenty minutes ago to say she was at HQ. Walter Clarke was still showing no sign of arriving at the point. Her prompts so far had been counter-productive, she let him ramble, allowed her own thoughts to wander.

She wondered about the other calls after last night's programme. According to Paul Wood forty plus people had phoned in. Most were being followed-up, checked out. She suspected it would be another instance of quantity rather than quality. That was certainly the case with Walter Clarke's outpourings.

She cut the old boy a glance, saw a cross between Captain Bird's Eye and Alan Sugar. Walter sat well back in an ancient wing chair, cup of tea balanced on his paunch; slippered feet an inch or two off the carpet. 'Yeah, Winnie was a good bloke.'

Churchill. She tuned out again. Thought of another good bloke: John Hunt. They'd chatted earlier when she'd asked him to chase forensics. She'd sensed he still felt a touch miffed because he was no longer her partner. Mind she also realized she quite missed the older man's unquestioning support. Talking of old men . . . She tuned in again.

'I know there's not much of it left, but I still like to go

back, have a look round. I can see it all in my head. I was born in number six, see, then after the war me and Betty moved to number twelve. The kids were born there. Top room at the back.' His smiled faded. 'Always thought I'd die in that house . . .'

His voice petered out. She tried steering his thoughts. 'You phoned us, Mr Clarke. Can you tell us again what you saw last time you were there?'

He stared into the distance, miles away, a lifetime ago. She wondered what was in his mind's eye.

Walter saw a scruffy little fellow with scabby knees and bruises from fights with his mates; he saw a good-looking kid leaving school at fourteen and learning a trade; a handsome young soldier with big boys' battle scars then a loving husband with pretty wife and well-mannered kids.

All these images Walter saw more clearly than his own reflection in the mirror every morning. He barely recognized the face that looked back with its deep lines, dull blue eyes. The once fine features were now coarse, misshapen. No one really looked at it any more. Only Walter and he hated it. Quite often these days, Walter had taken to leaving off his glasses. Soft focus was easier than hard reality. He was still proud, he could pretend. It helped him to turn a blind eye to the yellowing walls and nicotine stained ceiling in his room; the fussing and faults and over-friendliness of fellow residents and the prying and patronizing of the owners. It was more difficult to ignore the odours of age: a staleness, a trace of something less than fresh however fastidious the personal hygiene. He considered it a smell peculiar to aging flesh and it wasn't easy to ignore because some of it emanated from him. He knew this, was shamed by it. It was why he took refuge in the past.

Sarah gently removed the cup from its precarious perch on the old boy's stomach. His eyes struggled to focus for a few seconds, then: 'You know love, they should never have knocked them houses down.' Dust rose when he whacked the arm of his chair. 'They mightn't have looked much from the street but they were little palaces inside. People kept 'em spick and span in them days. And another thing, everybody knew their neighbours. Not like now when hardly anyone knows and nine times out of ten couldn't give a monkey's. It's why I knew who she was straight away, see.'

Sarah and Harries exchanged glances. Was that a pearl among a pile of verbal pig food?

'The minute I clapped eyes on her, I knew. They used to live round the corner, see. I've known her since she was a kid. Cheeky little sod she was.'

Sarah wanted no misunderstanding. She spoke slowly, clearly. 'Who exactly are we talking about, Mr Clarke?'

'I'm not deaf y'know. Nor thick.' He'd misunderstood.

She smiled. 'I appreciate that Mr—'

'I've told you once. Don't you listen or something?'

'We have to be absolutely clear here, Mr Clarke. I know you spoke to one of my officers on the phone, but I need you to tell me again now.'

'OK. But this'll be the last time. Why don't you people make notes?'

Harries shrugged, he was.

'I got the bus to Paradise. It's a nice journey. I like the bus.'

'When was this, Mr Clarke?'

'Do you want me to tell you or not?'

She'd swing for him in a minute. 'Yes. Of course.'

'It was the day they were talking about on the telly last night. It's what made me think of it. If you'd seen anything they said, call the police. So I did.'

'Right. Good.' Sarah bit her lip. 'So what did you see?'

'I saw the woman. The mother. She had the baby. She was walking along carrying the baby in her arms.'

'Did you speak to her?'

'No she was too far away.' He scratched the beard. 'She didn't see me. I did wave.'

'You saw her walking along. What happened?'

'Nothing.'

'Nothing? Where did they go?'

'I dunno. I weren't that interested tell the truth.'

'What time was this, Mr Clarke?'

'I don't wear a watch, love.'

'Approximately?'

'Must've been about lunchtime. One-ish? I was getting peckish. I went in The Swan. Had a pie and a pint. Never thought no more about it till I saw the news last night.'

Sarah wasn't convinced but could see no reason why he'd fabricate the story. More likely, he was mistaken. 'You can state categorically can you that the woman you saw was Karen Lowe?'

'If that's the name of the woman on the telly. That's who I saw. Without a doubt.'

'I thought you said you knew the family. That you saw Karen grow up.'

'I've seen lots of kids grow up, love. It don't mean I remember all the names.'

'But you're absolutely certain it was Karen Lowe?'

'No I'm making it up.' He scowled. 'Course I'm sure. What do you take me for?'

A cantankerous old git. 'You've been very helpful, Mr Clarke. Thank you for your time. We may need to talk to you again.'

'Don't suppose there's a reward or anythin'?'

'What do you reckon, boss?' Harries and Sarah were walking back to the motor. She reckoned a number of things, including the fact she'd forgotten to get back to Tom Lowe. The *Birmingham News* hadn't carried anything about a reward though so the old man wasn't just after a fast buck. Not that she thought he'd be in line for a payout.

'I think Walter Clarke's convinced he saw Karen Lowe.'

'But?'

'What does it amount to? He saw a woman he says was Karen Lowe carrying a baby across waste ground off Blake Street. He didn't speak to her because she was too far away. He thinks it was lunchtime because he was hungry. He didn't see where she went or what she did. It's not a lot, is it?'

'It's more than we had yesterday.'

'It's not enough.'

'Do you think he saw her though?'

'I think it depends whether he's long- or short-sighted.'

Harries frowned. 'But he wasn't wearing glasses.'

'Precisely.' And he clearly owned a pair. The indents on the bridge of his nose bore witness to that. Question was how much he needed them. There'd been no mileage further antagonizing the old man. She'd get a couple of DCs over with photographs, if he picked out Karen Lowe it would be a start. She couldn't see it herself though.

FORTY-THREE

Caroline King slipped the silver compact back in her Prada handbag. The mirror confirmed her make-up was flawless. She knew her appearance was immaculate: red silk jacket, black silk vest, skirt with a subtle black-and-white check. Crossing her legs, she tapped her nails on the metal desk. Mentally, she was pondering the equivalent of several ladders in her stocking.

First the run-in with Bob Grant. The ITN editor had been furious over her less than frank call to Sarah Quinn. He'd been on the receiving end that morning of an ear-bashing from Baker. Getting round the cop, and putting him straight, wasn't the problem. Grant's point was it should never have been necessary in the first place. She was under warning never to push her luck or his patience again.

Second, her own patience was at a premium. Quinn had kept her dangling in an interview room for well over an hour. Ninety-two minutes now she'd been running through potential exchanges with the Ice Queen: all heated.

Neither setback was the cause of most angst.

The main source was because she knew, or had been informed, where Quinn was, who she was interviewing and why. Her initial arrogant assumption that last night's broadcast had got a result was short-lived. It faded when she realized the break in the case could be an embarrassing and humiliating home goal. If the hurried call from her contact was correct the witness who'd come forward had put Karen Lowe in the frame. It was the last picture Caroline wanted to see.

'No white coat today?' Sarah, doing a Baker, dispensed with formalities and breezed in ferrying files and a mug of tea.

Caroline broke off a study of her nails. 'Sorry?'

'The white coat? That fetching little number you wear on your ward rounds. Lucky for you Charlotte Kemp was on the mend. The sight of you turning up like that could've given her a relapse.'

'Oh! How they laughed.' Sullen pout. 'I knew she was out of danger. I got a condition check from the hospital.'

'No, you didn't. There were none issued.' She slammed the files on the metal table. 'Did your informant supply that as well as everything else?'

'What informant?'

Sarah shook her head. 'When I find out—'

'Water. Bridge. Under. DI Quinn, if that's all you've got . . .'

'Sit down,' she snapped. 'How do you live with yourself? Lying, sneaking around, putting words in people's mouths. What a way to earn a living.'

'I don't lie. I don't sneak. I work hard.' Pause. 'And I get results.'

'Meaning?' She cocked a casual eyebrow. But only to mask concern. Had she had the nod about Walter Clarke? Already?

'My results speak for themselves, don't they, inspector?'

'Unlike Karen Lowe.' Sipping tea, she studied the reporter's face over the rim of the cup, then: 'Tell me, did it take long? Priming her? Making sure she was word perfect?'

'I'm a reporter not a drama teacher.'

'How much did you pay her?'

'Why don't you ask her?' She would but according to a neighbour Karen was staying overnight at a friend's in Warley. How convenient. Sarah wasn't surprised the girl was keeping her head down.

'You're playing a dangerous game, Ms King. One of these days you'll get more than you bargain for.'

She paused. 'As long as it's not a pig in a poke.' The brazen stare suggested the words had been carefully chosen.

'Stop messing with people's lives, Caroline.'

She rose, tossed her head. 'You try saving them, eh?'

'One more thing before you go.' She'd let the reporter reach the door.

'And?'

'That report last night? It was a pile of shite.'

Within seconds, Baker's head appeared round the door. He'd bumped into the reporter on her way out. 'What's up with Lois Lane, Quinn? Talk about hack in a hurry.' He sniffed. 'I hope to God you've not given her another sodding scoop.'

'No, chief.' Inadvertently, he'd given her the best laugh she'd had all week. 'I kind of told her she needs one.'

The prospect of spending quality time with Flo Carver held not a hint of amusement. Harries sighed as he killed the ignition and cast a glance at the house in all its pebble-dash glory. At least the net curtain wasn't twitching. He wondered what he'd done to earn the short straw. Was the boss paying him back for his lippy attitude that morning? He still thought it justified: she was the one who banged on about the be-all and end-all of an open mind. Walter Clarke hadn't exactly received her credit rating since the start. Was she really so petty? No. Course not. Or was she? What did he really know about her? The only thing he'd take bets on was her loathing towards Caroline King. He groaned, added a mental cringe. Had the boss cottoned on to last night's subterfuge? In the cold light of day, his Jamie Oliver impersonation had all the subtlety of a sledgehammer in a soufflé. Or was that his conscience kicking in? Surely she'd have said something? He'd watched her like a hawk, not noticed any shift in manner. *No, come on, get real.* He'd been tasked with seeing Flo Carver because the boss knew he could charm the fuzz off a peach, never mind sweet talk the old bat. It was nothing to do with payback time.

Sarah rang a number on her office phone. It was the last task on her daily to-do list. Other entries were ticked though mostly ongoing: gaps in the house-to-house; background checks, particularly on the Kemp family; follow-up calls; forensics, chase. Paperwork went without saying, or listing. A stack of written reports at her elbow were proof of that. Shoving it to one side, she reached for a can of fat Coke. Engaged signal again. No sweat, she'd give it a minute or two.

Lounging back in the chair, she propped stockinged feet on the bottom drawer, mused on how tomorrow's reconstruction of Evie Lowe's abduction would go. It was certainly an addition to the routine. She gazed at the baby's picture on her wall. Hard – in many ways – to believe it was a week since the kidnap. The police use re-enactments to jog memories and keep a crime in the public's mind. She turned her mouth down. Given the story was already getting blanket coverage, she wondered if it was worth the effort. Karen certainly wasn't

putting herself out. She'd refused point blank to take part. A
young officer would play her role while other squad members
interviewed everyone on the street.

Sarah drained the can, crushed it, binned it. Karen had better
be back tomorrow. She'd certainly got questions to answer.
Like what was she doing with Michael Slater in the Cinnamon
Tree? Apart from eating. And arguing. Still, as far as they
knew she hadn't committed a crime, they could hardly put her
under house arrest. According to the neighbour, Karen had
said she was desperate for a little break.

Sarah curled a lip. *Aren't we all, love?* Had the Slaters been
keen to get away too? Neither parent nor Michael had been
since for four days now. It wasn't an age, but even so . . . She'd
already jotted: liaise with police in Cumbria, on tomorrow's
list. It couldn't do any harm to check out the caravan. Thanks
to Harries they had an address in Millom now. He'd fed Flo
Carver a line about smelling gas through the Slaters' letterbox.
Sarah smiled. The old woman obviously watched too many
cop shows, knew full well he was after a snoop. She'd eventually lent him a key, made him work for it though. He'd come
away stinking of stale smoke and elderly cat. And several
dozen names and numbers copied from a phone book. Just in
case . . . Thinking of which. She straightened up, hit redial.

'Mr Lowe? DI Quinn here.'

'Thanks for getting back. I was beginning to think you'd
forgotten.'

She bit her lip. Sarcasm she could live without. 'Busy here,
Mr Lowe. Said I'd call about your offer of a reward? My boss
and I have talked it through. We'd like to see how the next
few days pan out.'

Slight pause while he gave it some thought. 'Sounds like
you expect a development, inspector?'

'Could be.' Fudge, fudge. 'We're following several lines of
inquiry.'

'Oh?' She heard the chink of ice on glass. 'I didn't get that
impression from last night's news.'

She laughed, made light of it. 'I'm surprised you believe
anything they say.' *You claimed you never watch the bloody
thing, smart arse. Unless . . .* 'Did you know Karen would
be on?'

'Of course not. Why do you ask?'

She wasn't sure. 'Just wondered.'

'It came as quite a shock actually. She looked . . .'

'What?'

Long pause. 'Sad. Lost. Frail. Not . . . the same as I remember her . . . at all.' He cleared his throat. 'Sorry, inspector. Someone at the door. Can we talk later?'

She hung up, pensive. Suspected the visitor was an invention. If she wasn't mistaken, there'd been a catch in his voice. Had seeing his daughter on screen resurrected painful memories of what he'd once had, and lost?

The mobile rang as Sarah, briefcase under arm, two Sainsbury carriers in hand, stepped into the apartment. Harries' culinary digs – not that she'd admit it – had acted as a spur. She'd blitzed the supermarket, bagged a bunch of stuff that hadn't even seen a tin and there wasn't a ready-meal in sight.

Slipping the case on the console, she ditched the bags on the hall floor. 'Adam, hi.'

'Hi, lady. You OK? I tried calling. And texting.' She heard in his voice that he'd watched the piece last night.

'Sorry, Adam. I'm fine. Just we're really up against it at the mo.' Her reflection in the mirror was proof of that. Grimacing, she glanced away.

'I kinda got that impression.' He obviously wanted to debate it, but . . .

'Look, I've just walked in, give me five. I'll call you back.' Plus the niggle that had been at the back of her mind all day had just started gnawing again. She'd try focussing on it while unpacking the food. It was one of those mindless chores like washing up, anything domestic come to that.

It was nearer fifteen by the time the goodies had been offloaded. The nagging thought still eluded her. She carried a glass of wine through to the sitting room, put Dylan on the CD player, sank back into the settee. The ring-tone woke her an hour later.

'Longest five minutes I've ever known, lady.'

'I dropped off, sorry.' She sat up, smoothed her hair.

'No worries. You're working a tough case. Strikes me it's King who should be apologizing. That piece last night was appalling. Are you going for a retraction?' He was like a dog with a bone. She'd let it go now.

'What's the point?' Bloody wine was warm.

'There were outrageous allegations in it, Sarah. Christ, it sounds as if you don't care.'

'I cared, past tense. It's out there now. I can't wave a wand and magic it away.'

'What about an apology?'

'Not worth the aggro.' She'd discussed it with Baker but felt forcing the issue would do more harm than good. King would get extra air time and public interest probably increase in a story best left buried.

'What about the viewers who think you cocked up?'

She rose, wandered to the window, watched the reflection on the waters of the canal. 'Come on, Adam. They're not going to lose sleep over it. If news doesn't involve people personally – they're more interested in the weather forecast.'

'And those who are involved?'

'They matter. Which is why I won't be wasting any more time worrying what the media's up to. The squad's working round the clock and it'll be police routine that leads to the killer, not some rubbish TV report.'

He paused. 'Are there any new leads?'

She told him about Walter Clarke coming forward, the interview at the rest home. 'He was adamant the woman he saw last Thursday was the same woman he saw on television, but later in the day when he was shown Karen Lowe's picture he said he couldn't swear to it.'

'Big help that. Still, even if he saw Karen there, it doesn't mean she did anything wrong.'

'Except lie.' *Again.* 'She's always sworn she was nowhere near the waste ground that day.' Her gaze followed a passing narrow boat.

'She came across pretty convincingly last night.'

'Thanks a lot, buster.'

'Not about you.' He laughed. 'No. I meant the way she talked about loving Evie. I keep seeing all those pictures of her and the baby.'

'The ones in the park?' She replayed the images in her head.

'All of them really. I wonder who took them?'

She narrowed her eyes. 'Have to go now, Adam. Talk soon.'

FORTY-FOUR

It had been too late to do anything last night and even now Sarah wasn't sure. She'd tossed and turned, wrestling with nagging thoughts, counting the hours. When the clock showed six, she rose, showered, slipped on a dove grey shift dress, left the apartment at seven. It took twenty minutes to drive to the *Birmingham News* offices. If the photograph had ever existed, the archives were where she'd find it.

She could have tasked a junior officer with the action but wanted to do it herself. She told the picture editor what she was after, but with only a vague idea of the year it might have been taken, she assumed it would take an age to locate. It took just over an hour. She'd known what to look for, but was still mildly surprised to find it. She was even less prepared for exactly what the print showed. She wanted a dozen copies, asked how long it would take.

By nine, Sarah was parked up outside Karen Lowe's block of flats. She needed another picture for her portfolio. She was pretty sure now she had at least the basis of a case, but it needed building, a few more bricks laying. She'd called the incident room, told Wood she was following a lead, kept it deliberately vague, asked him to try and keep Baker off her back. She was no maverick, but if this was way off beam at least hers would be the only time wasted.

It was late morning before she spotted Karen's approaching figure in the wing mirror. Teetering along the pavement, the girl toted a couple of Primark bags. Her hair was tucked under a baseball cap doubling as eyeshade. Sarah gave the girl a couple of minutes to let herself in, catch her breath.

'Morning, Karen.' My, she looked pleased, what little of her face was visible. The door was only open a hand's span.

'I was just on the way out, actually.' Was she capable of telling the truth?

'Course you were. So let's get on with it.'

Sarah trailed the girl into the sitting room, unsurprised she hadn't stood her ground. Leg to stand on and all that. Her sullen scowl suggested she had an idea why Sarah was there.

The room was a mess. Sarah moved a pile of magazines to the floor, took a seat, stared at the girl. Then stared some more. It had the desired effect.

With a diva sigh, she flopped onto the settee. 'I'm sorry, OK.' She snatched off the cap, flicked her hair out of her eyes. 'Those things I said . . . I didn't really know what I was doing.'

Sarah pulled a loose thread from her skirt. 'Stitching me up is what you were doing, Karen.'

'I didn't think—'

'Got that right.'

'Look, DI Quinn, I don't like you—'

'Thanks.'

'But I didn't mean to do it. Well, not that bad.' She lit a cigarette, sucked as if her life depended on it.

'Great. You just wanted to ruin my reputation a little bit. Nothing serious. I'm considering legal action actually.' Not. She wanted Karen scared, running scared. 'My solicitor's looking into it.' She let that sink in then gave her something else to mull over. 'That's not why I'm here though.'

'No?' She narrowed her eyes. Maybe against the smoke. Maybe a chink of light at the end of the tunnel?

'I want to talk to you about Walter Clarke.'

'Who?' Gormless expression.

'Walter Clarke. Old guy. Garrulous.'

'Garru-what?'

'Gobby. Likes to think he knows everyone's business.'

Mouth down, she shook her head.

'Lived on Blake Street,' Sarah prompted.

'Oh him.' Flicking ash into a foil tray. 'Thought he was dead.'

'No. He moved. Likes coming back now and again. Visits old haunts.'

'And?'

'That's when he saw you and Evie on the waste ground. Not long before you found her missing.'

'He's brain dead then.'

'I don't think so, Karen.'

'I wasn't there. You've got to believe me.'

'What? Like I'm meant to believe you've not set eyes on Michael Slater for months?' The girl opened her mouth, about to deny it. 'Don't go there, Karen. You were seen in the Cinnamon Tree.'

'Yeah, OK. I . . . he . . . his parents think I'm a slag.' She dropped her head. 'He gets it in the neck if he hangs round with me so we keep it quiet.'

'The argument was pretty loud by all accounts.'

'I was sick of it. Like he was ashamed of me or something.' The hurt appeared genuine. Sarah had a flash of sympathy for the girl. 'He's not Evie's father though. You can trust me on that.'

She didn't think he was. Not now. But she could use him as leverage. 'You come out with a lot of things . . . I'm supposed to take on trust.'

'Honest to God it's the truth.'

She raised an eyebrow. 'That's what Walter Clarke said. About seeing you and Evie.'

'He's mistaken. I was nowhere near the place.'

'I don't think so. And now we've got one witness, we'll get more. We're getting close, Karen. Very close.'

'You're gonna stitch me up. Same's I did to you, aren't you?'

'With Walter's testimony, I don't need to.' She watched the girl stub out the cigarette. 'Tell you what I do need though. That photograph of you and Evie in the park? The one in the report?'

'Yeah.'

'I want Walter to take a look at it.'

She broke eye contact, toed the carpet. 'Not sure where it is. Could take ages to find.'

'Five minutes.' Sarah tapped her watch. 'I have officers downstairs with a warrant.' She didn't make a habit of lying, must be contagious. For once she didn't care.

The girl left the room, returned almost immediately, sullen expression on her face and a photograph in her hand.

Sarah held hers out. 'I'll take the memory card too.'

'It's this area here. Can you bring it up at all, Jo?' Sarah was in the film unit at HQ. The darkroom technician Jo Sim was studying the picture, Karen and Evie the focal point. And the sticking point. As Sarah now realized, people saw a mother and baby – and didn't look beyond.

'Shouldn't be a problem.' Jo glanced up, smiling. 'I'll give you a bell, shall I?'

It had been Adam's words that prompted Sarah to take another look at the recording of last night's news report that she'd already viewed a dozen times. Thirteen. Lucky for some. At last her half-formed notion had begun to firm up, take shape.

Like she hoped the fuzzy image would when Jo enhanced it. The photographer had taken it unintentionally: a shadowy figure merged in with trees in the background, an observer seeing but unseen, a part but apart. It had been there all along and bugged Sarah since first watching King's item. Concentrating so hard on Karen's words, she'd barely seen the trees, let alone the wood.

With luck and a little technical wizardry, Jo should be able to put a face to the figure. Sarah had an idea she already knew the name.

'Tom Lowe?' Baker, arms folded, ankles crossed, leaned against the sill in his office. The enhanced print was on his desk, it was the only shot on which Lowe appeared. 'You're sure it's him, Quinn?'

Sarah had ditched the Lone Ranger act, outlined her thinking to the chief. Baker might talk bollocks sometimes but at least he was straight. He'd agreed that, with the building leaking like a faulty sieve, the developments should be kept on a 'need to know' basis. Withholding the information was important; drip-feeding it could even flush out the mole. Most of the squad would be kept in the dark. The line wouldn't be mentioned at the late brief. Baker would major on that afternoon's reconstruction.

'It's definitely him, chief. He was in the park that day. Whether with Karen or just observing I don't know yet. Either way he was lying.'

'Must run in the family.' Baker sniffed. 'And he's on his way in, is he?'

'Six-ish, he reckons.' She'd called Lowe's mobile. 'I told him we're keen to go ahead with the reward. He thinks we want to talk detail.' Powder dry and all that. No point forewarning him.

Baker snorted. 'I suppose he thought offering the dosh would give him brownie points, muddy the waters?'

She nodded. 'And maybe give access to inside information.' She reached for the pic on Baker's desk. 'I can't wait to see the lying bastard's face when I show him this.'

'There's a big difference between catching a liar out and nailing a killer, Quinn.'

Like I don't know that? 'I'm not saying he's the murderer, chief.'

Just that he had a lot of answering to do.

FORTY-FIVE

Tom Lowe had eventually reluctantly agreed to a recorded interview under caution. The new evidence hadn't been specified. Sarah had expected bluff, bluster, bullshit. Lowe had obliged, briefly. Leaning back in a chair, legs sprawled, he'd batted away the first casual queries. Then she'd taken the photograph from a slim file, slid it across the metal table in IR1. It was like a sucker punch. Lowe seemed to crumple, winded. The physical reaction was extreme. She was about to ask if he needed a doctor when he dropped his head in his hands and confessed to killing both babies.

She'd wanted to halt the session but he'd eschewed a solicitor. It was almost a relief, he said, not having to live a lie any longer. She'd let him talk, exchanged occasional glances with Harries, made the odd note on her pad.

It hadn't taken long. Less than an hour, less than that when the gaps and jagged sobs were omitted. The only break was Lavery bringing in tea no one drank. The mugs stood untouched on the desk. Afterwards, Lowe had been led away to a police cell, drained and seemingly dazed.

Now Sarah and Harries watched the interview back. The basic story was this: he hadn't meant to harm Evie, he'd wanted to hurt Karen, the baby wouldn't stop crying; he'd snapped and killed her.

Harries' fists were balled. She heard his muttered, 'Bastard.'

'I was scared then.' Lowe's voice faltered. 'I had to make

you believe there was a maniac on the loose. God forgive me, I took another baby. I can't live with myself any more. I'm sorry, so very, very sorry.'

The tape showed Lowe hunched over the desk, shoulders shaking. Sarah drew her lips together. Perhaps that was the point he realized the enormity of what he'd done.

And she didn't believe a word of it.

'When are we charging him, boss?' Harries must've been hanging round waiting for Sarah to emerge from Baker's office. It was gone eight. Past home time.

'The chief wants him to have a brief.'

'Did you tell him Lowe refused one?'

'What do you think?' She rolled her eyes. 'He's facing serious charges. The chief wants it done properly.'

'The guy confessed. What's Baker's problem?'

'Points need going over. What's your rush, David? Lowe's not going anywhere.'

Ten minutes later, Sarah was in the motor heading home. With Baker's blessing, she was playing a game. It was devious rather than dangerous, she was pretty sure they'd be on the winning side. She was convinced she knew the killer's identity now – and it wasn't the man kicking his heels in a cell at HQ. Tom Lowe was guilty of a number of misdemeanours, but not murder. As she'd pointed out to the chief, Lowe hadn't told them a single thing he couldn't have picked up from the newspapers or TV. And there'd been omissions, the doll and note left in Sarah's apartment for starters. So was he punishing himself or protecting someone else? Probably both.

It wouldn't do any harm if the real killer believed charges were imminent. The quickest way of achieving that was to release it to the media. They'd not issued the information, but she'd take bets it would appear tomorrow. It was the one time she didn't want to stop a leak – it could reveal who was pulling the plug.

As it happened, she didn't have to wait that long. Her mobile rang as she was parking. Caroline King. Could Sarah confirm a whisper she'd heard?

FORTY-SIX

Man held on baby deaths

It wasn't the lead, but it was on the front page. No surprise there, then. Sarah slung the newspaper in her office bin. Driving in, she'd heard the same line on the radio, assumed it made breakfast TV too. She drummed speculative fingers on the desk. Caroline King was freelance; doubtless she'd flogged the story everywhere. The extra cash must come in handy. It wouldn't come cheap keeping such a prolific informant sweet. But if Sarah was on the money, the contract would shortly be cancelled. The need-to-know strategy agreed with the chief meant only a handful of officers were aware Tom Lowe was in custody. Thinking it through Sarah had boiled it down to one man. Knowing who'd been feeding the reporter didn't make it easier. In fact it left a bitter taste.

She reached for the overnights, leafed through reports, answered a few emails, made a couple of calls, told herself it wasn't displacement activity.

The squad room was pretty hectic, twenty or more detectives, bashing phones, tapping keyboards. Media coverage of yesterday's reconstruction had prompted another influx of calls. Sarah walked in, glanced round, spotted John Hunt, headed over. Harries sat at the next desk.

She waited until the DS came off the line.

'Huntie, how're you fixed? Free to come with me on a house call?'

'Sure. No problem.' He'd already grabbed his jacket. 'Where to?'

'Small Heath. Karen Lowe's place.'

'Did I get the wrong end of the stick, boss?' Harries frowned. 'I thought *we* were going out there. You mentioned it last night.'

'I'm not discussing it now, Harries. I'll see you in my office when I get back.'

'So what . . . ?'

'There's a stack of witness statements that need reviewing, cross-referencing. You can make a start on that.'

'Ma'am.' Tight-lipped.

He looked like a schoolboy who'd been given lines, resentment was there, sure, and she thought she'd seen a touch of fear.

When the door opened, Sarah flashed a bright smile. 'Karen! Ever get that feeling of déjà vu?'

The girl didn't bother stifling a yawn. Her hair was mussed, cheeks pillow-creased. 'What time do you call this?'

'Wake-up time. Are you letting us in or what?'

'Do I have a choice?'

'That'll be the kitchen then.' Sarah still breezy. 'I could do with a coffee.'

'Sodding make it an' all.' She traipsed into the kitchen, bare feet sticking on tacky lino. She had on a baggy none-too-clean T-shirt and yesterday's slap. Maybe she was thirsty: she'd relented and was filling the kettle. 'So what you want this time? Come to arrest me, have you?' The tone was light, joshing. Sarah reckoned Karen was damn sure they weren't here to take her in, and why.

'You haven't seen the news then?'

'Don't be stupid. I only just got up.'

Sarah waited until Karen turned round. She wanted to see the girl's reactions, they'd be interesting, could be crucial.

'Your father's at police headquarters. He came in yesterday and confessed to the killings.'

'No!' She staggered to a chair; her face losing the little colour it had. 'It's not true. He couldn't have.' She sat on her hands to stop them shaking. Her shock was genuine – so was Sarah's.

She exchanged glances with Hunt. The DS turned his mouth down, held out empty palms. 'He says he did, Karen.' She watched as the girl rocked back and forth with tears streaming down her cheeks. It was the last thing Sarah was expecting to see. 'I'm sorry.'

'*You're* sorry? My father's been charged with murder and *you're* sorry?'

'He's not been charged.'

'Is he going to be?'

'If the confession stands. Yes.'

She shook her head. 'No way. I don't believe it. It can't be true.'

And until she had answers, Sarah wasn't sure what to believe any more either.

'What did you think, John?'

Sarah and Hunt were driving back to HQ, the DS at the wheel. She wanted his assessment of Karen's reactions. He'd been on the edge of the action recently, he'd look at it with a fresh pair of eyes, hopefully give a more neutral interpretation.

'Well, not having—'

'Come on, John. I don't want chapter and verse. Just your initial impressions.'

'She was devastated. Virtually incoherent.'

'Yes. She was . . . wasn't she?' She spoke slowly, lost in thought.

'What's on your mind?'

'Nothing really.' She shook her head. 'Forget it.'

'Go on, tell me. I'm interested.'

'I guess I had some preconceived ideas. But they seem to be turning out premature.' She just hoped they weren't going to die on her. 'I was convinced Karen knew about her father. I laid a false trail or two for her hoping to get at the truth.' Turning her head, she gazed through the window, spoke almost to herself. 'Maybe I gave the wrong directions.'

'You've certainly lost me.'

She smiled. He wasn't being obtuse. She was. 'OK, here's the deal: I'm pretty sure Tom Lowe's no killer. I'm equally convinced Karen Lowe knows who is. Yesterday, I told her we had a witness placing her at the scene.'

'I hadn't heard that.'

She filled him in on Walter Clarke's statement, then: 'It's unreliable evidence, John. I don't think he's lying. I think he's mistaken. I told Karen he was prepared to swear to it in court. I think she convinced herself we'd make up the rest and she'd end up inside. Total bollocks, but I didn't try convincing her otherwise.'

'Why?'

'She knows something, John. I've felt it off and on all along. I think she knows just about everything. I wanted her to talk. And I think she has, but not to the right people. And certainly not me.'

FORTY-SEVEN

'Can I have a word, ma'am?' Harries popped his head round the door of Sarah's office. 'Deborah Lowe's downstairs demanding to see her old man.'

Well, that didn't take long. Unlike her daughter, Deborah Lowe obviously kept an eye on the news. Sarah glanced up from a report she was trying to write. 'She can't.' *Not yet anyway.*

'She's kicking off, refusing to budge until she speaks to him.'

She saved the file. 'I'll go down.'

Deborah Lowe, still ranting at the front desk sergeant, failed to register Sarah's approach. Sarah observed the woman in action for fifteen seconds or so, then: 'Mrs Lowe. Good morning. How may I help?'

She turned, eyes flashing. 'I want to see my husband, that's how you can help. Have you seen this? It's all lies.' She was tugging a newspaper from her shopping bag. Sarah's copy was in the bin.

'I have. And we need to talk, Mrs Lowe. The sergeant here will take you through to an interview room. I won't keep you long.'

There was someone she had to see first.

Sarah made her way to the squad room. Harries was hunched over a keyboard, tapping with two fingers.

'My office, now.'

She turned on her heel, heard footsteps follow. The growing anger was directed at herself almost as much as Harries. She'd trusted him, taken him into her confidence, even let him into her home. No, scrub that. He'd tricked his way in with some cook and bullshit story. Her suspicion had started then, was confirmed last night. His betrayal felt personal as well as professional.

'Sit down. I'll come straight to the point. How close are you to Caroline King?'

He reddened slightly. 'Not with you, boss.'

She leaned back in her chair, fingers laced. 'I don't think you've been *with* me at all.'

'Sorry?'

'I thought I could trust you.'

'Of course you can trust me.' He frowned. 'I don't understand.' Confused. Uncertain. He was a better actor than she'd given him credit for.

'Then I'll ask again. How close are you to Caroline King?'

He swallowed, reddened further. 'We've been out a couple of times.' Breaking eye contact, he added, 'It's not relevant to the inquiry, ma'am.'

Screwing King? She snorted. 'Not relevant to the inquiry?' *The bastard's been screwing us both – one way or another.* 'Since day one, an insider's systematically leaked vital material to that woman. Information I deliberately withheld.'

'You can't—'

'I've not finished, Harries.' She took a sip of water. 'Someone on my team—'

'When you say "someone" . . . ?' There was quiet fury in his delivery.

'You were in on Tom Lowe's interview yesterday. You're the only detective who knew what went on in that room. Within a couple of hours, I had your *sleeping partner* on the phone asking for confirmation he was facing charges.'

'Now, hold on a minute.'

'No. You hold on.' Shouting now. It was rare for her even to raise her voice. 'The information wasn't just privileged, it's not true.'

'What?'

'Tom Lowe no more killed those children than I did.'

'But he confessed.'

'Get real, Harries. We'd have to have beaten him up to *stop* him confessing.'

'Why?'

She thought of the photographs, the video, the killer's notes. She pictured Karen Lowe in her untidy council flat, Deborah Lowe in her pristine house. She imagined Walter Clarke dreaming of his bricks and mortar. She saw Tom Lowe sitting alone in a police cell. And she prayed she'd got it right.

'It's what I'm about to ask. And I want you in on the interview.' Rising, she gathered a few files and her mobile. 'Don't get your hopes up, Harries. I'll still be putting in an official complaint. And believe me, if it's upheld by an internal inquiry, you'll be out.'

'Go ahead, ma'am. I've not broken your trust and I've never given away a confidence.'

'That's right. You got a good price for them, didn't you?'

Sarah watched Tom Lowe closely as he was brought into IR1. Strictly speaking, it was the first interview. Yesterday's session had consisted of Lowe talking while Sarah and Harries listened. The pattern wouldn't be repeated. She regarded this meeting as crucial: convinced Lowe was lying, now, however long it took she wanted the truth. He'd had a night to consider the consequences of his confession, more than twelve solitary hours to contemplate its impact on the rest of his life. She hoped it was enough.

'Are you charging me now?' He spoke before he sat down.

'Take a seat, Mr Lowe. We need to go over a few points.' Her approach was perfunctory and belied the importance she placed on the exchanges to come. She nodded at Harries who went through the rigmarole with tapes. She ran through the spiel herself, then: 'Tell us again what happened the day Evie was abducted.'

'Please, inspector. It's so painful for me.' Fresh out of sympathy, she gave him silence which he eventually broke. 'I saw the pushchair outside the shop.'

'Which shop?'

'I don't know . . . some newsagent's.'

'Describe the pushchair.'

'For God's sake, what does it matter?'

'It matters a lot, Mr Lowe.'

'I can't remember.'

She let it go for the moment. 'What happened next?'

'It was a spur of the moment thing. An aberration. I never meant to take her, certainly not to harm her. It's all so hazy now.'

'What was she wearing?'

'I don't remember.'

'Don't or can't?'

'Don't.' He shouted.

'I don't believe you, Mr Lowe.'

He misunderstood, maybe deliberately. 'OK. I think it was one of those Babygro things. And a hat.'

'Colours?'

He ran a hand through his hair. 'What the hell does it matter? She'd dead . . . I killed her. I killed them both. What more do you need?'

'The truth.'

He punched the table with the side of a fist. Harries jumped. She didn't react, continued staring into Tom Lowe's eyes, willing him to drop the lies.

'Why did you send the photographs?' The sudden change of tack didn't faze the guy.

'To hurt . . . to cause pain . . . I . . . don't . . . know . . . now.'

No, I bet you don't. 'And the notes?'

'To point you in the wrong direction.'

'Why implicate the mother?'

'It's usually the mother in cases like this, isn't it?' His laugh was brittle. The irony unwitting?

'It can be.' She paused, ostensibly to jot words on a pad. Ultra casual, she added, 'And the items you left in my apartment?'

What appeared genuine confusion flickered across his face. 'I don't . . . I'm not sure now . . .'

She frowned. It was clearly news to him. Was it possible someone else was responsible for the touching little scene in her hallway? She cocked an eyebrow? 'You were saying?'

'No comment.'

Keeping quiet was probably safer if he hadn't a clue where she was coming from. And on balance, she didn't think he had. *So who was the intruder?* She put it on the back burner for the moment.

'Why did you leave a note and a lock of hair on a reporter's windscreen?'

'No comment.' Either it was down to the killer or Lowe had been blackmailed into planting the material.

'OK, Mr Lowe. I'm charging you with wasting police time. Time I'd rather spend catching the babies' killer.'

'Bitch.'

Harries tried intervening but Lowe was faster. In the split second, Sarah realized what he intended, she turned her head. Lowe's fist hit the side of her face. A bruised cheek was preferable and less painful than a broken nose.

'Are you OK, boss?'

Harries belatedly had Lowe in a headlock.

'Absolutely fine.'

'I'll take him down, shall I?'

'No, we haven't finished. We've not *really* started, have we, Mr Lowe?'

FORTY-EIGHT

Sarah took up the questioning as if there'd been no interruption. Her face felt flushed, the cheek throbbed. She clenched her hands together to conceal the tremor.

'Why did you abduct Evie, Mr Lowe?'

'I'm so sorry, inspector. I shouldn't have hit you.' His voice was full of remorse. It was no answer.

'Why did you abduct Evie?'

He sighed, slumped back in the chair. 'I don't really know . . . It seems so senseless now . . . I think I just wanted to hurt Karen . . . I'd loved her so much, but she wouldn't let me anywhere near her . . . I guess I thought it would . . .'

'You're lying.'

'It's the truth.'

'You didn't take Evie. You didn't kill Charlotte. You're not a violent man.'

'I hit you, didn't I?'

'If punching me was meant to prove you have a violent nature, I could have told you it wouldn't and saved us both a lot of pain. You hit out because I was about to reveal the killer's identity, and you didn't want to hear it.'

She paused, gave him an opening to refute the suggestion. Harries' gaze was on her. Tom Lowe stared at the floor, slowly shaking his head.

'You wouldn't harm a child. You certainly wouldn't hurt

Evie.' Something in her voice made Lowe look up to meet her gaze. 'Not when she was your own child.'

The truth hurt. He covered his ears with his hands. 'Enough. Stop this.'

'It's a bit late to stop now, Mr Lowe. You confessed to two murders you didn't commit. Just so you could protect Karen and your own precious reputation.'

'You're wrong . . . so wrong, inspector.'

'Karen panicked and called you, didn't she? Did she tell you we were going to arrest her? You had to help her, didn't you? You had to look after Karen. She's your first child.' Another pause. 'And the mother of your second.'

Harries masked what could have been a gasp. Even to Sarah's ears her words sounded melodramatic. The moment on stage when the curtain falls on a hushed audience. But Tom Lowe had a different script, a role in another production.

'You're right, inspector. I lied to protect Karen. She is the mother of my child.' He paused. 'But Karen's not my daughter. And she didn't kill Evie.'

Lowe's admission was like a second slap in a face still smarting from the first. Sarah had been convinced her interpretation was correct. The Lowe's wedding picture in the newspaper archives had been the catalyst. She'd registered immediately the likeness between the young Tom Lowe and the murdered baby. She'd failed to see there was no similarity between Lowe and Karen. With hindsight no resemblance at all.

'Your wedding picture shows Deborah was pregnant, already carrying Karen.'

'It might show she was pregnant. It doesn't show who the father was.' Lowe sounded tired, sick and tired. 'Deborah told me I was the father and we had to get married. I wasn't just going to walk away. Christ, I was proud of fathering a child. Can you imagine?' The laugh was bitter this time.

'For years I treated Karen as my daughter. Why not? I'd no reason to doubt it. I even grew to love Deborah, a little. The marriage might have lasted if she hadn't lost more babies. It changed her, it was destroying her, I can see that now. She clung to Karen like a limpet, but the more she smothered her, the more Karen pulled away. Naturally, the kid turned to me.

'In Deborah's eyes, of course, it was anything but natural. I assumed her jealousy was because our daughter loved me more.' He shook his head. 'It was because she saw her daughter getting close to a man who wasn't her father.' His eyes glistened. Sarah balled her fists under the table. 'I found out when Karen was fifteen. I stayed in touch after I left. I still loved her as a daughter. Then.

'We hid it from Deborah, of course. Didn't meet that often. I came down for Karen's birthday. Deborah was supposed to be out. I dropped Karen at the house. Her mother was in. She ran at me with a knife. I thought she was going to kill me. Maybe she thought the truth would hurt more.'

She'd screamed at him in the street, Lowe told them. *Fuck off, pervert. She's under-age.* Neighbours had come out to watch the action. Deborah standing there, ranting, features distorted like some mad woman. *She's a bastard. Her father fucked off. Now you can fuck off – or I'll set the cops on you.*

Lowe was weeping openly now. 'I didn't believe it at first, but the more I thought the more sense it made. Her insane jealousy had been driven by guilt. Our lives had been built on a lie. She assumed I was as bad as her.' He traced an eyebrow with a finger. 'Maybe she was right.

'Once I realized Karen wasn't my own flesh and blood, I thought I wouldn't want to see her again. I was wrong. I wanted to see her more.' *But not as a daughter.* 'We grew . . . closer. I love Karen and I think she feels the same.'

'Meaning?' Sarah thought she knew, wanted to hear his explanation.

'She was aware the relationship would hurt Deborah. Maybe it was partly revenge, paying her mother back for a miserable childhood.'

'And maybe Deborah took her revenge too.' Sarah said. 'Only it was more than a pound of flesh, wasn't it, Mr Lowe?'

He didn't speak, maybe couldn't.

'She took your daughter, didn't she? Your wife abducted Evie – the baby she couldn't have. And then made damn sure no one else would have her.' He was sobbing. Sarah felt only disgust. Lowe hadn't killed anyone but if he hadn't acted the spineless coward the deaths might have been prevented. 'Isn't that what happened, Mr Lowe?'

'I don't know.' He dropped his head in his hands. 'I honestly don't know.'

Sarah did. Proving it was a different matter.

'How did you know he was Evie's father, boss?'

Sarah and Harries were taking a short break in the canteen. She sipped black coffee in the hope its bitterness would get rid of the foul taste left by the Tom Lowe interview. Just for a while, she also needed to surround herself with ordinary people; wanted to hear easy banter and believe basic decency was still the norm. But like the bad taste in her mouth, the fury and disgust were still with her. She was aware the bruise darkening her cheek was attracting sidelong glances but no one made eye contact. Maybe it was the vibes she was giving off. Doubtless the wisecracks would come when she was out of earshot.

'Did you hear, boss. I asked . . . ?'

She flapped an impatient hand. 'The real question's why I failed to work out he wasn't Karen's father.' She was still beating herself up about that.

'Is it a failure? You were nearly there.'

'Nearly isn't good enough. I should have made the connection earlier.' The impatience faded. She felt a quiet sadness, a resigned acceptance that the realization had come too late. 'It was obvious from the start the Lowes were never going to make the cover of *Hello* magazine. But I didn't see the depth of Deborah Lowe's despair. If I'd registered how disturbed she is Harriet might not have died.'

Harries was ripping chunks from a polystyrene cup, piling them on the table. 'Why did she do that, boss? Take a baby she'd never seen from a family she'd never heard of?'

'I imagine because there was no link. So we'd put the deaths down to a random killer.'

'She's sick.'

'That's what the lawyers will say.' Assuming it got to court. 'She's one smart woman, Harries. Where's our evidence? She's not left a shred.'

'Yeah, but Tom Lowe—'

'Isn't going to stand up in court and admit fathering a child by a girl he thought for years was his daughter. Everything he's done is to protect his pathetic reputation. He'll deny everything, she'll deny everything and as it stands we can't prove a thing.'

'What now then?'

'We'll do what the note told us. We'll ask the mother. Only this time we'll ask the right one.'

FORTY-NINE

Deborah Lowe perched on the edge of a hard chair. She glanced up, her smile a little wary, as Sarah and Harries entered. If Sarah was right, the woman should be close to cracking. There was no sign of it. She looked to be writing a shopping list; on the table was a completed crossword, two empty tea mugs.

Sarah sat opposite, she'd been working on several opening lines; Deborah supplied it. 'You've hurt your face, dear. How did you do that?' She reached out as if to touch the swollen cheek. Sarah recoiled, unable to hide an involuntary flinch. Appalled that a woman who'd killed two babies could show concern over a bruise.

'Your husband punched me.'

The shock tactic prompted a nervous tic: Deborah Lowe's signature shrug and shake. 'My word, that's unlike Thomas. Mind, I did tell you it was all a mistake.'

'Lies is what you said.' She took a deep breath, knew keeping cool was going to be tough. 'How did you know we were holding your husband?'

'It says so. In that.' She curled a lip at the newspaper.

Sarah picked it up, read aloud: '"West Midlands police are questioning a man about the abduction and murder of two babies in the city. It's believed the man blah blah . . ."' She slung the paper back on the desk. '*A man. The man.* So I ask again: how did you know your husband was in custody?'

She answered with the truculence of a six-year-old caught out in a lie. 'I got a phone call, didn't I?'

'Oh?' From Karen or Caroline King? This would be interesting.

'Some woman. Said she was a reporter. Asked me how I felt about it.'

'And what did you tell her?'

'The same as I'm telling you, it has to be a mistake. I can't understand it when you've got an eyewitness.'

'Oh?' Sarah cut a glance at Harries. Maybe he'd see the dangers now of leaking privileged information, how detrimental it could be to an inquiry.

'The reporter mentioned it. Said someone told you they'd seen Karen with Evie.'

'And who is this "eyewitness"?'

'She wouldn't say. Just wanted to ask me about Thomas.'

King hadn't been entirely stupid then. 'So why are you here?'

She looked nonplussed as if the reason was obvious. 'Well, you'll release him now, won't you? No harm done.'

No harm done? 'Two babies are dead.'

'Yes, of course.' Shrug. 'But it wasn't Thomas.'

'He's confessed.'

'Confessed? Confused more like.'

'What's it to you anyway?' They hadn't lived together for years. Maybe she was worried who'd foot the bills.

'Not a lot.' She sniffed. 'But it should matter to you when he's innocent.'

'So were Evie and Harriet.'

She carried on as if Sarah hadn't spoken. 'I mean, much as it grieves me, if you've got a witness who can put Karen at the scene, it strikes me it's her you should be questioning not Thomas.'

'You'd like that, wouldn't you?'

'Course not. But if she's guilty . . .'

'Of what?'

'Doing away with little Evie, of course.'

'Why do you hate her so much?' Enough to take sick Polaroid pictures and post one through her own daughter's door. She'd had the sense to plant the other one handily down the road from HQ. Ironic that Todd Mellor was the only person who appeared to have been telling the truth.

'I don't know what you mean.'

'Did you decide to punish her for her wickedness?'

'I don't know what you're talking about.'

'Oh I think you do, Mrs Lowe. She took your husband, didn't she? So you took her baby.'

Blood flowed to Deborah Lowe's face, mottling the pasty skin. She was clenching and unclenching her fists. The nervous movements of her head and shoulders which had either stopped or gone unnoticed were back with a vengeance.

'You're mad.' She spat the words. 'Thomas wouldn't touch Karen. She's his daughter.'

'He thought she was. That's what you told him. You deceived him all along, didn't you?'

For a few seconds, Sarah thought Deborah Lowe would crack. The woman cast shifty glances to the door; her breath a rasping sound. Then: 'Liar. Don't be ridiculous.'

'Then you told him the truth. You hoped it would drive him away but it didn't. It brought them closer. So close, she gave him a baby. Something you hadn't and never could.'

Rocking and keening the woman hugged herself tightly to stop the tremors running through her body.

'You couldn't stand it, could you?'

She wouldn't or couldn't speak. The silence infuriated Sarah more than the woman's pathetic lies. She itched to shake her, smash her evil face into the wall. Wanted to hear her plead for mercy, then whack her again. From a file on the desk, she slipped out two photographs. Bit her lip. The babies looked like broken discarded dolls.

'Take a look at these please, Mrs Lowe.'

She lifted her head, cast a cursory dry-eyed glance. Sarah rose, walked round the table, forced the pictures into her hands, wanted to force the reality into her head.

'Poor little souls,' Lowe said. 'Look as if they're asleep, don't they?'

'They're dead, you stupid bitch.' She'd never lost control in an interview room before. She closed her eyes briefly, walked back to her seat. 'They're dead, and somebody killed them.'

'Yes. And old Walter's told you who, hasn't he?'

She froze. Spoke very slowly. 'What did you say?'

Deborah Lowe didn't answer. She knew – like Sarah – she'd already said too much.

FIFTY

'I need to speak to her now.' Caroline King was on the phone, mentally spitting feathers. Her reserves of patience and pleasantries were exhausted. She could so do without this guy's patronizing manner.

'I've told you once, petal, she's not available.' DS John Hunt sounded as if he was about to hang up.

'Get her to the phone now. It's really important.' She'd been at Lea Bank earlier where she'd spent the obligatory three hours with Walter Clarke. The old man had refused to be hurried, Caroline had left feeling like a researcher on *This Is Your Life*.

'You can try later, love . . .'

'Look, I think I know who killed the babies.'

'Hold on.'

'Good timing. Put her through, John.' Sarah gave a wry smile. She'd wanted a word with the reporter anyway. Interview halted, she slipped into the corridor to take the call.

'DI Quinn?' Alert, energized. 'I've got some amazing—'

Yeah yeah. 'Did you call Deborah Lowe last night?'

'Yes, but, listen—'

'Did you mention Walter Clarke by name?'

'No.'

'Are you absolutely sure you didn't divulge his name?'

'Yes! But listen, I showed him—'

'No. You listen. I want you in my office in the next hour. And if you go anywhere near Walter Clarke again today, you'll find yourself in a police cell.' Looking through the spyhole, she saw Deborah Lowe leafing through the newspaper.

'Who the hell do you think you are? Didn't Neanderthal man tell you why I'm calling.'

'DS Hunt did mention it.'

'Well then. I think I know who the killer is.'

'I do know. I'm looking at the killer now.'

'Can I quote you on that?'

Bloody woman never missed a trick. 'No. You can't quote me on anything.' She leaned against the wall.

'You just can't stand it, can you?'

'What?'

'Old Walter came forward because he saw my report. You can't handle that.'

She heard the smirk in the reporter's voice. 'Old Walter, as you put it, is one strand in the inquiry.'

'It's the biggest break you've had.'

'And you might have blown the lot this morning.'

Silence. Sarah's efforts had identified Tom Lowe as Evie's father and subsequently established a motive for the murder. But without forensic evidence, it was all speculation, circumstantial. The case hinged on a confession. Several hours' questioning Deborah Lowe had failed so far. Sarah saw Walter Clarke as a way of extracting it.

'Look, Ms King, get over here soon as you can. I might have something for you.'

'An apology would do for a—'

Sarah hung up, smiling. For once the reporter was talking to herself.

'I'm sorry to bring you here like this.'

Though judging by the beam on Walter Clarke's face, Sarah thought her apology was probably unnecessary. Maybe he'd enjoyed the ride in the patrol car, the unaccustomed attention.

'That's OK, love. Ta, lad.' Sitting in her office now, Walter took a cup of tea from Harries.

She returned his smile. This cantankerous old man could provide the pressure to push Deborah Lowe over the edge. But Sarah had to be so careful.

'I understand you've been talking to a reporter this morning, Mr Clarke?'

'That's right, love. I thought she was one of your lot first off.'

'Did she tell you that?'

'Not in so many words. But you said you might be back and when she brought out more pictures.' He shrugged.

'What pictures?'

'Pictures of the Lowes.'

She groaned inwardly. Then wondered if Caroline's crass interference might prove useful. 'She showed you some pictures? Tell me more, Mr Clarke.'

'Yeah. It was then I realized like. It wasn't Karen I saw the other day. It was her mum.' He looked a little sheepish. 'Easy mistake to make. Anyone could've done it. Like peas in a pod, them two.'

'But you're sure now? It was Deborah Lowe, not Karen.'

'Yeah. It was mainly the picture of Deborah and the kiddie.' Sarah masked her surprise. The woman said she'd never set eyes on her granddaughter. 'Karen's just a kid really. It was definitely her mum, I saw.'

'And you'd know her again?'

'Definitely.' He slipped his hand in a jacket pocket. 'I've even brought me specs.'

Sarah spent five minutes in Baker's office bringing him up to speed. She'd briefed him every step of the way, knew he wanted to be in at the finish. When the chief left to take up a vantage point, Sarah proceeded to IR1

'OK, you're free to go, Mrs Lowe. I'll see you out.'

Scowling, the woman gathered her belongings. 'About time, too. You'll be hearing from my solicitor about this.'

Sarah smiled. 'I'm sure we will.' She led the way, glanced to check Walter Clarke was waiting in reception, primed and ready for action.

The old man's recognition was instant. 'That's her.' Pointing a finger. 'I'd swear to it. On my life.'

Judging by Deborah Lowe's reaction, recognition was mutual. White-faced, she staggered, clutched her chest, collapsed in an ungainly heap. Sarah knelt beside her, shouted at the desk sergeant to call an ambulance.

Don't die on me, you bastard.

Face dripping with sweat, distorted with pain, she beckoned Sarah closer. The idea of comforting her was repugnant. Deborah Lowe didn't want comfort, she mouthed what Sarah wanted to hear and asked her to pray for absolution.

Sarah's only prayer was that they weren't the woman's final words. She'd wanted a confession, but not on a death bed.

FIFTY-ONE

Caroline King sprang to her feet when Sarah entered the office.

'I can think of better ways of spending my time. What the hell's going on?'

Sarah walked to her desk, waved the reporter down. 'Give it a rest, will you? I've not got the energy.' She sank back in the chair, closed her eyes briefly.

'Are you OK?'

She suspected the reporter's concern was nowhere near as great as her curiosity. 'I'll get over it.' *Given time.*

'You said you'd have something for me?'

'What?' She tried dragging her thoughts from Deborah Lowe, the sight of the ambulance driving away, blue lights flashing.

'You said you might have something for me?'

Sitting up, she reached for a bottle of water. 'There'll be a news conference. Here. 4.30.'

'What? You got me here under false pretences.' Glaring, she rose, hoisted bag on shoulder. 'That's no good to me.'

'If I were you, I'd sit down. I've got things to say that may or may not make the press briefing. Either way, you won't want to report them.'

'Sounds like a threat, DI Quinn.' She sat. 'Go on then. I'll judge what I report. Not you.' She looked and sounded the cool professional, but broke eye contact first.

'In that case, I sincerely hope you display sounder judgement than you have so far. While you've been sitting here contemplating better ways to spend your time, I've been spending mine with a sick killer. Not just sick, Deborah Lowe's had a massive heart attack.'

'Brilliant. Can I—'

'Christ, Caroline, you're nearly as sick as she is.'

'No, I'm not. It's a great story. Divine retribution. Weird kind of justice.' Her eyes sparkled, she was probably seeing the headlines already.

'Divine retribution? It's a cardiac arrest. She's not been struck down by God. And if she dies she won't get sent down either. Justice? Try telling the Kemps that.'

'That's a point. Where do the Kemps fit into this? Why kill their baby?'

Sarah rose, walked to the window, perched on the sill. Holding the reporter's gaze, she said, 'Deborah Lowe was provoked by something she'd seen.'

'What? The Kemps playing Happy Families?'

'She'd never set eyes on the Kemps before snatching Harriet.'

'What set her off? Must've been pretty extreme.'

Sarah nodded. 'It was on TV. She didn't like it at all.'

'Go on then. Was it a late night film or something?'

'No. But it might as well have been.' She folded her arms. 'It was on the late news. One of your stories.'

Caroline's foundation had been carefully applied, but Sarah detected a sudden shift in colour. She aimed for an even paler shade. 'The fatuous piece about Karen being taken in for questioning. We didn't release anything. It was one of your "exclusives".'

'Bollocks. You can't possibly say my piece drove that woman to kill.'

'I'm not.' She paused. 'Deborah Lowe is.'

'Yeah, well she's mad as a box of frogs.'

'She was on a knife edge. And your report tipped her over.'

'But why?'

'That's the sort of question you should have asked yourself all the way along. How far should you go? When's the time to hold back? When you chase a story, you shouldn't be asking its price, you should consider its cost.'

'Here endeth the second lesson.' She curled a lip, the delivery was glib. But Sarah sensed the words had hit home. The reporter looked to be still weighing them up.

There'd been more time for Sarah to reflect. She knew the killing of Harriet Kemp wasn't clear cut. The cause and effect she'd outlined was too simplistic. Deborah Lowe had been living a life of quiet despair for years, her mind severely warped before seeing the report. But fearing Karen would implicate her, she said, had provoked a second death – to misdirect the police. In the next breath she'd claimed neither death was deliberate, that the smothering had been accidental. Clinically insane – or cold and calculating? The jury was out. At least Sarah hoped it would be.

She shared none of this with the reporter. It would do Caroline no harm to contemplate consequences which for the moment she believed she'd caused. She hadn't. She'd contributed casually to an outcome no one could have predicted or prevented. No doubt she'd arrive at a conclusion she could live with. For the moment, Sarah was happy to let her sweat. It didn't last long.

'OK. So why the hell didn't Karen tip you off about her bloody mother?'

'What with? She had no proof. The girl could hardly bring herself to believe it, let alone persuade anyone else. It was probably easier in a way for Karen when Harriet was murdered. Must've been tempting to believe both deaths were down to a random killer.' She paused, wanted to test the water. 'I wonder whether Karen will blame herself?'

'Why on earth should she do that?'

'Well, there was Deborah desperate to have another baby. Then there's Karen, barely out of school, and she's a mother.'

'Oh come on. Teenage pregnancies, single mothers. It's the norm these days.'

'Not when the baby's father is also the mother's.'

It took her a few seconds to work it out. 'What? Tom Lowe . . . ?'

Sarah arched an eyebrow. At least that was news to the reporter. 'No one told you he's Evie's father?'

She shook her head.

'Then I don't suppose you know he's not Karen's father?'

'How did you find out?'

Sarah was enjoying this. 'Partly good old-fashioned police work: the archives of the local newspaper, plus that piece you did with Karen. All those stills you used? I got one of them tweaked, and guess who was in the background? Even Karen didn't realize Tom Lowe was there until later.' Michael Slater her old boyfriend had taken the pics. He was currently on some religious retreat with his parents, according to Karen.

'OK. Smart bit of detecting. But Walter Clarke provided

the big breakthrough. And he only came forward because of my report.'

Sarah gave a lopsided smile. 'You can't have it both ways, Caroline. If you believe your pieces have that much impact then you have to accept Deborah Lowe was moved to kill.'

'Will you be releasing it at the news conference?'

She'd already decided against. Not to save Caroline from professional discomfort but to protect the Kemps from further trauma. They were the real victims in the case as far as Sarah was concerned. 'What's it worth, if I don't?'

'I can't stop you, DI Quinn. And I've got nothing that would be of any use to you.'

'Oh, I don't know.'

'I'm not with you.'

'No. But you've been with one of my officers.'

'DC Harries?' She laughed. 'Dear David, you mean?'

'He didn't come cheap then?' No amusement now. The voice was clipped, bitter.

Caroline frowned, seemed genuinely puzzled. 'You've lost me again.'

'Your cheque book? Must have taken a hammering.'

'Selling stories? Yep. He's a very close contact, the source of a few leaks.' Her lip curved in a smile. 'And I can state quite categorically: not one was connected to the inquiry. We shared sex, not secrets.' She arched an eyebrow. 'And I assure you, I never have to pay for that.'

Tight-lipped, Sarah watched as Caroline – trying not to laugh – reached down for her handbag. Knocking it over and scrambling for a few contents dented a gloating exit, but at the door she turned, threw in a last line. 'So, wrong again, inspector. David Harries is definitely all male, you've yet to find your mole.'

Late evening still in her office, Sarah freshened her make-up, peered at the bruise that would take days to fade and applied more concealer. As for the metaphorical egg on her face? She'd already apologized to Harries for her mistake. She took it as a good sign that he'd called her 'boss' throughout.

Messages from the hospital were mixed. John Hunt had called in to say Deborah Lowe's condition was critical but stable. The next twenty-four hours would be crucial. He'd been in the ambulance, caught garbled words as she slipped in and out of consciousness.

Sarah glanced at her watch: had a meeting with the chief in ten minutes. It would be a debriefing but she felt none of the usual elation that came with the end of a case. The conclusion of Operation Bluebird could hardly be described as successful.

If Deborah Lowe survived, lawyers would almost certainly argue she was unfit to stand trial. She'd probably be sectioned, spend the rest of her miserable existence in secure accommodation. Tom and Karen Lowe would be free to pursue their affair. Sarah doubted it. Even without snatched moments and dark secrets, wherever they went, whatever they did, long shadows would follow. As for the Kemps, their grief for Harriet would continue unabated.

And Evie? Her picture was still blue-tacked to the wall. Sarah rose, wandered over, kissed her fingers, pressed them gently to the baby's lips. Briefly she closed her eyes. *Suffer the little children.*

Best not keep the chief waiting. Walking back, she spotted a piece of paper under the desk. Was it from Caroline King's bag? She bent to pick it up, found the wording more interesting than the reporter's stories. The receipt was from a pre-printed pad, but the handwritten additions made fascinating reading. Top line was that Caroline Quinn had shelled out £500 to PC Dean Lavery.

Written proof was a gift from heaven. But had it fallen or had the reporter left it deliberately? Sarah would never ask and she reckoned for once it would be 'no comment' from Caroline.

She gave a bitter-sweet smile. There was only thing to do with a gift.

'Well, well, well. If it isn't Father Quinn.'

'Sir?' She halted mid-stride.

He waved her to a seat. 'All these sodding confessions.'

'Oh that.' She smiled weakly. Not that she'd screwed one out of Lavery yet. The detective's informer role was a given, but she had a strong suspicion he'd been the intruder at her apartment too. She reckoned a guy who'd consistently betrayed his colleagues' trust was capable of pulling off an act like that, gaining some sort of vicarious pleasure from it. She'd run it past the chief in a while, either way Lavery would be hauled in and questioned first thing.

'Yeah, confessions "r" us, chief.' She flopped in a chair.

'Let's hope it's not the last rites next.'

'Deborah Lowe might pull through. The hospital says she's stable.'

'Her heart might be.' He tapped his temple with an index finger. 'Her head ain't. She's doo-fucking-lally.' He talked about the chances of the case getting to court, but Sarah had been there done that. Her heart wasn't in it; her mind elsewhere.

'Come on, Quinn. You did everything you could.'

He'd done it again. Mr Empathy. Maybe inside that sexist macho exterior a New Man was struggling to get out. She gave a thin smile. 'Yeah, right.'

'The case started coming together soon as you made the Tom Lowe connection. Don't sell yourself short and don't beat yourself up. Mind, you should've listened to me from the start.' There was a glint in his post-lunch red-eye.

'Go on.'

'Told you having babies makes women go funny, didn't I?' He winked. 'Didn't realize it goes on so bloody long though.' *Yep, that New Man had a job on his hands.* She shook her head, realized that in Baker's clumsy crass way, he was trying to lighten her dark mood. And he hadn't finished. 'I trust you're not buggering off to have babies any time soon, Quinn.'

'I won't if you won't.' She returned the wink.

'Sod off, smart arse.'

'Just before I go, I've got something for you.'

'Yeah?'

'Our little local difficulty? The leaking policeman?'

'Not funny, Quinn.'

'I was wrong. It wasn't Harries.' She gave him edited high-lights of the conversation with Caroline King. Then: 'So dear David was more performer than informer.'

Baker turned his mouth down. 'Wouldn't mind getting in on King's act myself.'

'That'd be a bit part, would it?' Dead pan. 'Anyway you were wrong too.'

'Oh?'

'Remember what you said about receipts and not getting the informant gift-wrapped?'

'I did?'

She reached into her pocket, took out a small parcel. The gift paper was red; the scarlet ribbon was tied in a neat bow. 'You did.'

Baker unwrapped it and smiled. 'I was wrong again, Sarah. Calling you Father Quinn? Make that Father Christmas.'

Sarah? First names? In that case: 'Fancy a drink, Rudolf?'